CW01390942

The Prince and His Groom

About the Author

D.K. Wood is a twenty-year-old author, and this is their first full piece of work. Writing has long been their passion, and *The Prince and His Groom* has been the most important project to them to date, having taken its first form when they were seventeen.

D. K. Wood

The Prince and His Groom

Olympia Publishers
London

www.olympiapublishers.com
OLYMPIA PAPERBACK EDITION

Copyright © D. K. Wood 2024

The right of D. K. Wood to be identified as author of
this work has been asserted in accordance with sections 77 and 78 of
the Copyright, Designs and Patents Act 1988.

All Rights Reserved

No reproduction, copy or transmission of this publication
may be made without written permission.
No paragraph of this publication may be reproduced,
copied or transmitted save with the written permission of the publisher,
or in accordance with the provisions
of the Copyright Act 1956 (as amended).

Any person who commits any unauthorised act in relation to
this publication may be liable to criminal
prosecution and civil claims for damage.

A CIP catalogue record for this title is
available from the British Library.

ISBN: 978-1-80439-849-4

This is a work of fiction.
Names, characters, places and incidents originate from the writer's
imagination. Any resemblance to actual persons, living or dead, is
purely coincidental.

First Published in 2024

Olympia Publishers
Tallis House
2 Tallis Street
London
EC4Y 0AB

Printed in Great Britain

Dedication

This book is dedicated to my angel, Bonnie, my loyal
companion for her fifteen years on this planet.

Chapter One

Robbinn Falkonn Carbeu never really kept many friends. He found that people only hurt you as they left your life, and had held this opinion from a young age, even so as bright morning light filtered carelessly through thin gaps in expensively embroidered curtains to persistently hit the closed eyelids of the prince as he slept. Or at least, tried to.

He had always thought the sun to be obnoxious in every way – it ought to be far less bright. Each wall of his bedchambers was lavishly decorated with expensive, gold details in the shapes of wings and flowers and trees to tell the intricate stories of his family: the Noble House Carbeu – of their triumphs and winnings, how one relatively small family with a formidable army from an equally unsuspecting little island conquered the globe.

Prince Robbinn of Arkordouur's bedchambers were situated on one of the highest floors of the imposing royal castle, the entire building decorated with a gold and black scheme inside and out, accented with the richest of scarlets from the occasional well treated oak detail or the gleaming leather covers of books. It was enormous, yet pleasantly intimate, every spare inch of wall in these chambers was lined with bookshelves, each of which full to bursting with books of every kind: from wild fictions to personal accounts of battle strategy.

Each he had read at least once at the request of his tutors and parents, some had served as comfort on lonely nights, reopened so many times that he could essentially recite the words, others hadn't been touched since the initial readthrough, discarded as something useless to him. He had often found more comfort in his books than he ever did in other people, 'Books are a constant', if he were to give a reason. Not that his explanation wouldn't be sound, by all means it was true – no matter how many times he read them, his books would never change. Unlike people.

"Good morning, Your Grace." This voice was all too familiar, Clauude Harper, Robbinn's favourite servant since he was a boy. He had a slightly gravelly voice – it carried a well poised, well-trained tone, not too high in volume nor too quiet, and he would annunciate his words with all the grace and clarity of a nobleman, despite the fact that he was born into a crowded peasant village. Clauude was a tall, almost imposing, broad-shouldered man with a lined face, dark hair, and strong features; despite what may be expected of such a man, the large, bony hands he possessed were soft – perfect for dressing a prince with. He had, after all, done this job for the last twenty-four years.

Clauude placed a tray of tea, sugar, and milk, all contained in fine China, (intricately painted black and gold with similar patterns to the chamber walls), upon the side table. Prince Robbinn liked to take his tea sweet, it didn't seem to matter how sweet the tea itself was, he would ask for sugar to add to it without fail. Clauude floated to the window to open the heavy curtains and tie them to the wall, allowing the bright, obnoxious light of the morning to flood in and bathe the pale skin of the prince in waves of gold.

Finally, thin eyelids and long, brown eyelashes parted to reveal amber eyes as the body they belonged to gave a soft, quiet groan. He rolled over to his back, shifting himself to be com-

10

fortable again against the luxurious linen, impossibly soft woollen mattress with matching pillows, and mass of furs that made up his bed.

"Is it morning already? Gods, it feels as though I only fell asleep moments ago." He had a sweet, almost nutty sort of voice, matching his pale, slightly round but sharp jawed face, and soft chestnut hair perfectly.

"It would be so, my lord. Unless, of course, the summer has come early," Clauude replied, adding the last part with a small chuckle. The prince laughed too – interactions like this one were the precise reason Clauude was his favourite.

"Curse the wretched sun then, bloody obnoxious thing," said Robbinn over a yawn, as he sat up in his bed to stretch his arms high up above his head, in turn pulling the skin taught against his muscular back, pushing all the bones closer to the surface. "Is there anything I ought to have remembered for today?"

"Yes, my prince. There is a Suitor's Ball this evening, beginning at dusk. Your mother has also requested that you join her and the king for breakfast in the dining hall as soon as you are ready." Robbinn's face fell slightly at the words as they left Clauude's mouth.

"Of course, I thought I was far too happy this morning," he muttered bitterly. "Thank you, Clauude." Now slightly downhearted, he spun around to leave his bed and pour a cup of tea, with a splash of milk and two spoons of sugar. As he drank and padded to the window to observe the day, Clauude made his bed for him before proceeding to begin dressing his master.

The two made conversation throughout the process, and for what must be the hundredth time, Robbinn noted how methodical Clauude was when dressing him – he always began with his undershirt, followed by stockings which were secured at his

11

calf, then trousers to better accommodate for tucking them in, a belt, and finally an overcoat to delicately accentuate Robbinn's lean figure. He was broad shouldered like his father, King Falkonn VI, but with none of his bulk, however, that is not to say that Robbinn wasn't strong – for he could certainly hold his own sparring and jousting against most opponents – only that he didn't show it in mass.

Before long Prince Robbinn was dressed and had drunk his tea, now left with only the task of breakfast with his parents. He loathed breakfast with his parents with the passion of a thousand suns. As he slowly walked down the hallways, he admired the portraits hung on the wall in solid gold frames, all of them in the most beautiful swirling wing and feather designs to surround the monarch locked behind the glass for eternity. All of his direct relatives resided here, his father, his father's father and three fathers before him, all of them respected Carbeu men. Robbinn found himself wondering where all the women were on the walls, surely there had been a queen born of the Noble House of Carbeu? Or at least, a wife worthy of similar recognition? It all seemed rather silly to him, that in all these years, not one monarch was a queen. The prince was the third to bear the name Robbinn in the family, the second was the Glorious Robbinn II, his great grandfather; celebrated for his efforts in war yet fair judgement on common ground, and most of all his wisdom. Wisdom, the current prince had inherited and then some, based upon his performance in education.

The first of his name had been the very founder of the Noble House of Carbeu, the man who had forged his throne in steel with the hands of his ancient allies, who had conquered most of the globe from his small country. Robbinn, I had led his men to victory and power, discovering the five gods as he did.

Even when spectacularly dragging his feet, it unfortunately

12

didn't take him long to reach the ornate dining hall. Its ceiling was high, supported with gold covered wooden beams and painted to show a glorious black bird, his feathers shone with green, the tip flight feather of each of his four wings was a stunning gold and his eyes gazed at the room below, red with his fury – the symbol of house Carbeu, the Dreaded Skreghle. Twice the size of an eagle, the Dreaded Skreghle were enormous, some may even say dangerous, yet beautiful birds that were swiftly used as the animal symbol of House Carbeu after discovery. It was simple enough to see why the castle was decorated in the black and gold scheme with its red accents.

At the long dining table, sitting at its head, sitting up stiffly, and staring with his cruel steel eyes, was King Falkonn VI. Although his chestnut hair was greying, pulled half into a bun at the back of his skull, muscles deteriorating, his face heavily scarred, the resemblance he bore to his son was still quite obvious. The two shared so much of their appearance, (in fact, they seemed to share one of Falkonn's many scars – a shallow line tracing the left side of his jaw, continuing down his neck and finishing above the collarbone), that many visitors had assumed they were brothers – even the way their feet struck the earth was said to be the same. To the old warrior's left, slightly more relaxed in her form, glancing with her soft amber eyes, was Oleyyna Carbeu. Her flaming red hair was pulled into around half a dozen careful plaits lying tight against her scalp, golden threads woven throughout it to secure rings of the same colour. She had the same eyes as her son, the same soft skin and even the same clusters of freckles dusting her cheeks – it would appear that she had also passed on the soft quiet way her breaths came and the nervous gesture of picking at her fingernails.

"Good morning, Robbinn," his mother said as she smiled sweetly, her eyes creasing in the same way his did with the warmth of it. Robbinn had often found it far easier to look his mother in the eye than his father. When the golden sun hit Oleyyna's eyes they would shine like honey, her freckles would almost glow like stars and her eyelashes burn like fire – much the same as his did. There was a certain familiarity in finding himself within the loving eyes of his mother. Unfortunately, he could find nothing of the sort in those of his father. Falkonn's eyes would gleam in the sun like a sword caught by harsh rays as it was swung to spill precious blood, his creased with anger, not with smiles – Falkonn's smiles were rare and saved only for the deepest of pleasure that was killing, for the old warrior missed his days in battle.

"Good morning, Mother," Robbinn replied stiffly. Finally, he sat – to the right of his father and opposite his mother. He was abruptly quite aware of how tense his jaw and shoulders were, how straight his back was against the chair, where his eyes were cast. His voice trembled slightly as he carefully made an addition to his greeting. He was cautious of his tone, the way he glanced, even the way his hands lay upon the table. "Good morning, father." He hoped he hadn't hesitated.

"Good morning, son," Falkonn said dismissively. It would appear not. Robbinn quietly released the breath he hadn't realised he had been holding, his taut shoulders began to release slightly.

Amber eyes cast downward, at his intricately decorated plate. Similarly to the rest of the castle and its contents, it was black, gold and with red accents, far more attractive in the moment than the food presented delicately upon it, consisting of two slices of bread, lightly toasted each side, two small fish cooked in butter, and a cup of sweet red wine. Precisely why so much fuss was made for such an insignificant meal, Robbinn would never understand.

Nobody spoke for a while as they began to eat. However, such peace didn't last long at all, as his father stared with cold eyes and a hard expression before breaking the blessed silence with his rough, terminally aggressive voice.

"Son. Your tasks for today. You will study battle strategy, reply to any letters you have recently received, and write letters of thanks to the Lords and families who will be attending the ball tonight. Your ball." Robbinn dropped his gaze and swallowed hard. "And," Falkonn added sharply, "you will oversee some preparation. The decorations, silverware and so on."

"Yes, Father," Robbinn said monotonously.

"You will not disappoint us all tonight, understand?" Falkonn slammed his fist on the table to drive his point in further as he barked it out. Robbinn tried hard to hold back his flinch, and prayed Falkonn didn't see it.

"Yes, Father," Robbinn responded soullessly.

The old king's eyes narrowed dangerously in the direction of his beloved son, yet he didn't say another word.

Breakfast finished without further conversation and air left feeling thick, as though it would choke the three of them at the slightest notice, time passing like the drip of water with the melting of ice.

Excused, Robbinn made his way to the library. His personal library. Once more he dragged his feet spectacularly in an unsuccessful attempt to lengthen the time he took to get there. Surprisingly, he found that examining the walls as though he was seeing them for the first time was the best way to go about delaying his work. Robbinn gazed around each wall, observing the delicate gold patterns and intricate wooden carvings that told the stories of his family, always of their victories and their greatest ones at that. Almost startlingly, he found that there were more than the tales of which he was taught – there were battles he hadn't heard of, yet there they were, carved into walls. The founding of his family, the discovery of the dreaded skreghle and its naming as the animal to represent such a noble, powerful house. He made a mental note to look up these events at a later date.

It felt as though out of nowhere, the library was upon him. Robbinn thought it would only be fair to look at the enormous library doors, too. The castle had a certain uniformity in its decoration, besides each of them being expensively commissioned from poor artists. For example, every doorframe had perfect, gold wings, trees and flowers climbing it like vines in a forest clinging to trunks of ancient trees. The heavy oak wood of each and every door was stained black, and yet shone with diligent polishing. Even its panels had the image of a skreghle with a small crown floating above its head carved into the forgiving wood.

Robbinn gave his head of soft chestnut curls a shake to sharpen his thoughts and his smooth hand closed around a golden doorknob, forged to be the shape of the skreghle's head, a small, red jewel in place of a furious eye, and twisted it. With a satisfying click, the door pushed open to allow the prince inside. His shoulders sagged as a deep sigh escaped his lungs with relaxation. Despite his hatred for boring desk work, his library was one of his favourite places to be. The gold-plated bookshelves, the smell of the old books, the sound of pages shuffling, the warm, soft lighting – all of it made him feel so very at peace with the world. On numerous occasions he had mentioned how 'if ever there were a time to die, it would be now, with a book on my lap and that view from my window' to his friends, however few they may be.

He waded through the maze of bookshelves to reach his desk, carved from oak for his great grandfather, a man known

16

for his strategy, passed down to the next boy to bear his name. Legend would have it that countless battle plans of pure genius were formed and written at the very desk that currently bore parchment, ink, an assortment of quills and far too many books that the current prince wasn't yet finished with.

It was pressed against a wall, with a window just above which he could see rolling fields where the family's horses were kept, it was just as peaceful to watch them during quiet moments. Before sitting, he opened the window to let the smell and sound in. It was mid-autumn, and although it had rained during the night it was looking to be a sunny day. As the air rushed in Robbinn could smell the lingering rain and leaves, even taste it when he sighed, taking his seat. Instead of immediately setting to work, he decided to listen to the outside world around him: trees rustling softly, grass being disturbed by the breeze, quiet footsteps around the library behind him as servants passed to-and-fro, and the occasional snort of a horse from outside.

Reluctantly, the prince peeled his mind from its calm and retrieved his work for the day with a sour expression. He would begin with the letters, as they were the most tedious of his tasks in an effort to avoid doing anything close to as boring later on.

When one has written the names of every lord on the continent what must be a thousand times over, they're bound to begin to sound the same. Keenbreakker and Hardweaverr could turn to 'Keenweaverr' and 'Hardbreakker' with remarkable ease. Robbinn's beautiful looping, slanted handwriting flowed across each page like some well poised snake, addressing and thanking each lord and lady, signing each and sealing with wax, then moving them to the 'complete' pile to his right.

His mind swiftly dulled to the repetitive nature of the work, so much so that he near fell from his chair as a horse's shrill whinny abruptly ripped through the air, causing a ringing in his ears as he jumped and dragged ink across the parchment he was writing on. For a few moments he stayed, halfway out of his chair, panting from the panic before he could sit down again; though his legs still wobbled as he did so.

Following his tedious work, there was only a few other letters which demanded his attention, thankfully. Once more, his mind became dull and repetitive, writing to this lord and that one, offering his humble thanks. From sheer boredom, or as he would rather boldly put it, 'his mind attempting to save itself from what would surely kill it otherwise'; Robbinn's amber eyes would wander to the window, over the sprawling emerald fields, watching the horses go about their lives grazing and playing and grooming one another until he remembered what it was he was supposed to be doing.

It was during one of these stretches of time that he laid eyes on a man. A tall, broad man with white, shoulder length hair who captured Robbinn's attention immediately. He felt quite certain that he would remember a man as striking as this if he had seen him before – the white hair – pulled half tied at the back of his head, just neatly enough to appear careless and to keep it from his eyes – was after all, rather distinctive.

Robbinn stared out of the window as he trudged across the grass, carrying headcollars and ropes, his plain tan-coloured shirt rolled at the sleeve up to the elbow, showing his muscular forearms. He observed the slight swagger of the man's hips, and as he turned to face the castle to open the gate, the prince's cheeks grew hot with the faraway glance at his face.

By the gods, he was handsome, even at such a distance. He walked so calmly up to each horse and caught it with a headcollar, then led it to the others. From his window, Robbinn could just see the man's build – he looked like a warrior, muscled like the statues of the gods he worshipped, like he could swing a sword and cleave a dragon's head from its shoulders if he so chose.

The prince could scarcely imagine what the man must look like underneath, his cheeks burned with the thought, the hard dips and valleys of what his chest and stomach must look like, what his skin must taste like after sweating from the work he does. As he craned his neck for a better look, his thighs made contact with the underside of his desk – he had stood up without realising it, and had his hands on the desk as he leaned closer to the window.

No sooner had he noticed what he was doing, had he been struck with the thought that it was wrong. Why on earth was a respectable prince mentally undressing a man so quickly, and from such a distance? His father had warned him about what would become of men who enjoyed other men like that, and on numerous occasions told him the consequences if he, the prince, were to lie with another man in particular, needless to say – they were far, far worse than if he were to simply enjoy a barmaid for a night.

With a distinct feeling of shame, he returned to his seat, and with it his work. Yes, his work. What he was supposed to be doing before becoming distracted by a man, of all things. With a soft, clarifying shake of his head, Robbinn picked up his forgotten quill and brought it back to his ink, then the parchment where his looping, slanted handwriting returned. His father had often called his handwriting too feminine – 'almost womanly', he often snarled, as though it were a crime, the prince had thought bitterly. Putting the man firmly out of his mind, Robbinn returned to his letters, intending to finish them all in one fell swoop.

Finally, he reached the last letter to reply to. The name of a fighter sprung out at him, surprising him so much that he simply had to read the name a second time. The name of a great warrior, who had lived the most adventurous of lives protecting the kingdom. A legend. A legend whose name he hadn't heard for years.

The great Oseerys Daeemori. It would seem that after such a long life of war, the man had married and had a child. A daughter... A daughter he was now presenting to him as a suitor. Shit.

Chapter Two

Even as he moved on with his work to battle strategy, Robbinn couldn't shake the horrifying thought of having to possibly marry the daughter of a warrior, or worse, reject her. What if she liked him? What if any of those girls liked him? He couldn't think of anything worse than to be married. Precisely why he felt that way, he couldn't for the love of all the gods pinpoint.

After bringing his mind back to the book he was supposed to be reading for the umpteenth time, he decided to stand up and walk, (or rather pace) to rest his mind. With delicate hands he placed his bookmark in, returned his quill to its place, and smoothed his parchment before standing to walk. After years of standing and pacing the library when his mind grew clouded, the chestnut-haired prince had worn a track into the hard floor. Each time he walked the same path, winding around where his favourite books were held, back around his desk and making loops around the three bookshelves closest to it.

As always, he paced while deep in thought, but only for long enough to dislodge the fog, to get back to his work and have it finished as soon as possible. His feet landed in almost the exact same spots as they had when he was four years old – marks lengthening as his stride had grown longer as he had grown taller, when he became aware of the marks, he tried to match the steps of his young self.

Somewhere during this pacing he had been approached by a servant – a wizened man, voice so soft Robbinn wondered if he was even capable of raising it at all and so amused himself with ideas of him whispering during some kind of emergency – and offered refreshment. Therefore by the time he returned to the desk, there was a glass of water upon it, with a jug beside it should he wish for more. *How very thoughtful of whisper man*, he thought, chuckling softly to himself and brushing soft chestnut hair from his eyes.

With a huff, he returned to his seat and the book he had abandoned for being boring. As a boy he thought there was no sense for a book to even exist if it was boring, after all, who reads books that are boring? Princes do, Mother had once told him. 'And you will find that princes do many things that they don't want to do for the good of their people.' As she had continued. Head in hand, he thanked his former self for doing the letters first as he tried once more to finish the chapter on battering rams.

Finally, hours later, he had read all there was to read about battering rams and so was free to go about his next task. Before leaving, he chanced just one more look out the window, hoping to see… What was he hoping to see? The distant image of that man suddenly popped into Robbinn's mind, so suddenly in fact that it startled him. He was hoping to see his horse, not some man. With a shake of his head, and the sight of neither, Robbinn turned away to leave.

As he descended the castle stairs to the ballroom, and decorations began to appear his stomach began to sink. Further and further with each tapestry and flag until he was certain it must be in the ground by the time he got to the ballroom itself. And yet, once more he was surprised. When he laid eyes on the room itself, he felt his stomach drop at least another twenty feet. The at best imposing ballroom was gorgeous, lavishly decorated with the king's flag and colours, house banners covered the walls – the crest of every noble family to be in attendance was somewhere on these walls, each of them representing a girl he would have to dance and make conversation with, a Father he would have to thank (in some cases a brother to speak with), and most commonly a mother who's hand he would have to kiss with perfect poise and grace. His lips grew numb as the urge to vomit began to pool in his gut. Casting his eyes away from the main floor and walls, he took notice of the thrones at the head of the room – for his mother and father to sit on and watch as he would dance with each young lady who hoped for his hand.

These thrones weren't as grand as those in the main throne room, though that wasn't to say that they weren't beautiful. Placed on a platform, they were raised to loom over the heads of all, to allow the monarch to observe them with ease, much like everything else pertaining to the king, his throne towered even over that of his wife – for she wasn't his queen. Robbinn took to glaring at the spot where his father's head would reside, topped with a crown so heavily encrusted with jewels that it was a wonder his neck didn't break, he was certain that his wife – when he found her – would be his queen. Gods forbid he ever turned out like Falkonn.

With a resentment pooling over his dread, he ascended the steps to come face to face with the throne. Gold, of course, forged to form the most intricate of thorns and branches, as though a tree had grown that way and been turned to solid gold and given black velvet cushioning with green piping. To the left of it sat Oleyyna's throne, not as tall, nor as grand, but just as intricate and forged in silver instead of gold, her cushions were green and piped with the same colour. Everything about it was slightly less than what her husband had. Robbinn calmed down a little at the very thought of his mother sitting there and watching him dance like she had taught him to do, watching him take a woman's hand and waist to spin her ever so delicately around the ballroom. She would be proud.

Finally turning around, he looked over the ballroom – incidentally in the precise spot at which he would enter and bow to the guests later that evening – and decided that he truly couldn't care less how it was decorated. It was gothic with hints of gold, like everywhere else in the castle – perfect for a royal ball. Father told him to oversee the preparation, if he didn't change anything, that was surely a good thing.

Next he trudged down to decide on which silverware he liked best; telling the servants he passed that the ballroom looked perfect. Upon reaching the silverware cupboard, he found each set to be practically identical, rather frustratingly. Naturally, he picked one at random and told the nearest servant which he had decided upon, as though it were some weighted decision he had given long thought to, then asked if there was anything else he was needed for. He had never been more de-lighted to be told no than in that very moment.

With a refreshing air of freedom, Robbinn made his way out to walk in the grounds, once more taking in the glorious nature of the castle he lived in, he noted how clean everything always seemed to be, how the gold never seemed to deteriorate and every plant in the windows never seemed to die.

As he strolled, he came across Oleyyna, on a walk of her own, dressed in a glorious black and green gown, with silver details that almost looked like armour beginning at her shoul-ders and snaking down her back, growing branches like ribs to wrap around her and join at her middle; flaming hair still in its careful plaits, the tails of which lay on her shoulders with the wolf skin that formed the top of her thick, black cloak. His face immediately brightened at the sight of her.

"Hello Mother!" he called happily.

"Hello dear. I was going for a walk, would you care to join me?" she smiled through her response.

"I'd be delighted," he smiled warmly and took his place at her side as they traversed into the perfect grounds. Conversation was always easy with his mother. She was warmer, more understanding and a much better listener than his father; he would often talk over others and blatantly not listen to what they were saying, then have the audacity to make them repeat it.

"Are you looking forward to the ball this evening? I hear Lord Daeemori is bringing his daughter," Oleyyna asked pleasantly.

Robbinn cast his eyes, appearing gold in the sunlight, down at the damp grass beneath his feet. "… Yes and no. He was a great warrior, and it will be an honour to meet him and his daughter, but finding a wife is just as daunting of a task as it always has been," he muttered sheepishly. It wasn't that he desired to disappoint his parents, nor his kingdom, he simply couldn't find a woman that he wanted to spend his entire life with.

"I can imagine so, my dear boy. Having to decide whom you wish to marry after a single night of dancing and wine? I certainly don't envy your position. You ought to use as many balls as you see fit to pick." Oleyyna held her head high as she spoke, channelling her confidence over to her son. "Thank you, Mother. I appreciate your wisdom more than I can say," Robbinn sighed.

"It is the job of a Mother to help her children, my love." She paused, fighting with herself in consideration over her next words. "Unless it is not a woman you would rather marry. If you prefer men, I wouldn't hold it against you and I encourage you to please tell me if you do."

He was silent for a moment. His mother had just asked if he

was gay. How could she ask such a thing? The very thought revolted him, made him want to rip his skin off and discard it, the very mention of the topic surely brought deep shame to the previous kings that walked the path they were now.

"Father has made it abundantly clear how disappointing it would be if I did. I will choose a bride eventually; I just want to be sure." He spat the words at her, venom lacing every one of them, and tears beginning to sting his eyes. He shocked himself further by walking swiftly away, down to the stables, snapping that he was going for a ride and to have his horse ready at the nearest servant as he went.

Upon arriving, Robbinn paused in the doorway to the stable yard and took in every smell he possibly could, slowing his whirlwind mind to focus on each one. First was horses, quite obviously, the comforting, lingering smell of horses – a familiar scent that never failed to calm his heart before it settled his mind. There was the pleasant smell of straw and oats too, hay and something even sweeter lingering in the air, another type of roughage fed to the horses, he presumed. He could also smell the beginnings of a light rain while he hung outside – not that a drizzle would be at all unwelcome, riding in misty rain was always more peaceful than in the sun.

For a few moments more he listened to the hooves and footsteps of stableboys and girls, the scrape of pitchforks on stone and voices carrying a definite urgency, and the prince realised with a start that his peaceful stable was descending into mild chaos. He could hear the questions, the brushing of horses, the sweeping of floors, the occasional displeased call of a horse separated from his friend – with this realisation he began to feel the tension in the place.

After listening for a few moments more, he finally turned the corner he was hiding behind to enter the gorgeous stables properly and observe this chaos for himself – only to find himself face to face with the groom he saw outside. Or so he felt – there was a good six feet between him and the man. He froze, and time seemed to freeze with him. As though the earth itself was allowing him a good look at the man before him. He was tall, taller than Robbinn by at least a head, easily more, broader than him and with sculpted hands near enough the size of bloody dinner plates. He stared up into his eyes – the most beautiful eyes he had ever seen, eyes he was certain any woman would be jealous of – his left eye was a rich honey brown, his right eye shockingly icy blue. In his staring, he observed the kind, handsome and slightly weathered face, strong jaw – all dusted with freckles like the stars against his warm toned skin. He could look at that face for days.

The fantasy world he had stepped into came crashing down as the groom turned away again, either he hadn't noticed the prince staring at him or simply (and kindly) chosen not to address it; whichever of the two was true, Robbinn's cheeks still burned with the embarrassment of staring at a groom for gods knew how long.

He crossed the yard to his horse's stable, where a red haired, freckled stableboy was saddling him. Robbinn's bony hands smoothed the chestnut face of his horse – a fine beast by all accounts, tall and strong shouldered but with an accommodating back that was easy to saddle, a kind eye, large ears sitting proudly atop his head to lead into a thick, crested neck. He was certainly a stallion fit for battle, and had been trained to accept armour, swords, and banners around him – the beast's calm nature meaning he took it all in stride. Robbinn had named his horse Solmyrer, often calling him Sol for short.

It took the red-haired boy only moments more to finish and bring the horse out for the prince, who, remarkably calmer than he was earlier, thanked him graciously and took over handling of his gentle stallion.

Within moments, he was cantering towards the wooded portion of the castle grounds, Solmyrer's great hooves thundering against the grass below, hardly slowing as he broke through the tree line – Robbinn imagined it to be a wall of soldiers he was ploughing through instead of bushes, swinging the sword of his grandfather, jumping fallen bodies instead of ditches; purely for the fun of it in the moments before he brought his horse back down to walk.

The ride was soothing: he could hear Solmyrer's feet picking carefully through the underbrush, the occasional snapping of a twig, his horse's sighs and snorts, the leather saddle squeaking, birds singing to one another and the rustling up above him in the trees. It hadn't once escaped his notice quite how much more wildlife he saw while on horseback compared to on foot – if he was especially quiet, he would often see the deer picking through the undergrowth, regularly fairly close to him.

Amber eyes grew wide with awe and his breath slowed as a rabbit appeared, snuffling about the leaves on the ground; his wonder grew further as he caught sight of the eyes of a fox, hunting the unsuspecting rabbit. As he watched, his mind wandered like a dog without direction, fetching him the face of that groom. But, why? Why now? Why, while he was watching a startlingly red fox creep up on a rabbit, was he thinking about the groom? And worse still, why could he not shake the thought? Even as the fox pounced and successfully killed the fat rabbit? Even as he felt triumph for the little hunter as it carried its dinner back, he couldn't stop thinking about that man.

Upon his return, Robbinn was surprised, mildly confused and more than mildly fearful to find the king waiting for him.

"Walk with me, son. Back to the castle," Falkonn demanded.

"Yes, Father." He remembered to stand up very straight beside his father, and to keep to his elbow as they walked.

"About the ball. You will find a wife tonight, you will not disappoint me again." Confusingly, Falkonn gave a deep sigh and allowed his shoulders to sag the second his servants were out of sight. "I just hope you're not gay. I hope you've just fallen for a peasant woman, or a fucking barmaid, shit – even one of the servants would be better." Suddenly his tone frosted and hardened again. "I don't want to remind you of what would happen if you were gay – what happened to the last prince who was."

A tale Father had told him many, many times. Of a prince who declared his love for another man, a warrior, who was overthrown by a rival country, let in by his own advisors and held down to be murdered by his own people. A precautionary tale.

"And you know it's wrong, anyway. Just pick one of them, any of them, it doesn't matter," muttered Falkonn with another sigh.

Robbinn paled.

"Yes, Father."

Worse still, he thought of that groom again as his father walked away. He thought about those eyes and how they filled his stomach with butterflies.

He could not be gay, that would be wrong.

But that man was so very handsome.

Chapter Three

His hands trembled with the pounding of his heart as Clauude helped him into his suit. Gloved hands twisted buttons into place down the front of his tunic, each of them coated with gold, matching much of its thread. Robbinn swallowed thickly, taking yet another deep breath as he glanced to the window at the pinks and oranges thrown carelessly across the sky with the setting of the rich, golden sun. Beautiful sunset.

He listened for a few moments to the horses pulling their carriages in towards the castle, to the noblemen and their families stepping out, to their voices as they were invited in. His eyes closed as the belt being pulled tight around his waist drew a soft gasp from his lips.

"Apologies, my lord," murmured Clauude.

"No, no. It's fine." Trembling hands picked at fingernails in his lap as his ever-efficient valet moved on to his soft chestnut hair. "In fact, I wondered if I might leave some of my concerns with you?" Robbinn asked slowly. The older man huffed a soft laugh.

"Yet again you amaze me, Your Grace. You never need ask before sharing something with me, and yet, here you are, as ever showing kindness to me. You are always welcome to share concerns with me, and I shall take any of your secrets to my grave." These words pulled a smile to his lips, meeting Clauude's eye through the mirror before him.

"Then I thank you." His gaze abruptly dropped to his feet.

"What if I find nobody? Out of all these girls – women – none of them appeals to me enough to marry?" his usually quite level tone began to wobble, and his words became rushed. "What if – what will Father think? And the kingdom? Gods, what if people start to talk? And Mother, what would Mother say? I'd never be able to show my face anywhere again, not even—" his breath caught in his throat as he thought of that groom, looking at him with disgust. He couldn't tell why, but the thought made his heart ache. Clauude paused his work, looking at Robbinn with concern in his eyes.

"Not even the stables."

With his crown set firmly upon his head and everything about him looking perfect, Robbinn sat between his mother and father at a table upon a platform which raised them above the guests for a small, delicate meal before the dancing. Falkonn stood, his crown flashing in the chandelier's light, his heavy, black, knee length cloak swirling behind him to address his guests. He even went to the trouble of putting on a convincing smile for them.

"Beloved guests, on this most wonderful evening, I would like to welcome you to this suitor's ball, and thus introduce my son, Robbinn." The handsome young prince stood, as though he hadn't done this countless times at his other suitor's balls, and gave a gracious smile while trying hard not to notice just how many people there were in the room, "Who will be King Robbinn the Third – although not for many years, I hope!" The king laughed, as did the polite guests. Robbinn did not. Nor, he noticed, did Oleyyna. Regardless of whether he noticed or not, the king went on. "I would like to wish all the young ladies in attendance tonight the best of luck, my son would be lucky to have any of you as his wife."

Now it was Robbinn's turn to speak. He swallowed hard,

ignoring the sweat forming on his palms, the heat creeping up his neck. "Thank you, Father, for such a fine introduction. I would also like to extend the hand of welcome to our guests, and the hope that each of you has an enjoyable evening. And although I can choose only one, I wish each of the ladies in attendance tonight the best of luck," Robbinn said with false confidence.

"And now let us all enjoy this meal," the king waved a hand, and music began to play from the next room, "and leave here as friends, if not family by the end of the night." Finally, the king and prince retook their seats to applause from their guests as the delicate meal was served.

It was custom that the meal was light – this way everyone could dance well into the night. Thankfully, this also meant that Robbinn didn't have to worry about eating enough to please Falkonn. His eyes remained firmly on his plate as he picked at his food – the pit in his stomach was opening again, and not to graciously accept the fish it was given. Thankfully, he managed to finish it, with the help of more wine than it probably should have taken.

It took hardly an hour for every guest to finish eating and – led by the king – enter the ballroom where the music was loudest, the most noticeable to the prince being the glorious cello echoing through the enormous hall. It would have been enjoyable if he wasn't expected to marry one of these women. The very thought made him pale even further.

Falkonn began the dancing by taking Oleyyna by the hand and leading her to the middle of the room for a well-practiced waltz. She smiled her first smile of the evening when dancing with her husband whom she clearly loved deeply, and judging by his own expression, he loved her too. Robbinn reluctantly drew his eyes away and approached the nearest woman: she had flaming red hair just like his mother's (a fact that deeply disturbed him, for all he could see in her was Oleyyna) and blue eyes, wearing a pale lavender dress that didn't compliment her complexion nearly as well as Oleyyna's did her. The Keenbreakker crest sat proudly on the chest of her father, who held her shoulder.

"My dear Lady Keenbreakker, would you do me the honour of a dance?" Robbinn asked as he extended a gloved hand with a gracious smile which was quickly accepted by the noble lady as he glanced at her father, from whom she seemed to have inherited the red hair. Though she was rather pretty, her father looked like an oversized weasel with darting, watery eyes that did not seem to settle on anything for more than a few seconds, not even the prince.

Somewhere between meeting her and their feet finding the dance floor Robbinn had been told the lady's name, however with his anxiety reaching such a crescendo he had little hope of remembering it. Once all three royals were on the floor, the other guests had their signal to find a waltzing partner until the prince greeted another lady. Robbinn slowly worked his way around the room to meet every single guest, face after face he smiled at, hand after hand he held, waist after waist he took, woman after woman he danced with – and nothing. No flutter of his heart, no feeling that any of them would fit. Not one of these women was more memorable than the last, eyes and names faded easily into nothing.

That is until his eyes came to rest on a familiar face. Oseerys Daeemori. Standing there behind his daughter. He was far, far taller than Robbin had expected, with the broadest of shoulders, arms that were still muscled, showing that the man still swung a sword at his age – his skin was pale, but one's eye would be immediately drawn to the startling scarlet of his – his hooked nose, chiselled cheeks and black hair would swiftly fall to insignificance when drawn into the churning abyss of his eyes.

Finally Robbinn drew his eye from Oseerys to invite his daughter to dance. She was tall too, easily as tall as him, with the broad, muscular shoulders of her father. It startled him so much that he hardly noticed that her arms followed the same mould, nor did he register that her skin was darker than her father's, only that the singular feature they seemed to share on her face was the eyes – hers were the same deep scarlet. Upon regaining his composure, he asked the lady her name.

"Oserys, Your Grace." Her voice was strong, but smooth. "Spelled differently."

"Might I ask you for a dance, my Lady Oserys?" Robbinn asked, his hand outstretched.

She seemed pleased that he didn't mention her father, though he swelled with pride behind her as she took the prince's hand. It didn't escape his notice quite how uncomfortable she seemed, both close to him and in the dress – it was a rich, emerald green which complemented her complexion and eyes rather beautifully. She almost looked ethereal. Somehow, seeing someone look equally uneasy helped him, he felt far less alone as he whisked her towards the dancefloor.

"Do you not like to dance?" Robbinn mused. "Not really, no. But Father says I must try." Oserys smiled falsely through her reply.

"I see. You look as though you've swung a sword more than once, maybe you would be more comfortable if we were sparring." They laughed quietly together. Finally, he was connecting with a woman!

"Perhaps we both would." Remarkably, she had seen through him in an instant, this woman knew he was uncomfortable dancing with her and at least suspected as to a reason why, judging by her knowing smile.

"I suppose I ought to invite you back, so we can test our skills?" he asked.

"I'll hold you to that, prince." Oserys smirked.

With that, a promise had been made. One he was more than willing to keep, and rather excited to do so. He was happy, having found an acceptable woman to connect with – perhaps he had finally found the one to marry, if he allowed himself such foresight. However, when he pictured the idea of a wedding to Oserys and what followed, he was startled by the feelings of intense guilt, and furthermore disgust. These strange feelings pulled his mood down once more, especially as he took the hand of the next pretty woman – noticed her dress, her perfume, the powder in her hair and the stiff way she gripped his hand, like she would surely die if she didn't crush the very bones within it to powder.

On and on the ball went, in much the same way, hours later Robbinn had danced with nearly every woman in attendance, one of the last being a piggish sort of woman in a pink dress that seemed to squeeze the life out of her. She seemed friendly enough, and was rather sweet to attempt conversation with, but ultimately just as unsuitable for him as all the others.

Just as the waltz was reaching its peak, high pitched screams rang out above the music: Oleyyna's at the top of them all, followed by the clash of metal and frantic footsteps, by the time Robbinn could look he saw the two Daeemoris: the man running to shield the king while his daughter held a sword to that of another man.

Somehow, she looked more at home fighting off an assassination in the middle of a ball than she ever had while dancing – the room watched with bated breath as sparks flew between

35

swords as Oserys fought the nobleman, she was fast and vicious, not once did she let up, give him a second to recover, only advanced more and more. The crowd watched her figure tense as she dealt blow after blow to the would-be assassin before he dropped his weapon, giving her chance to swipe his legs out from under him and stand on his chest when he fell, pointing the two broadswords at him.

"I would advise that you stay there," Oserys spat. As she held the man there, her father and the king rushed over to question the man. Robbinn released his dance partner to join them, his eyes coming to rest on the face of one Huxell Hardweaverr; a once handsome, desperately thin man with long black hair, hollow cheeks, and startlingly blue eyes. Startlingly blue eyes which were fixed on the woman who overpowered him in a sickeningly hungry manner.

Laughter suddenly rang out in the silent room – the king's deep voice, coupled with the sound of him slapping the old warrior at his side on the back. Clearly, his own assassination attempt was rather amusing.

"Only you would teach his daughter to fight like that, Daeemori! Well, the news that she shared your name should have been indication enough!" Falkonn chortled. The rest of the room stayed silent as the king continued to laugh, either he didn't notice or didn't care that he was the only person who found it funny. "You must be proud. Lady Daeemori, feel free to kill that man where he lies on my behalf, I will honour you and your family for protecting the crown."

"With all due respect, Your Grace, I wouldn't want to get his blood all over the floor." The room gasped as she spoke back to him with confidence. "May I throw him from a tower instead?"

"Brilliant idea! Come, lords! See how a Daeemori deals

36

with an assassin!" Robbinn couldn't tell if his father was being sarcastic. He had rarely – if ever – shown respect for a woman who wasn't Oleyyna, and yet here he was treating this woman like his favourite knight! He couldn't think what was possibly so special other than her behaviour and name to command such respect, but surely there was something? He hardly recognised the man following this young woman as she dragged a grown man up the highest tower of the castle with the intention of pitching him off it. The other men in attendance followed with them silently, leaving women in the care of Oleyyna – it was almost like a sick sort of parade, 'Come one, come all to see this man fall to his death!' Robbinn's stomach suddenly felt tight and his lips tingled. He desperately wanted comfort, but his mother was three flights of stairs down from him. A face came to mind, a face which brought him just as much comfort as Oleyyna's – the face of that groom. The idea that a man's face, let alone a man who's name he didn't know, brought him comfort made his eyes sting with the threat of tears.

Far too quickly the group reached the highest tower and its balcony where statues of the five gods were mounted around them, each one of them watching. Daeemori faced the bound, writhing, sobbing man to the sheer drop he was to fall. The men watched with bated breath as she took a silver dagger from within her skirts and put it to his throat.

"Please – your majesty – I'm sorry, this was a mistake! Please, have mercy!" Bawled Huxell, desperately.

"You forfeited your right to mercy when you pulled out your sword. With all the gods as my witnesses, Huxell Hard-weaverr; using Oserys Daeemori's hand as my own, I sentence you to die." Robbinn felt his heart in his mouth as his father sentenced the man to die. In his mind he knew this was right, a deterrent, but the man's wailing desperation made him believe otherwise.

"Kill him, dear lady." Falkonn drawled in an almost bored tone.

Huxell's wailing and babbling was cut short as the dagger split his skin, cutting deep enough to render his voice to a horrific, desperate gurgling before he was shoved off the balcony. The statues of the five gods were all facing the sight, as though their eyes were fixed on the execution taking place. Hardweaverr seemed to fall forever – until the sickening dull thud reached them all. Robbinn was certain he wasn't the only one to close his eyes at the disturbing sound.

Bafflingly, the entire group acted as though nothing had happened. Led by Falkonn, they returned to the ball, expecting Robbinn to finish dancing. With a deep cup of wine, he swallowed the urge to cry, vomit and scream all at once, and then took the last woman by the hand. She noticed how pale he was, the redness of his eyes, the coldness of his hands and seemed to know not to speak too much. For this, Robbinn was grateful and tried his best to remember her name so he could write to her at a later date, perhaps to thank her, perhaps to apologise.

Finally, as the moon began to sink into its bed of inky sky, the torturous night came to a close – all the nobles remaining in attendance climbed back into their carriages pulled by their strong horses, and the prince fled to the castle roof.

The very moment he was under the eyes of only his gods he began to cry, great ragged sobs which shook his entire form and ripped his throat raw, made his eyes sting and his lungs hurt. He threw his head back to wail into the face of Ydmirr, the god of war – pleading with him for guidance. To his surprise, the statue to which he bore surprising resemblance, blinked. With the grinding sound of stone, Ydmirr moved to look better at the prince, returning its great sword to its scabbard as it stepped down from his plinth.

"Robbinn, of The Noble House Carbeu. Heir to the throne of Arkordouur. You call to me for guidance. What is it you need?" Its voice was smooth and deep, keeping to a soft sort of tone as he observed the pitiful prince who wore an expression of the truest bewilderment.

It took a moment for him to answer, to collect his thoughts enough to reply, coming out with one question in a very small, almost hesitant voice.

"What's wrong with me?"

Chapter Four

"Wrong with you? There is nothing wrong with you, my child," Ydmirr said, a curious edge to its voice.

"How is that possible? I can't do anything right, will I ever please my father?" Pleaded Robbinn.

"Why should you? Why does it matter what he thinks?" the statue asked patiently, tilting its head.

"Because… Because he's the king! And—And my father!" Robbinn said, searching for emotion of any kind in its face.

"He is a human man," said the statue simply.

"What does that mean?" His chest still heaved with the effort of his distress as he furiously wiped tears from his face. "That means," the statue took a deep sigh, "he is human, and no titles make his opinion matter more than that of another man." Robbinn gaped. Here was the God of War himself, telling him that his father's opinion didn't matter.

"But—but why can't I find a wife? Will I ever find a wife?" he began to stumble over his words as Ydmirr shifted back to his statue position. He turned back once more.

"No. You will never find a wife," said the statue, plainly. Robbinn was crushed. He felt despair crashing in, knocking into him like waves on cliffs in a storm as the words left the statue's mouth.

"What?" Robbinn's voice was empty, but trembled with his devastation.

"Why do you look so destroyed, dear child? Not having a

40

wife isn't a bad thing. Explore, that is my guidance for you."
With that, Ydmirr's statue returned to its original position as
solid stone once more.

When Clauude brought Robbinn his morning tea as the sun
rose once again the next day, the prince had refused it – inform-
ing him that he wouldn't be coming down for breakfast that
morning, either. It didn't escape the man's notice the way tears
had tugged at his prince's voice, almost choking him at times.
In accordance with his wishes, Clauude passed on the message
to Falkonn and Oleyyna; much to the former's fury.

Falkonn's rage seeped through the entire castle like a nox-
ious gas, souring faces and pushing servants into hiding away
for fear of execution. Yet again, Robbinn hadn't found a wife.
The hope that he might have found one in Daeemori had been
shattered when he watched her butcher a man without remorse
nor fear of the gods over her shoulder. He was unsure if he
could ever look her in the eye again, despite connecting with
her so well at the time.

Regardless of the rage her husband would be saving for
her, Oleyyna brought a tray of food up to her son's locked door.
She knocked gingerly on it, and waited. When Robbinn didn't
reply, she knocked again, louder this time.

Once more she was ignored.

"Robbinn, dear, please eat something, you need it."
Oleyyna pleaded to the unforgiving wood before her. This time
Robbinn knew his soft sobbing came through the doors, as he
heard his mother's breath tighten with tears of her own. He
could all but feel her pain through her voice, like snakes stran-
gling prey, her distress gripped his heart – tightly enough to
crush it into countless pieces. Robbinn heard her place her hand
on the heavy oak door.

"I want to be here for you, my sweet boy," she whispered.

There was no doubt that Oleyyna loved her son more than life itself, but that didn't mean she knew how to help him now. Tears rolled down her red cheeks as she listened to her son try to stifle his sobs, clearly trying not to worry her, most likely so she would leave.

"I will leave your meals at your door, please eat something." Her voice held a note of desperation. But, as promised, she left the prince alone.

Days passed in much the same way. Oleyyna would bring him meals and knock softly at the door to no response from her dear son, and she would leave once more. At every return she found the food she left to be entirely untouched, every single time. Not once did it become easier to ignore his food, he knew Oleyyna would see that her son had once again not eaten, and her heart would ache more with each passing day, yet he couldn't bring himself to take it.

Past the enormous black and gold doors, the prince retreated further under the mass of furs on his bed, curled up against the world around a pillow as he wept harder still. His throat was already raw from his sobbing, now his breath wouldn't come, and his stomach ached as his lungs desperately drew in more air.

He knew very well that Falkonn was more than angry with him, he knew he had to deal with it, although he avoided all ideas of life and responsibilities and what he ought to do altogether at that moment as he screwed his eyes shut. Ridiculously, the face of that bloody groom swam into the darkness of his mind, and proved to be unshakable. He could think of nothing but him, which was preposterous, for he had never even spoken to the man! *Come on, Robbinn,* he thought bitterly, *you're being stupid, you stared at him once! From six bloody feet away!*

Eventually, after hours of battling the abyss of his mind and

42

sting of his tears, he crawled out of bed and pulled himself towards a bookshelf, reaching for one of his time tested favourites. It was a story about a handsome young prince, cursed to take the form of a monster and to live in exile, only to slowly lose his mind in the decades he spent alone. That was, until a beautiful, headstrong young woman entered the castle after her father was imprisoned by the beast, offering to take his place instead. Over months of tiptoeing around him, she began to work at coaxing the man back out of the beast, which eventually came to fruition when he asked for her hand in marriage, which upon her acceptance, brought the handsome face of the prince back.

Somehow, Robbinn resonated with the prince in his story. Much of the comfort came from the smell of the rough, old parchment and long dried ink, the soft, worn leather while he was warm in his bed, and yet the way the prince in his story felt trapped struck something within his core even more this time around. Amber eyes glanced to the window to find it a deep, dangerous grey with the threat of rain. Robbinn huffed a bitter laugh. *How fitting*, he thought.

Now that his crying had eased off, all the prince was left with was a feeling of emptiness along with a throbbing headache. He was lost, despite countless voices all telling him the true paths, he was still walking them as though blindfolded. At each and every turn he found himself hopelessly lost, there was no path that felt right, no path that led to light – he was navigating woodland with naught but whispers to guide him from death's waiting jaws. And to top it all off, it was going to rain soon.

Rain could be comforting. But when one is wounded inside it can tear down the last defences. Woefully he turned page after page of words he knew by heart as though he willed for them to

43

change – but of course they never would, that was what he liked most about books. They would never change, no matter how many times he read those words. He turned the final thick page, its ink slightly smudged, edges of the parchment worn to fibres, and immediately flicked the book back to the start to read it again.

Over the course of the afternoon, Robbinn brought down more of his favourite books, one about a girl with cruel sisters who finally receives her retribution when her foot fits a glass slipper; one about a little girl in a red cloak who takes food to her grandmother and is swallowed by a wolf and one more about a mermaid who sacrificed her voice for the love of a prince, but flung herself off a ship to be turned into bloody sea-foam. The last one he found to be quite objectionable – for mermaids were vile, bloodthirsty creatures that were hardly capable of being civil towards each other; the idea of one falling in love with its main source of prey was simply absurd. In fact, mermaids were so objectionable, that the males avoided them unless to mate, and even that was observed to be with decided reluctance. Their cousins, known as sirens, were far more likely to be the subject of a story like that, but he supposed when it was written that the difference wasn't known.

Regardless of the bitterness of fact, Robbinn sought comfort each and every book. The leather's softness from the oils on his hands, the smell, even the old ink and parchment, the sound as he turned each page. He wasted hours lying there, reading words he already knew, stories he could recite by heart, comforting himself. That is until he was brought to a realisation. These books told of an ideal, the right way to go about love, but they didn't feel truly right. Now that he thought about it, had they ever felt right? Or had they always been someone else's story, but never for him? Did it ever feel real, or was it always a work of fantasy?

No, now that he thought about it properly, it had always felt like something that was never going to apply to him. The words of another that would never be his to repeat. A fairy tale was never for him to relate to, never something he wanted to be like. He had never before realised he was supposed to. Other children would dream to be the lead role, little boys were supposed to dream about being the hero, but not Robbinn. The idea of the tales had always felt absurd, he never thought about being centre stage – how could Ydmirr possibly tell him there was nothing wrong with him? There had to be something wrong.

Rain finally began to tap at his window. Slowly, at first. Then faster, fast enough to lose its gentle rhythm, but not fast enough to be considered a downpour. Robbinn's heart began to ache with the weather. A different kind of ache than before – now the very earth he walked on felt sorrow and despair with him. Before it had been bearable. Now it was desperate. Infuriatingly, his vision once more blurred with tears; tears of hopeless longing for something – anything – to make him understand. Within his chest the racing heart began to send signals of rage from his very core to the tips of his fingers, he turned with a swell in his lungs to fling open the window and roar his frustrations into the pounding rain. The clap of thunder didn't frighten him, instead he glared up at the clouds with murder in his eyes which he didn't seem to sense.

For a reason he couldn't explain, Robbinn looked down. His furious gaze landed on that groom, his white hair, strong posture and dark clothes, bundles of fabric in his arms. With that sight alone his anger was quelled, and his tears dried on his cheeks. The man was walking out to the horses in the field before they got too wet. Robbinn watched as he opened the gate to let himself in, shut it again, and greet every horse as he placed a waxed blanket over the back of each one—to keep the horse as dry as possible, he presumed. The horses seemed to love the man, especially an enormous black one which followed him everywhere like a lost puppy, perhaps his own? He thought it sweet.

Wistfully he watched as the man did his job and walked down the path, out of sight once more. His light heart fell. And yet, he found himself still watching, almost as though he thought that by willing it to happen, the man might reappear. To his delight, he did! Leading four horses, each wearing a waxed blanket and following him happily. He stayed within sight all the way to the furthest fields where he released the horses. Not one of them galloped away as though desperate to leave his company. No, each one stuck around for something out of his hand before walking away.

Gods, he could spend hours watching the man interact with those horses, if he could. He had already forgotten about his anger, his frustration, his pain just by watching for a few minutes. He just couldn't bring himself to look away as this man tended the horses. He felt so calm.

But...

Everything he had ever been taught started to protest. He felt the conflict bubble in his chest like molten iron, hotter and hotter as the man walked out of sight. Disheartened, he looked at his bed, covered with a thick layer of books, and wondered what he could do, when it struck him like a slap to the face. He connected with Oserys Daeemori II that night. He could write to her! He had writing supplies and a windowsill to lean on, and a pygmy dragon to send it with!

And so, he set about gathering his quill, some parchment, and his ink, then climbed up to sit in his windowsill, with his back against the wall and side against the glass as rain contin-

46

ued to beat against it.

Quickly he wrote out the beginnings 'Dear Oserys,' then brought his hand to the next line. And momentarily found he had absolutely no idea what to say. He had never written a friendly letter before, how was he supposed to do this? Was it something that came naturally? Something he should learn? He groaned.

"Pereggnir's tits, why can't anything just be fucking easy?" Frustrated, he rubbed his eyes and cast them back out into the rain. Bloody hell, he wished things were easier. The blank page was horribly intimidating – his hand hovered with his uncertainty. Gods, this was agonizing. In desperation he tried speaking possible combinations of words aloud to see if they would fit the looming expanse of blank parchment.

"'I write to you because'... fuck, that's awful. No. Maybe 'I want to know if you can help'? Absolutely fucking not." Robbinn's frustration escaped his lips as a tense growl, the clenching of his fists, and luckily no stray drops of ink on his parchment.

He gave a huff and tried again.

"'Dear Oserys,' um... 'I hope this letter...' no, this... correspondence? Yeah, that sounds better. 'I hope this correspondence finds you well.'" He was writing as he spoke this time. "That's a start, right?" He glanced up to the great expanse of nobody to whom he had been speaking with a hint of excitement and the beginnings of a smile on his face.

He promptly closed his mouth and furrowed his brow once more.

"Think, Robbinn, think! For fucks sake, you know advanced battle plans, but you can't write a fucking letter? Pathetic, honestly."

Following his dismal start, writing to Oserys only became

easier as he went on, the tone becoming far less formal. Or at least, so he hoped. Sitting back against the window, he read back his relatively short letter.

'Dear Oserys,

I hope this correspondence finds you well, and in due time. Unfortunately it is an unsound mind with which I write, and in other circumstances I would not write at all, but in these particular ones I believe you to be the only person I know who would understand. I face a bewilderment; the likeness of which I have never before faced.

I feel that we made connection the other night, one I would like to build upon, if this you find to be agreeable. If you do, please send your returning letter. I hope to hear from you in the near future.

Yours with faith,

Robbinn.'

"Not awful, not brilliant." He hummed thoughtfully, but it came out as more of an annoyed growl. "Whatever. I'll send it anyway." He carefully folded and addressed the letter, sealed it and attached it to the leg of the raven sized black dragon, named Zekeyus, who had been sleeping against his thigh. It gave a bubbling yawn as it stretched down on its front legs, curling its pointed tail, and opening up its transparent wings; then it chirped happily up at him and hopped up to the open part of the window.

"That's for Oserys Daeemori the second, up in the North. Okay?" the tiny dragon gave a whistle of its understanding and climbed out of the window and flew away, beating its little wings to gain height. "Good luck, little one."

Startlingly, he felt much better after sending the letter. Like he had a friend, someone to confide in, other than an ambiguous god. Slowly, he turned his head to rest against the glass to

48

watch the horses in their field. There were all kinds of horses out there, his own Solmyrer in a fenced off paddock which he shared with one other. How he wished to be as happy as that horse, playing with his friend; a large black horse who had the same blaze on his nose and white sock on the right hind leg as Solmyrer – it was as though an artist had simply painted the horse a different colour. The pair of them tore up and down the field, bucking and kicking and squealing at one another, evidently quite excited by the rain.

Robbinn's head tilted, soft chestnut hair falling into his eyes as he wondered just who the handsome black horse belonged to, what his name might be, why it was only him that Solmyrer was in the field with.

For the first time in days, Robbinn crossed to the elaborate handle in the corner of his room that would summon Clauude, and pulled it. The bell was rung downstairs, and in a few moments his favourite servant would appear to carry out his wishes.

A gloved hand knocked at his door in predictable time, and was promptly opened. Clauude looked relieved to be at his door, almost eager to do something for him.

"Clauude, would you inform the stable hands that I shall be coming down for a ride in about two hours, and I should like a guide for it?"

"Of course, Your Grace. It would be my pleasure." He smiled and gave a polite bow. "Would that be all?"

"Would you just draw a bath for me as well?"

"I would be delighted, Your Grace. Would you prefer me to notify the stable hands first, or to start your bath?" "The stable hands first, if you wouldn't mind."

"Right away, Your Grace." With another bow, he turned and strode away; Robbinn was certain he skipped halfway down the corridor as he went about his duties.

Before long, Robbinn was sinking into a warm milk bath, with the petals of various sweet flowers believed to promote good health and healing littered on top. With a new feeling of lightness, he allowed himself to draw further under the cloudy water, eventually dipping his head of soft chestnut hair under. The world and its duties and stresses disappeared as his amber eyes closed and the water covered his ears. *Far more peaceful,* he thought.

Chapter Five

Pale skin softened, dried, and covered with fine, rich coloured clothes; Robbinn began his walk down to the stables after convincing himself not to take just one more glance outside, just for the possibility that he might see the man bringing his horse in. In all the walk was relatively short; he hardly took the time to stare at the ornately decorated black and gold walls, or the high ceilings that made him feel like an ant walking through a theatre hall.

Outside the rain was stopping, slowly giving way to a deep, reddish mist as it often did in these lands when pixies were preparing for their hibernation. The little humanoid beasts would dig up blue and purple mushrooms and drag them along the floor of forest and field alike, spreading red and orange clouds of spores for the next generation to eat. Those that weren't eaten by foxes, wolves, carrier dragons, and kelpies, that is.

Robbinn trod carefully once he got outside and made his way to the stables, the last thing he wanted to do was irritate a pixie by stepping on it, or its mushroom, for as he learned as a boy, contact with one of them would cause him to break out in hives.

The enormous stable yard came into view. Just on its own, the housing for the royal horses was near the size of a palace; more than once it had been used to compare the scale of dragons, mostly of the Northern Greater variety – usually black, alabaster, or purple in colour, with wingspans that could darken entire cities as they would pass overhead.

With an edge of excitement, Robbinn entered the stables. In stark contrast to the last time he was there, it was calm and quiet; save for the sound of horses eating and snorting. In fact, he was unsure if there was anybody there at all. He called out to the place – he had, after all, requested a guide.

"Hello?" He paused, listening. "Is there anyone here?"

"Yes, Your Grace!" A slightly startled, deep, velvety voice carried through to him. The voice hardly even needed raising to carry to him. "I'm just bringing the horses round now."

The sound of two horses plodding around the corner to where he stood, waiting patiently. His eye first met his dear Solmyrer; the horse's kind chestnut face and deep brown eyes meeting his master's as he gave a soft nicker in his recognition. It took a few long seconds for him to set his eyes on his guide. His rather tall guide. Old, faded, tunic with a royal uniform waistcoat overtop. Broad chest. Wide, muscular shoulders. Big, sculpted hands. Finally his amber eyes met the blue and honey brown in those of his guide. To say Robbinn was floored would be a stupendous understatement. Utterly flummoxed. So much so, that he could hardly say anything to his companion, at least not until his kind, friendly expression turned to one of concern.

"Forgive me, sir, is there something wrong?" the man asked tentatively.

"No," he answered far too quickly, far too shortly before gaining control over himself once more. "No, there's nothing wrong. I don't believe we've ever formally met, have we?" "We haven't, Your Grace. My name is Luciaan Ciniswood." He smiled politely, (Robbinn noted that it was slightly lopsided due to a scar on his left side), still slightly cautious.

"It's nice to meet you, Luciaan. And who might your handsome companion be?" he stumbled over the words, tripping himself up and feeling his cheeks heat up. His own Solmyrer pulled at the hand holding his reins in an attempt to get to his master's side, prompting him to finally step forward and take him. Stepping back he saw that Luciaan's cheeks had grown slightly pink at the mention of his horse's name. He rubbed the back of his neck nervously.

"His name—well." He hesitated. "He's called Pereggnir."

Robbinn's eyes widened with shock. He should be offended, call for the man to be executed for such blasphemy and yet he found himself amused.

"Pereggnir, as in the goddess of death?" he almost giggled at the idea, his lack of rage clearly helping to calm the man before him.

"The very same, yes." The great black beast began rubbing his eye into Luciaan's shoulder. Robbinn glanced at him, noting that he was Solmyrer's regular field-mate, and was practically his twin, save for base colour. Both horses had a handsome roman-nosed face a white blaze and a single white sock on the right hind leg.

"I must ask why?" Robbinn struggled to hold his face level.

"I thought it would be funny, piss a few people off." The man shrugged. "And did you succeed?" "I have the scars to prove it." The man chuckled. A wonderfully smooth, warm sound that compelled Robbinn to join without him realising.

"Then I suppose it to be a good name!" He smiled, watching his companion relax considerably. Before he could admire the man for too long, he caught himself and almost reluctantly ushered the conversation forward. "I suppose we ought to get on, I doubt the horses will let us stand around for too long."

"Of course, do you need assistance mounting up?" His handsome face brightened at the mention of horses; certainly a

53

man in the correct profession.

"If you could just hold his head, that would suffice, thank you."

Mere moments later the two were settled in comfortably worn saddles with great, energetic beasts beneath them – side by side, it becomes obvious that Pereggnir is considerably taller than Solmyrer, with a far longer stride. He plodded along lazily beside his black companion's energetic marching. It was Luciaan who broke the silence first as they came to the first gate.

"Did you have a route planned, Your Grace?"

"Just my usual one, unless you have any better ones in mind? I fear I know these far too well."

"I could take you on my own personal favourite of the many routes, it is quite an interesting path; if we're lucky there's occasionally unicorns, on very rare occasions there's a little pack of dragons that roost in one of the bigger trees." Robbinn's eyes grew wide with delight at the idea of not only unicorns, but dragons too.

"That sounds like a tremendous idea, lead the way good man!"

To the sound of hoofbeats, the smell of rain and sight of the beautiful red and orange mist of spores which would surely stain the horses' legs, the pair set off at a trot. Luciaan took him down a quiet path, clearly known to just him and the wildlife – in truth he could hardly even call it a trail, it was so hardly worn. Solmyrer held his head high, looking around at his surroundings with interest, this was a first for them both. Pereggnir and his rider on the other hand, looked perfectly ethereal in the late afternoon light, on familiar soil.

Trotting along soon warmed up the horses' muscles enough for canter through the forest, past the pixies that scarpered at the sight of them, stirring up yet more deep warm mist of mushroom spores. Before long Robbinn noticed that he had never felt so at ease in the world than this moment – charging through undergrowth as he had imagined battle, with a friendly companion, with the smell of recent rain filling his nose. They turned a corner and slowed back to walk, Luciaan muttering a soft 'this is where the unicorns tend to be', with a soft wink and a finger pressed to his lips. Slowly and quietly the horses picked through the underbrush, lowering their heads to sniff and snag mouthfuls of grass on their way, eventually coming into a small clearing with a pond at the centre. Robbinn looked around excitedly as Solmyrer stuck his head up and gave a low, wavering nicker at a unicorn.

Robbinn had presumed himself to be more excited by the idea of seeing a group of dragons but gods he'd never seen anything quite this beautiful. The thin golden horn atop its head stood proudly, easily a foot in length, and it was far taller than he had expected, from this distance it looked only slightly shorter than Pereggnir, who himself stood as tall as Robbinn at the shoulder. Its fine equine body was covered in short, perfectly white hair that he could swear sparkled like untouched snow and had bright blue eyes which watched Solmyrer gently, returning his low, wavering nicker.

At his side, Luciaan smiled. He only just caught it as Pereggnir stepped forward, taking the man into his eyeline. After only a moment's hesitation the unicorn meandered over to the pair, coming nose to nose with Pereggnir, nuzzling for a few moments before turning its attention to Solmyrer. Thankfully there were only a couple of squeals exchanged before the two started to groom each other as though they had been field mates for years. His eye met Luciaan's with a beaming smile.

"Thank you for this, truly! Nobody has ever given me an experience quite like this."

"You're very welcome. We're lucky with this guy, he's pretty friendly with horses, we might get even more luckier later on at the dragonwood tree."

Robbinn's eye slowly moved to observe more of the man; his strong jaw and slightly long nose, mostly the claw mark scar down the left side of his face, not the deepest he's ever seen but not shallow either, certainly enough to interfere with the movement of his lips, causing his lopsided smile. In fact, he found it quite endearing.

"I suppose we ought to test our luck then, shall we?"

"As you wish, Your Grace." With another fleeting smile, he turned away; muscle pressing firmly against the thin skin of his neck. Hoping he was out of Luciaan's eyeline, Robbinn bit his lip before preparing to follow.

The unicorn followed for a little while, but eventually lost interest and left to pick blue mushrooms from a nearby oak tree. Calming forest sounds of birds, rustling leaves and footsteps of horses melted into the background as the two began an idle conversation, mostly about horses and Luciaan's experience with them. He learned that the head groom was only a few years older than him, and had been working at the castle stables since his early teen years, and had lived on the grounds since his promotion to head in his late teens. Nobody knew the horses quite like the man beside him, he trained most of them and oversaw everything to do with their care; Robbinn was particularly fascinated to hear that Luciaan's adoptive mother bred horses for royal use, making him even further involved in them all.

His voice was soft and fond when he spoke about his job – he had a genuine care and passion for the beasts. Like many people Robbinn also found it easy to bond with horses, but his own enthusiasm was nothing in comparison.

Further down the path trees began to thin, the smell of rain and horse and him mixed with distinctive smoke. Smoke in a forest nearly always means dragons. Once more Luciaan put a figure to his lips with a smile and a wink before leading him forward to see the enormous dragonwood tree. The trunk alone was as wide as a horse was long, bark blacker than soot, it towered over the tallest surrounding trees, with branches like thick, giant snakes; the surrounding ground scorched and smoking, some embers trying hard not to die out. Not that Robbinn was looking at the tree itself, he was far more interested in the group of almost horse sized black dragons roosting there. An entire murder of dragons, right there! When he managed to quiet his mind he could listen and hear them clicking and purring to each other, the occasional snap of their jaws in their little conversations. Luciaan's smile broadened at the sight of the prince so enamoured with the dragons; he did enjoy showing them off to those deserving of them.

Unfortunately the pair couldn't stay for too long, for the dragons began to show too much interest in them and their horses, so Luciaan took the lead and brought them elsewhere. It was equally beautiful wherever they went, Robbinn could smell the rain, the horses, even a faint hint of the groom beside him, if he focused. Along the calm, slow walk the idle conversation returned – Robbinn found that speaking to the man became easier and easier as he kept on, but also found it easier to allow his eye to drop to the muscles in his neck, to follow them down to collarbone and from there to the shape of his shoulders through his clothes. His imagining was just beginning to get interesting when a loud, firm voice in the back of his mind began to shriek at him to stop.

What's wrong with you, he thought bitterly, *what kind of a future king thinks that way about another man?*

57

And with that lingering disgust with himself, he forced his eye to the vegetation he was passing, not the handsome man to whom he was speaking.

Eventually, the path gave way to a winding river, and just as they stopped to offer the horses a drink, rain began to fall; tapping lightly at the trees and river to begin with, but soon giving way to a heavier downpour. The change in weather brough with it the smell of smoke from the dragons, making Robbinn swell with joy.

Somewhere by the horses' feet he saw a plant closing itself up entirely in response to the touch of a raindrop; his eye followed it up a nearby oak tree as it crept and choked up it's trunk, every so often a leaf extended would coil back into itself and hide under a purple fungal ledge.

"Hm. I thought the rain had stopped." He whined, cursing himself moments later for something so pitiful. Thankfully, Luciaan gave a soft chuckle as he leaned forward to pat his horse's neck.

"We don't have to go back just yet, if you'd rather stay out there's a nice, roofed path we can take back?"

"That sounds like a wonderful idea, thank you." His smile returned as he met Luciaan's eye. His beautiful eyes. Eyes he couldn't hold for more than a few moments at a time without feeling heat rise in his cheeks. Before too long Luciaan walked his horse on a couple of paces in front of Robbinn's; leading him deeper into the wonderful green of the forest, the horses kicking up more spores to stain their legs. The further they advanced, the taller trees became and further their branches reached towards one another, almost entirely sheltering the floor from the rain while creating the glorious percussion sound of the rain beating against the leaves. Silently he thought how lucky he was to be hacking out in such a beautiful place. He also briefly thought about how he might like to be buried somewhere like this, for a reason quite unknown to him.

With a soft shake of his head, Robbinn returned his attention to the horse pulling against his hands.

"Looks like he might want another canter, there's a long stretch in a little bit, it's got good footing if he wants a good blast. It'll practically lead us home." Luciaan explained softly, turning his head to lock eyes with Robbinn – time seemed to stop for the moment the man looked into his eyes. For that moment he couldn't speak, far too lost in the colour of his eyes – the ethereal bloom of icy blue in the brown one – to have a prayer at forming words yet couldn't drag his own gaze away. He nodded instead, feeling his cheeks heating up.

Luciaan smiled a handsome smile and tossed his head in the general direction of the path ahead, adding a little "Come on then!" as his horse broke into trot through the forest. Solmyrer followed his friend with apparent glee, being unable to stop himself giving a small half-buck.

Before long the path Luciaan had spoken of came into view, a well-used, muddy path that royalty were clearly rarely taken on – the thought of which made Robbinn swell with delight. His heart sang as Solmyrer and Pereggnir were allowed to gallop, evidently still quite energetic despite the long ride. Dark, sticky mud clung to the horses' legs as the occasional drops of rain fell onto their shoulders and down the backs of their rider's necks as though commanded that way by gods who were swiftly cursed for the effort.

Together they finally broke free of the tree line into pouring rain both had forgotten was there, hearing their horses' hooves beginning to splash in the swiftly forming puddles of mud. All the small population of pixies that had been previously seen had by now scattered to take shelter from the downpour, after all, a beast only a few inches tall could easily drown in even the smallest of puddles. If he squinted, Robbinn could make out their little bodies huddled together under leaves. It wasn't difficult to imagine that a fox or two could be sharing his den with a family of them right about now. He smiled at the thought.

By the time the two of them reached the stables once more they were both thoroughly soaked; Luciaan's thin tunic clinging to his skin in places – it was all Robbinn could do to avert his eyes in a far too bashful manner. Regardless of his companion's embarrassment, Luciaan smiled his handsome smile, so truly that it reached his voice.

"Well, Your Grace, I hope you had a good time?"

"I did! So much so that I'd like to come down and ride out with you again tomorrow, if you have no prior engagements." Slowly he turned to look at the man again, seeing his wet hair clinging to his jaw.

"It would be my pleasure to ride out again with you, sir. Would you like to take Solmyrer again or another horse?"

"I shall give the poor beast a rest from carrying my weight around, actually. Surprise me!"

"I'll hold you to that, sir." He gave a small smirk, nearly stopping Robbinn's heart in the process.

Chapter Six

Robbinn returned to his fine bed with a new appreciation for his home and its surroundings, so much so that he decided to bring a book to bed with him; one he had read cover to cover before now. With a small hum as he settled into the soft pillows and the lamp beside his bed lit, his careful hands opened 'An encyclopaedia of dragons' to the first page.

"Everything we know about every dragon we know of," he murmured to himself, a smile already beginning to form on his lips. Now this was the kind of learning he could get into, even if he had already memorized most of the common species. Each marvellous species of dragon was unique, and as such each had its own page including an illustration, its size class, danger rating, intelligence rating and current level of domesticity: the same classification as was found in the kingdom bestiary.

Before too long he sent for a cup of mulled wine and a small plate of savoury pastries to accompany his evening of indulgence and announced that he wouldn't join his family for dinner tonight, either, but that he would be down for breakfast the next morning.

As a young boy it wasn't an uncommon occurrence for him to imagine what it might be like to ride a dragon, especially after hearing the legends of people of the north who had lived there for so long that they had been able to form actual bonds with the beasts. He paused, halfway through reading about the Northern Greater Dragon, commonly known as the Greater

Deathcaller; as he remembered where he had sent Zekeyus, his Pygmy Dragon, a few hours ago. To Oserys. Who is in the North. How on earth did he forget that? He felt as though his childhood dream was within his grasp. The next logical step was to get to know Oserys better, and he had already sent the letter, but it may take days to get a reply.

With a slightly put out sort of huff, he returned to his reading. Northern Greater Dragons had been known to seek out volcanoes under mounds of snow and ice to sleep in to escape the unforgiving climate – and yet over thousands of years they had chosen to remain where they recognize as home. Reading on told him that the creatures could live for centuries, sleep for decades and maintain a bond with local communities for their entire lifespan.

He spotted a small note added to the bottom of the page, written by hand on far younger parchment than the rest of the book, it read 'Dear reader: please note that we of the northern communities have discovered that the Greater Deathcaller is especially tolerant to coexistence with other dragons, such as the minor deathcaller (or Northern Minor Dragon), or the many aquatic and boulder dragons that live around them. We have also found that they will never feed on other dragons, without exception. A Deathcaller would rather starve than eat another dragon. – Oserys Daeemori I'

Robbinn tilted his head curiously. He had read about countless instances of dragons cannibalizing each other in the past, but here was a species that demonstrated the intelligence to refuse. He hoped to ask Oserys about them, should she reply.

With a relaxing evening behind him, Robbinn left his chambers to meet his parents for breakfast feeling delightfully high spirited – pleasantly surprised when it didn't falter as his father caught his eye and glared.

"Remarkably *chipper* this morning, are we?" he growled, leaning over the table like a panther to get a good look at his face. Robbinn only stumbled on his mood very slightly.

"Yes, Father. Yesterday was quite enjoyable, I found that the feeling can linger."

Oleyyna chimed in before her husband could bite.

"That sounds lovely, son. What did you do? You seemed to be out for a while."

"I went out hacking, actually! I took a guide with me, spotted some dragons!" He smiled warmly at the memory as he settled at the table.

"How lovely, what kind were they?"

"Black roosting dragons! There was a whole murder of them in a dragonwood tree, they were quite calm!"

"How lucky! They can be rather skittish, can't they?" she hummed her praise, glancing at her husband who sat glowering at his son from his end of the table, his crown casting dramatic shadows over his brow. Remarkably, Robbinn was unshaken by it as he often would be. Perhaps he had finally grown into himself enough to feel confident enough to pay him no mind.

"Yes, these were quite used to seeing people on horseback, apparently. We saw a unicorn, too! He even came up and greeted Solmyrer! I've never seen a creature quite as beautiful as it, I'd like to go back and see him again. Hopefully he comes back today!"

"That would be nice, wouldn't it?" she smiled as Falkonn coiled himself up for attack all over again, his face pulled into an ugly sneer.

"So, instead of taking care of your duties, you've been off sightseeing?" he snarled, voice dripping with venom.

"Actually I wrote to the Lady Daeemori yesterday, my dragon should be getting to her sometime soon, hopefully she will agree to meet me in due time." He refused to meet Falkonn's eye as he spoke, finishing his breakfast quickly. Following this apparent bombshell, (his father's jaw hung open moving wordlessly, his eyes wide with stupendous shock), Robbinn picked up two bread rolls, stuffed them in his pocket and made for the door – only just catching his father clenching his fist. As he swept gracefully from the room, he heard hushed but heated voices as his mother tried to calm her husband; followed by the enraged slam of Falkonn's great paw on the heavy table, rattling the whole thing with his strength.

Outside it was finally pleasant enough to shed a layer of his outercoat on his way down to the stables, though not quite enough to discard it – the smell of rain still lingered threateningly in the air.

His eyes met Luciaan's, and his heart skipped a beat. The man smiled warmly at him as he led two horses up to the mounting block to meet him. One of the great beasts was his own Pereggnir, and instead of the chestnut Solmyrer there walked a proud looking flea bitten grey with a handsome roman nose, long legs, and a degree of fire in his eyes. Robbinn had never ridden this horse, but knew exactly what his name was. He knew he liked that look in his eye, too.

"Is that Clyde?" he was unsure if he was smiling more at the horse or the man leading him as he approached. Luckily, Luciaan smiled back. Smiled that oh so handsome smile that made his heart skip beats and his breath catch in his throat.

"It is indeed! I'm surprised you can tell him apart from his twin, Cloud. But then again, you are a pleasant surprise in general if I may, Your Grace." He could swear he caught the tail end of a curl in his lip as Luciaan turned to look more directly at him.

Robbinn said nothing for a moment as he felt his cheeks

64

heat up, undoubtedly turning an embarrassing bright red colour. "Is that so? I might ask you to elaborate on that later."

"Your wish is my command, sir." Something about the way he said that made Robbinn feel all giddy and warm all over. Of course, this feeling made very little sense to him.

Disregarding it, he closed the distance between them to mount up and take a moment to stand up in his seat, testing the stirrup length. He was delighted to find they were perfect, as though Luciaan had put some thought into preparing this horse for him, taking note from his own saddle to get it right. Thinking about it, he suspected that this action was the first thing anyone had done for him out of thought for him – everything else had always been because of his position, never alluding to anything about him as a person. Not even the other grooms would pre-lengthen his stirrups for him.

"I brought along a couple of rolls for us both to share, I hope you don't mind?"

"Not at all, Your Grace. In fact, if I may, doing that is probably the most thoughtful thing anyone of noble birth has done for me. So thank you, truly."

With another shared smile and heated cheeks they set off around the same journey as the day before, this time sharing a snack on the way and offering the unicorn a carrot Luciaan had 'forgotten about' in his pocket, (although Robbinn dared to suspect he had taken them with him on purpose, based on the look on his face.). Despite seeing them yesterday Robbinn was still in awe of the dragons in their tree, surprisingly undeterred by Clyde's slightly hot response under him as they passed, only lingering a little this time.

By the time the pair of them returned, their riding had quite comfortably taken up the entire morning – the sun was high with midday, and Clauude had ventured out to meet him, asking if he would be joining his family for lunch. With a particular stroke of genius, he decided it would 'piss his father off more' if he proceeded to avoid him after using the idea of writing to and meeting with a noblewoman like some kind of weapon. He asked instead for it to be taken to his library, where he planned to spend the rest of his day.

He bid Luciaan goodbye and arranged yet another ride out for the following day. Of course, he planned to watch the horses through the window from which he had first laid eyes on his new friend. As he walked, offhandedly he remembered how similar to one of his favourite romance novels this was, only he would have to be a woman for it to work...

When he reached his library, noticing all over again how beautiful it all was with all its expensive decoration. He was greeted by a loud series of excited clicks and whistles from Zekeyus, his pygmy dragon when he finally reached his desk which promptly melted his heart. Zekeyus jumped up and down on the spot, desperate to leap onto his master's shoulder and place the letter into his hands, but knew to wait until invited. Although that isn't to say that he had to wait for long – Robbinn opened his arms for the little reptile to barrel into him mere moments after seeing him.

"Back so soon, Zeke?" he scratched the beast under the chin as he chirped, rubbing his head into Robbinn's warm neck. "Let me see what you have then!" Upon command, the letter was dropped into his waiting palm. Sitting proudly on the parchment's overlap in black wax was the Daeemori's family seal. His heart began to pound – blood rushed to his ears, his hands began to tremble. He couldn't tell if he was more nervous or excited as he picked up an ornately decorated letter opener in his long, thin fingers and pried the thing open. His eye fell to the neat, legible handwriting of Lady Oserys II.

'Dear Prince Robbinn,

I hope my own writing finds you well, and with such I hope you are feeling in a better state than the one you wrote me in. Although delighted to see your dragon arrive, I was disheartened to hear that you were experiencing an unsound mind – I know quite well what this feels like, and please do believe me when I say it is something I would not wish upon anybody.

I am happy that you have reached out to me and do quite agree that we made a connection – one that I would very much like to further, if that is something you would still like to do. Would you be available for me to visit you in two weeks' time?

Yours with faith and hope,

Oserys'

Robbinn had to read through it at least three times before he comprehended what she was saying. Good Gods, she was happy to visit him! *Father would love that,* he thought bitterly. By now Zekeyus had fallen into some well-deserved rest on his shoulders, against the warm of his neck. Just as he began to ponder how he might respond, a small chirp came from the window. There stood another pygmy dragon, wearing a collar and tag that read 'Wessel. Oserys II'.

"You must belong to her. How convenient... Take your rest, little one." His tone turned questioning as he examined the beast – Oserys' carrier dragon was much more solidly built than his own, he looked far more like a miniature version of a Northern Greater dragon with thick legs and shoulders, full use of all four legs and strong, muscled wing joints. Robbinn tilted his head as the beady yellow eyes watched him closely.

"Hm. Not so little, I suppose." Robbinn wasted no time as he pulled out more parchment, his quill and ink to write his excited response.

'Dear Oserys,

Thank you for your prompt reply. The date you have proposed is perfect, I am excited to see you when you arrive. I shall have the wing adjacent to my own prepared for you, if this is acceptable.

Yours with sincerity,

Robbinn.'

The small letter was sealed and attached to the dragon currently taking his well-deserved rest. It would be sent soon enough.

For the remainder of Robbinn's day he remained in his library, surrounded by tales of good triumphing over evil, of love conquering all. Stories he once enjoyed, but recently felt like an ideal he couldn't meet. He joined his family for supper when he was reminded – thankfully with his wife's hand softly on his own Falkonn found no energy to bite at his son with. It felt like the most peaceful meal they had experienced in years, each family member appeared to be quite settled.

Finally, an oddly exhausted prince crawled into his bed, snuggling under the mass of fine pelts and sheets that kept him warm, hugging his pillow as though his life depended on it, and fell asleep the moment his eyes closed.

It had been a while since his last dream, but he knew this one felt strange. He was cold, alone, in the dark. He was aware of his movements, but he wasn't making them happen. It was as though somebody was controlling his body for him, instead of just feeling slightly disconnected, he felt fear. He paced in his dark, cold, shrinking space. Then suddenly, out of nowhere his father's voice shook his very bones, screaming at him with rage. But then everyone else he cared about: his mother, Clauude, Ydmirr – Luciaan – they all joined in with Falkonn, berating him relentlessly, and he couldn't understand why. He couldn't understand just what it was he had done to them, but before he had more chance he was falling fast towards the ocean.

The moment he plunged into the icy water, his eyes snapped open with a gasp. His body was covered in a thin film of cold sweat, his chest heaving, eyes stinging, and cheeks wet with tears. Immediately sitting up he ran trembling hands through his hair, trying to calm his breathing, but it only got worse. Robbinn was hardly aware of what he was doing when he stepped out of bed in his nightclothes and bare feet and made clumsily for his door.

Before he knew what he was doing he was flinging open the small, inconspicuous door at the side of the castle and running at full speed across the grass to a small cabin beside the stables. The head groom lived there so that he could have access to the horses at night. There was a candle burning inside, illuminating the window. Robbinn chased that light as though his life depended on it and finally reached the door to knock on it desperately. He didn't have to wait long before Luciaan answered and his beautiful eyes came to rest on the shivering, panting, pale prince. His face pulled into a mixture of true bewilderment and quite obvious concern.

"M—My lord? What are you doing here?" he stuttered, but didn't give Robbinn time to answer before beckoning him inside. "Come in, quickly. It's warm in here."

Finding himself without words nor energy to respond, Robbinn allowed himself to be steered inside. Luciaan's home was small, hardly big enough for the two of them to share, but remarkably cosy, with only two rooms inside, a kitchen and a bedroom – the latter he was led into to sit on the bed. It wasn't as big as his own, but it was easily big enough to accommodate two people if necessary. The furs covering it weren't as expensive as his own either, but they appeared to be more than enough to function, they were far more well-loved than his own. Luciaan sat him down on the bed and took the spot beside him.

"There… Now, what's wrong?" Luciaan asked patiently, offering a kind, reassuring smile as the pitiful prince caught his breath. He was clearly still quite shaken.

"I—" he swallowed thickly. "I had a—" he stopped abruptly. *How fucking pathetic of you.* But his desperate need for reassurance took hold faster as he met those kind, patient eyes.

"I had a nightmare, Luciaan." He mumbled it in the end, hoping the man wouldn't think less of him. "You were the first person I thought of."

"Your Grace—"

"Please, please, call me Robbinn." He was pleading with the man now. Begging to be seen as a person, not a prince.

"Robbinn." Luciaan repeated softly, reaching out to touch his face with an enormous hand, brushing away tears and guiding Robbinn to meet his eye once more. He found no judgment. He found no resentment. He found compassion. "It's okay. You're safe here, I won't let anything happen. I promise."

Those words were like the softest of blankets to the still trembling prince. He was safe. Luciaan spoke once more, following what appeared to be the most remarkable intuition he had ever personally witnessed.

"I think no less of you for coming to me, Robbinn. I'm here for you." He nodded against the warm hand on his cheek, his own moving to cradle it there before he could stop it.

His amber eyes locked with Luciaan's, seeing how beautiful the honey brown and icy blue actually were all over again. He was leaning closer before he realised what he was doing, and it was far too late to stop when he was suddenly kissing the man and to his shock being kissed back. He briefly thought he shouldn't be doing this, but it felt too good to stop – he was wrapped in strong, safe arms, kissing a man whom he trusted wholeheartedly.

Fuck it.

Chapter Seven

Robbinn wasn't sure how long he had spent in Luciaan's arms, snoozing in that warm comfort, but it must have been a while because before he knew it dawn had broken, and his comfort had to move.

"M'sorry," he mumbled sleepily, "horses have breakfast soon, you can stay here if you want to." With a yawn Luciaan stretched and stood as Robbinn whined pitifully.

"Father would kill me." He caught the man's hand before he could move away and met his eye once again to show his sincerity. "But thank you for this, I shouldn't have come but truly, thank you."

"S'no trouble, honestly." He rubbed tired eyes with his free hand and smiled. "You're welcome here whenever you want."

Robbinn practically glowed under his offer paired with that smile.

"I apologise if I have to take you up on that too often."

"There's no limit, don't you worry Robbinn."

Before he became too sluggish with whatever this feeling was, Robbinn stood, remembering he had to get back inside and quickly; he absolutely could not be seen.

"I ought to go, I don't want to get you into trouble."

Before too long Robbinn had stalked his way back inside and crept along the corridors – it was far too early for any servants to be around just yet; except perhaps Clauude, who took his role very seriously.

As he carefully passed his parents' chambers he heard voices and paused to listen, finding the door slightly ajar and light starting to spill out, he decided (admittedly against his better judgement), to glance inside.

Once his eyes had adjusted, his gaze settled on the form of his parents, wrapped in one another's arms, swaying from side to side as they sang quietly to each other. He wasn't sure how long he was watching for, just that he felt something warm in his soul that he hadn't felt before looking at his parents. He knew that they loved each other of course, but he had never seen something that indicated they were in love.

Robbinn had never heard what they were singing before, it must have been one that they knew from their own youth. They alternated between soft whistling for the other to sing verses about swearing that their love would guide them home, protect them in the waves of life and keep them warm at night. His mother's voice was beautiful and familiar, it felt as though she were bathing him in golden sunlight – gods only knew what it made her husband feel. Robbinn had never before heard the man sing, and it was far more perfect than he could have imagined, the roughness on the edge smoothed by the musical whistle from his wife, and came with none of the aggression Robbinn had thought to be permanent.

In that moment, time was slow and calm – as though the power of such fierce love could sway the very cosmos itself. The room was warm and light, so full of deep, true love; love Robbinn abruptly felt he shouldn't be watching, and was about to pull away from the door when his parents turned, and his mother's face caught his eye – what he saw was unmistakable. She gazed up at her husband, eyes full of hope, safety, affection – love.

Robbinn quickly pulled away and hid just out of sight, not

quite deterred enough to leave just yet. Apparently the song was over, which made him feel slightly sad as he had missed so much of it.

Oleyyna sighed. It wasn't a happy sigh. Something about it caused a knot to form in Robbinn's stomach.

"What is it, my dear?" The soft tone leaving his father's mouth felt foreign to his son, hidden just out of sight.

"You know very well what it is." There was no bite to her words. Something was troubling her that was clearly known to the two of them. "Why must you keep it from him?"

"Our son has enough of his own problems to worry about me. Not that I think he would."

What on earth are they talking about? the prince thought to himself.

"He's unprepared. If we tell him, he'll take ascending far more in stride."

Ascending? As in, ascending to the throne?

"Are you joking? He'd go mad. I don't want to tell him just yet."

"Darling Falkonn, you're dying. It pains me to say it, you know it does, but you don't have long."

"I know. He isn't ready to know just yet."

"He'll be less ready if you wait for too long. You're already playing a dangerous game."

Falkonn heaved a great sigh.

"I know. I'll tell him after he meets with the Daeemori girl."

His lips felt cold. Falkonn was dying. And fast, by the sound of it. He could hardly breathe as he raced back to his chambers, narrowly avoiding being seen by anyone.

Clauude came up with his tea a little later and Robbinn asked him to forewarn the other members of staff that he would be expecting a visitor in two weeks' time.

Overwhelmed by what he had just seen and heard, Robbinn decided to stay in his chambers, alone. His father was dying. According to his mother, he didn't have long either. And he saw his mother looking at the dying man with so much love.

He wasn't sure how long he had sat there in his bed, thinking, when it occurred to him. After he had replayed that look in his mother's eyes a thousand times in his head; after the shame of kissing that man had washed over him again and again did it finally click that he was desperately in love. There was no other explanation for what he was feeling – it was love. His heart near enough burned with it, this—this love.

"Ydmirr told me to explore. Hm," he muttered out loud to himself. "Explore. What did he mean? He said there was nothing wrong with not having a wife. He has a wife. The goddess of—the goddess of death." Suddenly this news felt like a divine signal, to look through history. Ydmirr told him to explore, now his wife was roaming the halls.

"That settles it. I'll start with the library, then the kingdom when Oserys is with me," he said to nobody but himself. Something about saying it out loud made the whole idea feel more final. For the moment, he pushed down the thought of his father dying. At least, until he was more prepared to deal with it.

Robbinn decided to start with the main library, rather than his personal one. Between his slender fingers he held a candle, outstretched just enough to light his way in the dark labyrinth of towering bookshelves, each lined snugly with book after book after book. It reminded him of walking through a forest at night on a path he didn't know very well.

He remembered that copies of the scriptures were kept deep in the belly of this place, away from damaging light and oils. Legend and subjects had it that the books held here were the second ever copies, although his father had maintained that they were the originals. The gods themselves weren't exactly much help, they had little reason to care about what was written, nor the memory to keep certainty of who said what and to whom. They were, after all, quite ancient beings.

Robbinn quietly removed the chain binding the book in place and opened it to begin reading about his gods. He read of the legendary tale of Pereggnir and Ydmirr's courting over countless battlefields, striding towards one another amidst the fighting, the blood, the screaming to share stolen kisses as though they were in the middle of a secret romantic garden; stories told of how they would dance among the dying men. Strangely, it seemed as though Pereggnir was the one to lead, which was odd considering she was a woman, and given today's custom. But it wasn't as though it didn't seem to be true, the other gods all seemed to confirm it – all but Pereggnir herself, as none had seen her in decades, she never was one to visit her statues.

The other goddesses Vyxena the goddess of life and Ydnias of thunder visited their temples and statues far more frequently than any others – it wasn't uncommon to find their statues in different poses in the mornings. If one were to ask a goddess for guidance, it was more than likely she would provide it.

But not Pereggnir. However, death worked in strange ways. He paused, his stomach dropping at the thought of his father's swiftly approaching demise as it followed the previous.

He took that as a sign to investigate the other gods.

Vyxena first. She was described as a woman with fiery red hair that reached her back, honey-coloured eyes and a strong figure; all her statues reminded Robbinn of his mother. Although their personalities did not match in the slightest, where Oleyyna was soft, kind and understanding, Vyxena was cruel.

She was the one who cursed innocents to lives of torture, of pain, feebleness, and sickness. She was the goddess who chose which children to be born without lungs, or which would be born with illnesses which would see them agonized for their few days of life. For it was not her sister, death, who chose when people died, she merely collected their souls and saw them through to the afterlife; it was life who decided that. Decided what they would become.

It was life who had cursed him like this. Cursed him to never love a woman, to constantly disappoint his father.

His hands gripped the delicate pages tightly as his hot rage flared within him, filling the hole that had dropped from him at the thought of his father's death. It bubbled and churned like lava in his chest as he read on, reminding himself of things he had only before learned in passing. Some part of him was glad that he never took his religious study seriously, as finding this now, when he truly needed somebody to blame was rather satisfying.

His eyes abruptly flicked over to the page on Ildyr, the god of the Ocean and Vyxena's lover. The god of the Ocean was vicious, destructive, and unforgiving. He was furious and churning and endless in a way that no other god quite managed to match. His statues had steely, harsh eyes, broad shoulders, and tight lips – reminding the prince of his father's appearance. Which, he thought, was quite an amusing coincidence, given that they too were fiercely in love.

According to his book, aside from being notoriously difficult to please, Ildyr created a great many ravenous monsters like merfolk and sirens to lure men into the crushing abyss of his embrace – the ferocious kraken and its smaller cousin being some other notable creations. It seemed that near enough every one of his ideas were devised purely to kill humans, the kelpie being Robbinn's least favourite. It lived in the moorland areas, hiding in the lakes waiting for a human to lure onto its back when it wore a pretty horse's form, only to drag them to the depths to drown and be feasted upon with freshwater sirens. He liked horses more than he did most people, and had often thought he may be one of the unlucky men likely to be tricked by one.

And thus, the god of the ocean was cast onto the pile of gods Robbinn held a grudge against, leaving only Ydnias, the goddess of thunder and Ydmirr whom he had not looked over in detail.

He knew very well of his own resemblance to Ydmirr – one of the few areas he and his father differed were the softness of his brow and his jaw, which he had inherited from his mother, but made him look strikingly similar to the god of war. Had he been born a peasant, or to any other than a fiercely protective royal mother, he would have been flung off the roof before he had taken his look at the world; the kingdom he belonged to saw any babies that resembled Ydmirr as omens of coming war, and thus promptly killed them. More than once when he had visited his people he had been called lucky. More often than not he had been spat on, had rocks and cow dung thrown at him, once he was even pissed on by an incredibly drunk, angry man from a second storey window. His brow furrowed with his fury at the memory.

Needless to say; he didn't visit his people very often any more.

Regardless of the issues the resemblance brought him, Robbinn thought quite highly of Ydmirr. He was not the easiest to work with as he could be difficult, abrasive, violent, and jealous; but he was a remarkably understanding being when appropriately pleased. Supposedly, anyway.

Robbinn had never had such an impression, although that could be because he was the first baby boy to resemble him that was not immediately executed in centuries. He didn't know for certain, but he certainly didn't want to find out.

Ydmirr's tales were mostly of the way he influenced humans to hate one another, whispered misunderstandings into their ears and caused miscommunications resulting in fighting. Fights often resulted in death, in the kingdom of Arkordouur. The streets were a breeding ground for loathing and discord – a place where poverty and excess met like a pair of ill-mannered stallions over a mare. Each man, woman and child felt as though they were hard done by the gods and by their status owing to the king's wealth – there was little to go around, but Falkonn seemed to relish in making things worse as he hoarded the lion's share of taxes like a dragon sat on his pile of gold. Of course, the reasoning he gave placed the blame on Robbinn's shoulders. A very brave knight once spoke up on behalf of the poor, asking why he needed so much of their money as he lounged in his throne like a serpent.

"Why, I need to train up my army, of course! My son, after all, is an omen of war, is he not?" The greedy king had hissed through a slimy sneer, looking at the boy as he had done it. When the public heard of this, there was outrage. The king, now utterly blameless, was henceforth able to pass through the kingdom in utter bliss, allowing his son to be verbally assaulted and fucking pissed on by angry men. He vividly remembered the look in his father's eye as he effortlessly shifted blame onto his young shoulders simply for the crime of sharing features with a god.

Even now, years after, he trembled with rage as he remembered it. He was but a powerless boy at the time, a boy who did as he was told, who sat there and took it like a good little prince when his father blamed him for the kingdom's struggle.

With an angry grunt and a thump of his clenched fist on the desk, he returned his attention to the delicate book in his grip, turning the page to Ydnias – the Goddess of Thunder. Until, that is, he became very abruptly horrified with himself.

He never hit things in his anger – Falkonn did that. Granted, his anger was very rapidly becoming a force he wasn't sure how to control, but he had never done that before. Becoming Falkonn was his worst nightmare, but he was starting to share more and more of his personality. The thought frightened him horribly. Many a time before now he had vowed to himself to never become his revolting father, but he refused to let himself begin to fall into the pattern with a single moment of rage.

In desperate need of distraction, Robbinn returned to the book and the legend that was Ydnias – the Goddess of Thunder. She was ruthless and unforgiving, but gave as much as she took. There were many parables of how she and Ydmirr were close friends, making fierce warriors out of one another. Interestingly, she was depicted as a tall, strong woman with dark skin, black hair, and pure white eyes – an appearance he abruptly found to be familiar, but from where he wasn't quite sure. It was said that women born resembling her were strong, fierce, and independent. Many supposedly had become formidable warriors in other nations – Falkonn would never allow a woman in his army. Perhaps Robbinn's would be different.

Before he knew it more than half the day had passed and Clauude came knocking with soft shortbreads and a few questions for him, mostly pertaining to the room Oserys and any of her staff would be staying in. He felt a sudden surge of gratitude for the distraction from the depressing truth that his life was controlled by gods and nothing he did would change that. In truth he didn't know what Oserys liked, nor had he ever been visited by a lady for more than a day, so he had absolutely no clue what he was doing. Regardless, he put on his princely confidence like makeup to hide uncertainty instead of blemishes and followed Clauude to observe the work done.

The suite was large but intimate and private, decorated as lavishly as the rest of his home. It seemed fine, but he didn't exactly know what women needed for an extended stay. Therefore he decided that any more detailed questions about women would be put forward to his mother, who knew far better than he did.

Once he was finished with his duties, Robbinn walked down to the stables to visit Luciaan for a short talk. Despite how wrong he felt about it, Luciaan's company already felt like a drug to him that he was swiftly becoming addicted to.

"Hi Luciaan." He leaned on the stable door as his muse was grooming the horse inside – the proud grey Clyde.

"Hello prince! Still up for a ride today?"

Robbinn blinked.

"Oh! Yes, yes I am! I do apologise, it has been quite an exhausting morning, the Lady Daeemori is visiting me in two weeks, I had to start preparing her wing early."

"That sounds like fun, I've heard she's nice."

"We got on rather well at the ball – it's just as friends to begin with."

"Of course, I hope things go well with her." Something about his tone suggested he did not want it to go well. Was it perhaps a hint of jealousy? Robbinn decided not to question him further and just go to enjoy his ride.

That night he stalked silently through the castle halls, dodging creaky floorboards and slipping past staff to edge out of sight of all the windows to see Luciaan again. Tentatively, suddenly remembering his disappointed voice earlier, Robbinn knocked on the head groom's door.

It opened momentarily to reveal his very tall, very handsome... something. Lover? Friend? Person-he-goes-out-hacking-with-but-also-sometimes-kisses? Surely there was a word for this but he certainly didn't know it. The slightly soured expression he wore melted into something far softer as their eyes met – reminding the prince of a comically oversized, besotted puppy.

"Come in, quickly."

"Thank you," he muttered as he stepped inside, taking in the enchanting aroma of Luciaan that made every inch of him tingle with something he didn't quite understand.

"I missed you." Luciaan whipped around as though Robbinn had blurted out that there was a unicorn in his house, or something equally as outrageous.

"What?" But he didn't seem angry as he stepped in closer.

"I missed you. While I was working. I... I think I might like you." Robbinn took a step this time.

"I like you too."

"I don't know what to call it – this feeling – you make me feel like there's hope for good in the world. It's like I'm on fire with it, but in a good way! I've never felt like this before. You make me feel a dangerous sort of safe, Luciaan."

He knew what to call it. Of course he did, he'd already decided it was love, he just couldn't say it yet.

"Dangerous?"

"I feel like if you were by my side I could look the gods in the face and tell them to fuck off."

Yet.

Chapter Eight

Before he knew it, two weeks had passed and Oserys was due to arrive that morning. A chilly, wet, miserable morning as the orange leaves were truly beginning to fall – before too long winter would be here.

Silently he hoped that Oserys wouldn't be too forward, as he had been rather friendly with Luciaan in the nights since his confession. Luciaan's response had been that he didn't know how to use words like that, and he had offered to show him his feelings instead. That had been the night he discovered exactly why pleasures of the flesh had been quite strictly forbidden – so naturally he had been to do it again. And again, and again. Sleeping with Luciaan had quickly become just as addictive as his company and he just couldn't get enough, and to make things worse it felt more than good enough to be worth the shame that often followed.

Luciaan also liked to leave reminders of what they had done in the form of bitemarks and bruises – which he truly did love, but generated another conflicting feeling when he caught himself biting his lip at the sight of one through the mirror as he ran long, pale fingers over it. Thankfully he owned numerous high collared items of clothing to hide them, and could trust Clauude to ignore them.

Robbinn stood by the great oak door with a well-rehearsed smile which hid his anxiety rather beautifully, buttoned in tight-ly to his tunic with a long cloak over his shoulders as he await-ed his guest, Clauude and Luciaan beside him. In the pouring rain. For what felt like hours.

Eventually – or more accurately half an hour later as the rain began to look more like a storm – Oserys atop her enormous jet-black steed followed by presumably her handmaiden on a smaller horse rode up to him.

"Your Grace! I do apologise, I seem to have brought Northern weather with me!"

"Lady Daeemori! How wonderful it is to see you, regardless of any storms! Come in out of the rain, Clauude will show your handmaiden to your suite and our head groom here will take your horses and see them settled."

"Thank you, I'd like Arriella to share the suite with me, if that's quite agreeable?"

"Of course, we thought you might prefer that, there is more than enough room for the both of you."

Seemingly well within her comfort zone, Oserys truly radiated command – even Robbinn felt obliged to follow her lead, as did Luciaan when she turned to him.

"Warden here has cooked oats twice daily at home, usually warm if he's been worked in the rain just before, he doesn't get on with other horses unless you have a very boisterous stallion he can bully," she gestured to her horse as she dismounted and handed the handsome beast off, Arriella doing the same behind her, "otherwise put him next to Arriella's mare Daisy. Both of them are used to access to fields all day, all night."

"Right – uh... I'll put him in with my horse, mares are kept in a different barn. If you'd like a ride, let someone know and I'll saddle them for you." He actually stumbled a bit on his words. Robbinn leered at him while nobody was looking.

"Thank you, I'll remember that. What was your name?"

"Luciaan, my lady. Luciaan Ciniswood." He bowed his

head politely as his hands were occupied by horses.

"That's a nice name, rare isn't it?" She had an odd expression as she spoke to him – entirely unreadable. It unnerved Robbinn slightly.

"Certainly around here. I think Mother wanted me to stand out."

"She definitely succeeded. I won't keep you, but if my horse is well cared for I'll see to it you're well rewarded."

"Thank you, my lady!" Luciaan bowed his head once more as he turned away and Clauude did the same, leading Arriella and helping her with her mistress' belongings.

Now alone with his guest, Robbinn could look at her properly. Half of her hair was pulled into similar plaits to the ones his mother wore, flat against her scalp and pulled into a loose tie at the back of her head where the rest of it hung free, a couple longer ones with dark green cord and silver thread woven in. She wore no skirts, instead tunic and trousers with lacing down her leg, presumably all fur lined, considering her home was so cold and wet. The cloak about her shoulders was a similar deep green to the cords in her hair, lined with thick grey fur, presumably from a wolf. She stood tall and strong, easily as tall as he was, a stunning broadsword hanging at her hip. The weapon truly shone with her power, undoubtedly a devoted blade. Robbinn hadn't made such a connection with any training swords, the closest had been his pathetic letter opener that other's couldn't lift.

Robbinn felt his cheeks heat slightly with embarrassment at his humiliatingly pitiful weapon in comparison to hers, for it meant she had already proven herself worthy of it. They were similar in age, and that meant she had probably been relatively young when she did that. He very abruptly remembered the suitor's ball. She had not only thwarted an assassination attempt, but killed the perpetrator too, without hesitation.

He began to lead her through the halls for a quaint little tour before meeting with his parents and seeing her to her suite for rest.

"I must thank you for coming here, I know my letter was written with great haste."

"Not at all! I was delighted to hear from you, it's a pleasure to be here – we got along so well at the ball. I thought so, anyway."

"I quite agree! I believe we agreed to spar, while you were here?"

"We did! I do hope that plan doesn't change?" she smiled pleasantly, seemingly quite excited.

"Of course not, I'll show you to the training grounds perhaps tomorrow? You've travelled a long way, I'd imagine you'd like to rest?"

"Yes, that would be lovely – after all, as comfortable as my dear warden is, a long ride is still a long ride."

"I understand, if you would like to ride any of our horses in the coming days to give him a rest too we have a vast number of wonderful steeds, many of whom I have personally ridden and can attest to their attitude, we have lots of beautiful hacking routes that I'm sure you'd enjoy." He added almost excitedly.

"That sounds rather lovely, would I be right in saying natural beauty is one of the main reasons the castle was built here?"

"It is! The natural wonders of our surroundings are rather enchanting, although I must warn you to be careful of the lakes, we have a few kelpies and freshwater sirens that live in them; even a dwarf kraken that isn't easy to convince not to eat you."

"I'll remember that! We have a great many species of aquatic dragons at home, but they're quite skittish of people, so it isn't often a worry. Would I be able to observe any kelpies from a distance? I've never seen one in person." She sounded quite excited by the idea of seeing one. After all, the kelpie was quite a rare beast. Oserys didn't hold his eye as they spoke, instead she took in her surroundings – the magnificent paintings of kings and warriors passed, the tapestries, and the ornate decorations.

"Quite possibly, I shall pose the question to Luciaan for you, he knows every route like the back of his hand." He added the last part hastily, almost as though justifying speaking to the man. Hopefully Oserys wouldn't notice. Or at least if she did, she wouldn't say anything.

"Thank you, I appreciate you going out of your way." She bowed her head as she spoke, marking her respect.

"It's my pleasure! I'd like to make your visit as pleasurable as possible, my dear lady."

It took just over an hour to finally reach the throne room where the king, his wife, and his advisors sat like gargoyles, risen at least a foot from the ground to allow them to look down on everyone in the room.

Robbinn drew himself up to his full height in a display of faux confidence he hoped would fool his father. It did however, surprise him when he had to swallow something hot and angry in the back of his throat at the idea of facing the man.

Saving that for examination later, (although he knew that 'later' truly meant never), Robbinn strode into the throne room with his guest in tow.

"Father," he began although he faltered at the astounding sight of his father looking horribly ill, but he continued regardless: "This is the Lady Oserys Daeemori, second of her name, heir to the Daeemori legacy. She has kindly consented to visit me for unofficial business, as we would like to get to know one another. If memory serves, I believe you two met when she

86

thwarted the attempt on your life at my ball."

"We did," Falkonn hissed, looking down his nose at them with a horrible expression – almost as though he was attempting to smile, "thank you, son. Lady Daeemori, it is a pleasure to see you here again."

Oserys gave a low, respectful bow. "It is a true honour, Your Grace. Prince Robbinn was very kind to invite me here."

"He made an excellent choice! You are a formidable woman. But I shall not keep you, after such a long journey you must be exhausted – go and rest, we shall speak more another time."

"Thank you, Your Grace."

"Thank you, Father."

With that they bowed once more together, and left the room. Finally after ascending countless stairs Robbinn brought the beautiful Oserys to her suite.

"My chambers are just across the way if you need anything, I thought being close might be more desirable."

"Thank you, prince. I'd like to ride out with you tomorrow morning if you have time, I like a horse with some blood, and I rather prefer stallions to anything else."

"Absolutely, I shall see to it you have something suitable. Shall we meet out here just after daybreak?"

"That sounds perfect, thank you."

"If you need anything do just ring for a servant, and someone will come, for now please do get some rest." With that he smiled, bowed, and turned to leave as the door closed behind him.

Immediately he raced down to the stables, careful to hide just inside the tree line to avoid being seen.

"Luciaan?" he called out into the deserted stables.

"I'm here." Luciaan stuck his head out from inside a stable with a smile. All the horses were out, and the stableboys dismissed.

"I was just coming to let you know," he leaned on the stable door. It was empty, freshly mucked out. Bored hands smoothed the metal edge beneath them. "Oserys wanted to ride out tomorrow. Before I forget I just wanted…" he trailed off, staring at Luciaan. He was covered in a light film of sweat, sleeves rolled up, unbuttoned tunic just enough to help him stay cool. "—to say she wants a stallion. Tomorrow morning. She said something with blood."

Luciaan propped up his pitchfork against the wall and unlocked the stable door with a small, subtle smile. Robbinn stared up into his enchanting eyes and promptly forgot about absolutely everything else.

"Is that so?" his huge hands settled at Robbinn's slender waist, making him feel hot all over. "I think that can be arranged."

He made a pathetic little whimpering noise as Luciaan opened the stable door between them and guided him inside, shutting both the top and bottom parts behind them. Before he knew it, his back was pressed against the wall, heart racing and every inch of him starting to tingle. Summoning some confidence, Robbinn walked his fingers up Luciaan's chest to tease the remaining buttons holding the tunic in place.

"However might I thank you, oh wonderful groom of mine?"

"I can think of something. It's just us in here, maybe you can help me release some tension." Robbin smiled, wrapping his arms around those strong shoulders as he leaned up to kiss the smile off Luciaan's lips.

"I think that can be arranged."

Now this, Robbinn thought to himself, *was the best way to test out horse bedding*. While it wasn't the most absorbent of materials, straw was comfortable and warm under his back, and eventually his knees as he drooled into it face down. In that moment he could think of nothing but the overwhelming pleasure Luciaan drove into his body with unimaginable rhythm, the feeling of fingers digging into his hips, the sound of his breaths, the smell of sweat and straw. Nothing else mattered.

By the time they finished, it was almost evening, but they didn't move immediately. Instead, they decided to lie there, Robbinn curled into Luciaan's side, an enormous arm around his shoulder, as he traced nonsense patterns into his partner's skin.

"I'm glad we met that day." Luciaan spoke so softly that Robbinn almost thought he had imagined it. He craned his neck to get a better look at the dopey, adoring expression on his face.

"You are?"

"I am. Makes everything worth it now."

"What do you mean, everything?" he tilted his head with the question.

"A lot of things I haven't told you yet." Robbinn frowned and opened his mouth to retort. "I haven't told anyone, before you think badly." He chuckled softly at the look on his prince's face.

"I see." There was silence for a moment. "What if I told you something I've never told anyone?" he offered hopefully, "And you don't have to tell me even then, but I'd like to know."

"I'm not willing to make a promise. I'll tell you eventually. Probably. Just not yet, I don't feel close enough to you."

"Excuse me? Did you miss the part where you just fucked my brains out?" he scoffed, starting to get irritated. Robbinn certainly felt close enough to Luciaan to share that sort of thing.

"No, that's—ah – that's not what I meant." He looked away, frustrated, and promptly looked up at the roof.

"Go on then." Robbinn folded his arms, glaring.

"I mean more that it's been a while and you still don't have a name for this. Whatever we are. I like you a lot, Robbinn. But I've lived with being gay long enough to know my worth. At least some of it."

Like the sound of a cup shattering the realisation that Luciaan didn't know Robbinn loved him so much it made his very bones ache dawned upon him. He knew it, he knew it like he knew his own name. He just didn't know what to do with the shame it brought him, with the feeling of such intense failure and hatred towards the gods that made him everything his stupid fucking father told him was the worst thing he could possibly be. He knew he loved the man he was snuggled up against. He just couldn't say it yet.

Luciaan abruptly turned his head back towards him, to look at him properly with sad, almost tortured eyes.

I know nothing of your secrets, my love, he thought, staring up into icy blue and honey brown with his lips parted to speak, yet no words came. *Your past is an enigma. A book locked away, only to be obtained by the most worthy. And worthy I am not.*

"What are we to you? Are we courting? Are we friends? Am I just someone you go to rant at then have sex with? Are we something to you?"

We're everything. His heart screamed it like a dying animal, as though his words were both the knife killing it and the salve healing it.

And yet he couldn't say it.

"Luciaan," he paused, stumbling on his words as he searched for the right ones, "I'm so confused. This is so new for me, I'm sorry if you think I've led you along. I think this is something. I still don't know what to call it. I just know I don't want to lose you."

That seemed to be enough. For now, at least, as Luciaan's eyes softened again and he leaned over to kiss him on the forehead.

"Okay. That's enough for me. I know it's hard, it was for me, gods know what it must be like to be a prince and navigate this."

"Your patience with me means more than I can put into words, Luci."

"I'll tell you what, let me show you something that helped me sometime. Maybe later this week? If Oserys wants to come she can too."

"Really? I'd like that. I'll ask her if she wants to tomorrow." He smiled, now rather more than tired. Despite his comfortable, even blissful position, he did have to move soon. Gods forbid he was seen by someone who might report back to Falkonn.

Reluctantly he sat up and leaned over Luciaan, propping himself up on one arm to brush hair from his eyes and lean down to kiss him just once more before he left and mumble a small, sincere 'thank you' into his lips.

Once he managed to drag himself away from Luciaan, Robbinn made his way back up to his chambers. During his walk he was surprised by a feeling of hope as he thought about Oserys. She could be the end of this awful feeling of inadequacy, the fear of his kingdom's reaction if he was openly gay. The thought of marrying her made all of that go away. He could possibly gain public favour as something more than the omen of war. He may even be able to produce an heir to his throne! Robbinn almost skipped with delight as he took himself up to bed.

As Oserys was staying opposite him, he passed her door on

the way to his own. A fact that wouldn't have mattered, had he not heard voices. Two voices, Oserys and her hand maiden presumably. What they were saying he couldn't tell, but suddenly he found himself wanting to know. He bit his lip and decided to listen anyway.

Robbinn pressed his ear against the door, being careful not to cause it to creak. He held his breath as he listened to them muttering quietly to one another.

"I'm so lucky you picked me," Arriella's breathless voice muttered.

"It was always going to be you, my love. I have this with nobody else, and I want it with nobody else." He heard Oserys shuffle in the sheets.

"Don't be silly – what about –"

"Fuck them. Fuck everyone else. Fuck everyone but you. In the bad way, at least. Fucking you is quite enjoyable."

Arriella laughed, finally. Robbinn's heart dropped. His fingers went numb, and his eyes started to sting. He knew his heart belonged to Luciaan, yes, but he was praying that Oserys was a suitable woman, if only to please the kingdom. Or rather, his wonderful father.

At a loss, Robbinn pulled away from the door and muttered a single word to himself as thought after horrible thought began to race through his mind like spooked horses.

"Shit."

Chapter Nine

Through the looming threat of tears Robbinn forced shaking hands to obey him as he opened his chamber door. Suddenly he couldn't breathe, he couldn't see properly, every wall was closing in on him. His heart pounded like a drum of war, thudding so hard against his ribs he felt it in his ears. He didn't understand what was happening. He felt the prickle of sweat on his back as his whole body started to tremble and tears started to roll down his cheeks. In desperation he clawed at his tunic collar, dragging it away from his throat as it closed up, trembling legs starting to give out from under him.

Some time passed like this, gasping for breath, and crying, gods he couldn't stop crying, to the point that he felt sick – there was no way for him to track how much time had really gone by. But it felt like an eternity before he could drag himself into his bed and hide from the world under his covers.

By the morning Robbinn felt at least a little better, crawling out from under the relative safety of his covers to face the world full of disappointment, cruelty, and shame. But at the least, he was going to be out hacking this morning. Perhaps he could simply ignore what he heard last night and try to be friends with Oserys, to begin with at least. Finding the best in things was something he had found more and more difficult in recent months, and this blow now seemed to him like the icing on an awful cake.

When he stepped out of his chambers Oserys was waiting

for him, twisting the last of her silver buttons into place at her wrist. Once more she wore no skirts, but a similar black, laced pair of trousers to the ones she wore the previous day and a rather elaborate green tunic – it was intricately decorated with gold and silver thread around each seam, leading into a woven pattern across her chest that reminded him of twisted thorns made from metal ribbons. All of it met in the centre, resting on her sternum where there was something Robbinn had never before seen. He didn't know what it was – a flat, ovular, shiny, black object with some degree of carving on it, extremely careful, delicate lines. It was about an inch and a half in length, secured with all that metal like a protective charm.

"Good morning, my lady! Did you sleep well?" he greeted her politely, trying hard to forget about what he heard by gazing at her hair, which this morning rested in two plaits, close to her head which finished halfway down her chest, decorated with silver rings.

"Good morning, Your Grace! I slept wonderfully, please do give my thanks to whoever prepared these chambers for me." She smiled, giving a soft bow of her head as her request is laid.

"It would be my pleasure! Do you still want to ride out with me this morning?"

"Of course! I hope your groom has found something suitable for me."

"I'm sure he has, although I suppose the only way to find out is to head down." He extended a hand in the direction of the stairs leading to the ground floor. "My father is expecting us for breakfast, but he always eats late so we have more than enough time."

"What an honour!" she smiled, taking on a joking tone as the two walked together. "Do all your guests get such special treatment?"

Robbinn laughed.

"They would if I had any."

It was a chilly, wet morning just like the one before – the first hints of winter were truly starting to show. It wouldn't be long now until the whole grounds were covered in a blanket of snow and his chambers would be more blanket than space. He liked winter visually, but not the cold. He hated the cold so much that it was completely unfathomable that Oserys lived in the cold all year round.

As they approached, Luciaan led out two proud looking flea-bitten greys with handsome roman noses, long legs, and a degree of fire in their eyes and Robbinn almost squealed in delight as his head groom introduced the horses to his guest.

"Good morning my lady, Your Grace. These are Cloud and Clyde! They're full brothers, Clyde is a year Cloud's senior but they're very similar. They're nice as a pair to ride out, but I'll warn you that they can feed off each other."

"What handsome boys! I must thank you, these two are exactly what I like in a horse. Do you have a favourite of the two?"

"I like them both for different reasons, Clyde is far more proud and won't go through puddles, but Cloud is bolder and more explosive. I think Robbinn likes Clyde more, is that right Your Grace?" Luciaan met his eye with a twitch of his brow as he remembered. Gods, Robbinn was so very in love with this man.

"Yes, that's right! Be warned that they both jump like deer, which feels very odd for the first few times." Robbinn smiled fondly at the two strange stallions as he took Clyde from Luciaan's hand. "I'll be taking my favourite, if that's agreeable."

"Please do! I'll be perfectly happy with Cloud." She nodded happily, stroking the great beast's nose.

Although he hadn't seen much of him, Oserys' horse warden was enormous, far taller than his own Solmyrer, only a little bigger than Luciaan's Pereggnir; a formidable black stallion who looked like he could kill a man in a single strike and know exactly how to do it efficiently. For a horse, anyway.

Without much further fuss, Robbinn and Oserys mounted their steeds and headed out at an uncomfortable jogging pace, as evidently being out together was far, far more exciting than whatever their riders were asking.

"My lady, might I ask you something?"

"You might, depending on what it is."

"Have you ever seen a unicorn?"

"No," she tilted her head thoughtfully. "I can't say I have."

"We might get to see one if we're lucky! There's a very handsome one that frequents a certain spot, I thought it might be a nice one to visit now?"

"How exciting! I'd love to go there, even if we don't see him." Her eyes lit up with excitement as they picked further along the path, deeper into the forest.

When the time to finally allow their horse to break into canter it was utterly glorious – the brothers beneath them raced each other, tossing their heads and kicking out behind them. Oserys seemed more than happy on horseback – she sat tall and strong with a beautiful smile on her face as the beast under her used every ounce of his strength.

Looking over at her like this he suddenly realised why Ydnias' appearance was so familiar to him following the ball – Oserys resembled her. Which of course made a great amount of sense, given the aura of power she commanded. He liked that about her; she was strong and respected without even trying to be, it all seemed to come with such wonderful ease. Some part of him wanted to be jealous of her, as he had to fight for many to see him as something other than an omen of war, but that part was quiet when he remembered that Oserys didn't seem to view him that way at all. There was no resentment in her expression when she looked at him, no disgust at his apparent weakness, but above all she treated him so much like a person. That particular quality being something he adored about Luciaan.

Before too long the path opened up into a now very familiar clearing with a large pond at the centre, where the horses knew to stop after so long of the same. Robbinn spoke in hardly a whisper.

"If we're quiet, he might come and say hello – we'll have to wait until he feels comfortable."

No sooner had they settled in for a long wait did the unicorn appear, in better health than ever. His golden horn and perfectly white coat near enough glowing, his blue eyes twinkling with intelligence as he gave a short little whinny. Cloud and Clyde called back and he approached, slightly unsure of the new human but comforted by familiar horses.

Oserys all but glowed at the sight of such an elusive creature walking right up to greet her steed. She didn't try to touch him, or greet him in any way. She just watched with adoration for something so beautifully pure, untouched by fear or evil, something that indicated perfect health in its environment.

Neither of the two spoke until the unicorn wandered off to something more interesting.

"Unicorns can only be conceived under a new moon, in an area with perfect conditions. There must be perfect food and water sources, no possibility of predation, no disease to the vegetation, and most importantly almost no humans." She paused, glancing around at the stunning area around her. "Having unicorns is quite possibly the best thing to promote the health of your land. You must be so incredibly proud!"

"I am indeed! I read the diaries of the founding Carbeu king, he mentioned having the castle built where it was because of the unicorns here, and decided it essential to keep them here. He specifically named it a bad omen to the kingdom if the unicorns disappeared." He was eager to tell her about him as king Robbinn I was a man of true legend.

"You were named after him, were you not?"

"I was indeed! Him and Robbinn II, the great warrior. Father had hoped that I would be like them. Just another thing for him to be disappointed in me for, I suppose."

"My father wanted a son. He didn't let his wife dying while giving birth to a daughter stop him from raising one." She sounded fond where he was bitter.

"Was it difficult for him?" grateful for the opportunity to speak on common ground.

"At first, when I was very young. He's never expressed disappointment in me though, but if I hadn't taken to the training as well as I did things probably would've been very different. What about yours?"

"I was a disappointment from birth, pretty much. He hoped I'd come out the spitting image of Ildyr, not an omen of war. I think as I've grown I've come to look just enough like Father to infuriate him, but still close enough to Ydmirr to be considered a bad omen."

"That must be awful." She didn't try to defend Falkonn, which surprised him. She seemed to just hear and understand his feelings. He gaped at her.

"Y—yes." In his shock he sort of trailed off, realising he didn't need to justify himself to her. "It is awful. It feels like he loathes my very existence, even if he doesn't say it."

"He doesn't have to say it, does he?" she offered politely.

"You took the words right out of my mouth." His lips

twitched into a weak smile. Frantically he searched for more to say, without the need to justify himself he was suddenly quite out of his depth. "Thank you, for listening to me. Would you tell me more about your father? He is quite legendary as I'm sure you needn't be told."

"It would be my pleasure! Father and I have a rather strong relationship, once he healed from my mother's death. I'm grateful that he left the pain he had from that out of my upbringing. It was harder for him to accept that he wouldn't get a son to carry his name, but he still raised me to fight the way he would've with a son. He never once made me feel like I disappointed him, more so that my sex was an unexpected difference, but he assures me he loves me very dearly. I only heard that my gender was difficult for him through a particularly nasty servant who liked to make little girls cry who promptly lost his job." Her voice was fond and happy when she spoke of her father, only slightly bitter as she remembered the servant.

"Would you say you have made him proud?" Robbinn asked carefully.

"Yes," she replied with an edge of pride showing in her face and voice. "He told me so the day I earned the loyalty of this blade. I was thirteen when I did it, he told me he was at least sixteen when he won his first sword."

"May I hear the story, if you don't mind sharing with a spoilt prince like me?" Oserys huffed a small laugh as she sat back in her saddle, casting scarlet eyes up into the canopy as she feigned pouring over such a little question.

"Of course, you may, prince." She smiled. "Settle in, it's quite a long story for one so old."

Robbinn felt himself rise in his seat just a little, like a child snuggling himself up in bed but insisting he is paying attention to his bedtime story. If she had truly won the blade, nobody else would ever be able to lift it until she died.

"It was originally my mother's sword – I'm told she too was quite the warrior – and it was owned by her for years after she died. I went every day to try and move it but no luck, it didn't trust me yet." She didn't look at him as she spoke, instead kept her gaze forward on the path before her. "It didn't stop being hers when she died, I think they had been a pair for many, many years. Perhaps it was 'grieving', I don't know. The day its jewels went dull again I could lift it, but it still wasn't mine: as I'm sure you know, owned blades help their masters to lift them. From that day I trained with it, I trusted it, I even took it to my chambers at night."

She paused, smiling as she took a sip of water from the skin at her hip. Robbinn listened like he was reading the best book of his life, and he was just about to get to the exciting bit.

"The day it did decide to trust me started as normal. I woke, ate, then trained. That particular day I was practicing mounted swordsmanship, so I was riding my darling warden out in our land when highwaymen pounced upon us; intending to rob my father and kill or kidnap me into something unimaginably awful. I killed them all, without hesitation. There was a moment when it all felt so good, cleaving flesh from bone with every strike and spilling the guts of men who truly intended to harm me – I admit I lost myself in it – somewhere in that moment my very soul fused with the sword. And from that day, she belonged to me." Some of the jewels in the hilt glowed softly when its master spoke so fondly of the day. Robbinn, however, felt sick. He had never before taken a life, and yet here was this woman talking about it like understanding how to communicate with a horse for the first time. However instead of telling Oserys this, he swallowed it and took to congratulating her.

"Gods, what a legendary tale! And you were so young, that's incredible, dear lady!"

"Thank you! I shall admit that winning over the blade didn't dampen the guilt I felt for killing them. That felt like a mighty sin, until I visited the Temple of Ydnias, near my home. She visited me that day and told me I would be welcomed into her halls after my death. That made me feel much better about it." She admitted almost sheepishly, glancing back as though to reassure him.

"I see! Even the Daeemori family is human after all!" he joked. "Might I ask if it gets easier?"

"With practice, yes. Strong faith also tends to help, the gods are quite fair." She nodded, understanding he needed to speak about it quite desperately.

"I see... Thank you. Before I open myself to similar, might I ask you just one more thing?"

"I don't see why not." She turned to look at him properly this time.

"What is that? On your chest there?" He pointed feebly to the strange ovular object woven into her chest piece.

"Oh, this?" She seemed surprised, lifting her hand to touch it. "It's a dragon scale, carved with sigils. Supposed to be good luck, wards off evil."

"A dragon scale?" his eyes grew to the size of dinner plates as he stared at it. "The beast this came off must have been enormous!"

"A Greater Northern Dragon, this particular one was on the larger side of mega class." She gave a small, proud smile; head turned just a little away from him. Robbinn stared at her, mouth hanging agape. How on earth could he have forgotten that Oserys lived in the North, where the Northern Greater and Minor dragons were native! She must see them almost every day at home, hell, she may even have one as a pet! Surely he had realised this before, which must be where he was getting this sense of déjà vu. When he thought back, he remembered that while writing to her and reading about dragons he had in fact been clubbed over the head with the very same realisation.

With a pleased hum, he looked around his glorious, verifiably perfect woodland and turned to his guest.

"Thank you for enlightening me, it must mean a lot to you." He paused for a breath, noticing how easily it came. Robbinn felt almost as at ease with Oserys as he did with Luciaan. "If you have any questions, please feel free to ask me! I have taken up far too much time on this ride interrogating you, yet you have committed no crimes!"

"Thank you! And yes, it does mean the world to me. I'd bring cities to their ruin if this was taken from me... If the subject isn't too sore, I'd love to know what the king is really like in the flesh. I've heard many rumours, but I'd like to hear from you."

Robbinn was slightly taken aback by this question. He didn't know these rumours. As far as Robbinn was aware, he was the unpopular member of his family, Falkonn was the revered king...

But the way Oserys spoke about these rumours suggested that Falkonn wasn't as loved and respected as the man so often insisted he was...

"He's... How do I describe him? He has exceedingly high expectations, but he can be cruel and vindictive. He prefers to show things rather than say them, things like pride in me—"

"I'm sorry, I know I'm interrupting, but do you mean your father has never told you he's proud of you?" she sounded baffled by the idea that he had implied Falkonn had never once told his son he was proud of him.

Which of course wasn't true.

Was it?

Devastatingly the more he thought and searched for an example, the less he could find one. All of a sudden the white hot rage he kept finding in himself reared its ugly head and told him this was why it was here.

"No," Robbinn answered slowly, "he hasn't ever said that to me, now that I think about it. He's told me how to make him proud, how not to disappoint him." Gods, the more he tried to justify it the worse it started to sound.

"I see." She spoke as though that were all she needed to hear about the king.

"When you see him, don't show weakness. He'll see it. He always sees it."

"Understood. I wouldn't normally, but for the king I shall have to bite my tongue. He shouldn't treat you like that."

That statement made Robbinn feel strangely validated.

"Good... Would you like to come with me on a trip later this week? I'm not sure how far it is, Luciaan wouldn't tell me, but he told me to invite you. That more than likely includes your handmaiden, Arriella."

"I think that would be lovely, thank you." She smiled once more.

Chapter Ten

Cloud and Clyde raced each other home not long after their riders' conversation faded into something far less serious. Thundering hooves signalled their arrival and prompted Luciaan to stand outside to meet them, on the back of his own horse Pereggnir to walk the puffing boys off. He had a dog at his horse's heel, a large black sighthound that Robbinn had never seen before.

"Who's this, Luciaan?" Robbinn asked, looking kindly at the dog as he rode up, Oserys beside him patting her steed and dismounting.

"My dog, Bonnie. A friend borrowed her for ratting, only just had her back. Say hello if you want, she's relatively friendly. Can be pretty aloof though." Luciaan gestured to the dog – Bonnie – as he leaned over to put headcollars over the horse's bridles and tie their ropes to Pereggnir's saddle.

Robbinn didn't need asking twice – he squatted down and offered his hand out to the long, elegant dog. She looked at him, considered, then trotted over with her tail wagging and sniffed his outstretched hand. Robbinn briefly considered the idea that she could smell Luciaan on him as she let him pet her. Only the man's amused hum broke his thought.

"She likes you, Your Grace."

"Ha, I like her too! I shall have to come down and ride more often, just for an excuse to see her." He grinned up at Luciaan while his back was to Oserys. Of course, he meant an excuse to see Luciaan, not his dog.

When he stepped away, Oserys greeted her too, and received similar reception which made Robbinn feel an odd sort of sad as Luciaan commented on her remarkable mood that morning, but he didn't understand why he felt that way. Carefully he stored it in that dark corner of his mind for examination at a later date. Which of course, if he had anything to do with it, really meant that he would try his hardest to forget about it.

With the attitude of a man heading for the gallows Robbinn trudged up to the dining room with Oserys floating along beside him, the absolute picture of serene beauty after a few moments to freshen themselves. Even as a man with little appreciation for women, Robbinn had to admit that she was one of the most beautiful creatures he'd ever laid eyes on. Her cheeks and lips were slightly pink from the exertion of a good gallop, and she had fixed her hair so that the top half was plaited and the rest laid down in perfect ringlets over her chest, littered with a few thin plaits with silver rings and green cord. But her eyes were what held the most beauty.

He couldn't tell what it was, but something made her scarlet eyes shine like rubies formed with dragon fire. Such a striking eye colour was incredibly rare in most of the world, including the continent the Carbeu family ruled over to the point that many with red eyes were considered demigods before statues in enough of the gods' likeness were formed that they could visit them and dispel this thought.

Oserys could be a goddess though, with beauty quite as perfect as hers.

Falkonn and his wife sat at the head of the dining table, waiting for Robbinn to bring his guest. He sucked in a breath that was far too hard to take and drew himself up to his full height, projecting similar calm to Oserys as he led her into the room. Head held high, trying not to blink too much. Suddenly the white-hot rage that had been giving him such courage was gone, hidden away at the sight of such a terrible beast. Silently he hoped it would return.

"Good morning, Father, Mother. Oserys and I would like to thank you for sharing your time with us for breakfast." He smiled, hoping his nerves wouldn't show as he offered Oserys the seat closest to the king. She appeared far less at ease than she was earlier, but remembered polite conversation and even gave a courtesy to both of Robbinn's parents.

"It's an honour to be invited to your table, Your Grace." Her head, usually held up proudly remained low and submissive, which was an odd sight to say the least.

"We're glad to have you, aren't we Oleyyna?" He gave a twisted smile that didn't suit him, looking over at his flaming haired wife.

"We are indeed! And such a fine woman you are, my son has good taste!" Oleyyna smiled politely from her fine cup of tea.

"Certainly he does! Come my girl, sit!" there was something off about his father's eye. Where usually he looked stern and steely, he was full of strange warmth, and something else a little wilder. The way he waved his arm to beckon Oserys into her seat was strange, too. Almost frantic.

"Thank you, Your Grace." Regardless, or rather, since she didn't know any different, Oserys sat with a gracious smile. Thankfully she had far better control over her emotions than he did – she seemed angry when he spoke of Falkonn's behaviour to her.

"Tell me, dear girl, what have you been up to this morning? My servants tell me that this morning has been quite an exciting one!" he poured her tea as he spoke and pushed a plate of fine cheese and thin breads towards her. Robbinn sat quietly beside her, taking tea and a plate of berries.

"Prince Robbinn invited me for a morning ride out in the grounds, it was a wonderful way to begin our day! I must add that the land is as beautiful as I have read about!"

"Did you see the unicorns? I'm quite proud of them!" Robbinn stared in total disbelief, wondering who in all the hells this man was and what he had done with his father. He was moving far too fast, far too jaggedly like a clumsily handled puppet.

"We did! And the tree dragons, too! It was a truly magical trip, I must admit!" she all but glowed, fitting right in as her king watched with wide, staring eyes. He almost looked like a cornered animal, instead of a lion waiting for the right moment to pounce.

Something was wrong with him, perhaps this latest in a series of assassination attempts at Robbinn's ball had finally driven him into paranoia. Or maybe it was the illness that was slowly killing him causing such strange behaviour.

"How romantic, I took my dearest Oleyyna on a similar route in our courting days, didn't I dear?" His whole body turned instead of just his head towards his lovely wife. She didn't seem unnerved by his odd mannerisms.

"You did indeed, I remember it fondly. The unicorns were truly what sold me, given that they only occur on perfect land. I do believe you asked me to marry you in a clearing known for unicorn births." She smiled fondly at her husband, though her eyes betrayed a hint of anxiety.

"I did indeed, dear woman!"

At that precise moment one of Falkonn's trusted guard burst in, panting heavily as he ran to his master's side. Aldredd Haardwing, the man was called. The king's face went further than pale, in fact he almost looked a sicky shade of green.

107

"What is it?" he demanded sharply as the tall, broad, black man leaned in to whisper in his ear. Falkonn looked as though he was going to be sick right then and there. He gripped his wife's hand under the table as he spoke once more in a low, only just level voice. "There was an attempt to poison me this morning. One of my tasters is dead."

Oleyyna gasped and covered her mouth, tears welling up in her wide eyes.

Aldredd spoke very fast with his deep, velvety voice as he bent down to be eye level with all the table's occupants.

"That's the third this week. Kitchen staff are being rotated to try to narrow it down, but nearly everyone has been checked. I'll keep you updated on our investigations, but we may have to move on to wait staff."

"I want you here at my side, at all times. And I want someone you trust outside my bedchambers at night, too." Falkonn hissed back, sounding more and more unnerved by the moment as he gripped the man by his shoulder plate. "Do you understand me, Aldredd?"

"I do, Your Grace. I'll have it seen to immediately, there are others stood outside for instruction."

"Go, make sure they know what they're doing." With that he drew back, into his seat and into himself, leaving Aldredd to run back out and Robbinn to wonder just how many assassination attempts his father had survived. And in turn, how many would he survive when he became king?

It would seem being a man that many wanted dead eventually took its toll on all. Even the revered king Falkonn. Oserys looked firmly down at her hands, folded in her lap. Robbinn never asked what the rumours she heard were. He resolved that he'd have to ask her, eventually. And that he would have to say he knew about her and Arriella.

Shit, he thought mournfully to himself; *this week is going to be hard.*

The rest of his breakfast passed in a blur, he couldn't even remember eating anything, but he was showing Oserys to his personal library when the fog finally cleared enough to question her a little more.

"My lady, forgive me, you mentioned rumours," his voice was hushed, to deter any hungry ears, "but I don't recall asking what they were? We'll be safe to discuss them in here, my library is only populated by myself and my most trusted servant, Clauude."

Quietly he showed her to his desk while he sat in the windowsill that looked out onto the fields where Luciaan was working, clearing the grass of droppings left by the horses ready to go out tomorrow. He had never before had need to learn about the keeping of horses, but he could listen to Luciaan ramble for hours, and very often did, so much so that he picked up more than a few things.

Oserys sat carefully in his old, sturdy chair and ran her fingers over the desk where many grooves and carvings of over four hundred combined years of hailed monarchs. The secrets the piece of furniture held were second to none. It wasn't every day that someone got to see something like that, as Robbinn soon realised. Finally, she dragged her eyes up from the fascinating desk and met the prince's. She sucked in a deep breath and spoke in a calm, level voice.

"Rumour has it that he's mad, mostly. Blinded by suspicion and paranoia, looking for any excuse to execute somebody. I never gave them any thought until that ball. The way he laughed... it made my bones go cold." She visibly shuddered, but continued. "Many are insisting he's going to lead us into war. That he's using you as an excuse to be reckless with his connections. The king was a dangerous man when he was young, prince. Even he can't escape consequence."

"That explains the assassination attempts then, doesn't it?" his mouth felt dry and his throat too tight. He didn't speak for a moment, just long enough for Oserys to wonder if he was going to speak again at all, but when he did his voice was quiet, but not calm.

"Do you think he's mad, Oserys?"

"I do. So does my father. There's a reason he refuses to be a part of his guard, and that I refuse to be part of his army." She spoke too quickly. He didn't think she was lying though.

"Do you think he's going to lead our kingdom to war?"

"Yes. I'm not sure when, possibly upon his death, possibly upon your coronation. War is going to break, his paranoia and ruthlessness and idiotic behaviour as a younger man made it so, and he's going to drag everyone else down to all hells with him."

Robbinn paused for a moment, his thoughts racing like spooked horses. *I have a good hand.* He contemplated silently. *I could secure her allegiance. But if she says no… I couldn't have her killed.*

"Oserys, I'm trying to find an appropriate wife. You are the only woman so far that has been suitable for me." She opened her mouth to speak, but he held up a hand to silence her. "But, I heard you and your handmaiden speaking last night. Your heart belongs to Arriella. It would be wrong to take that from you."

Serene, untouchable Oserys was quite visibly panicking, but remained silent so long as his hand was raised. Robbinn swallowed thickly.

"I could never love another as I do my head groom, Luci-aan. To save us both a lot of trouble, we could marry anyway, keeping our truths secret."

The woman before him visibly relaxed, seeing he wasn't about to have her executed or hold it above her head.

"I… I think that would be a good idea," she said slowly.

"Of course, we ought to get to know each other, first. We should be certain about each other." Robbinn spoke matter-of-factly, not looking Oserys any more.

She didn't respond right away, despite him being quite kind about everything, his knowledge of what he presumed to be her secret seemed to have shocked her.

"I quite agree." Oserys finally said, her voice quite distant.

"Don't worry, I won't tell anyone," he said quickly, mouth going slightly dry as panic began to set in about his approach. "You have my word." He finally offered, kindly. Or at least, he hoped it was kindly.

Her head shot up, scarlet eyes settling sharply on him. He didn't dare look away now.

"Really?" she sounded desperate. It seemed to be now or never.

"Really. Here," he picked up his dagger without thinking, and drew it across his palm, cutting into his flesh without flinching, then pointed it in his companion's direction. She offered out her hand willingly, and he drew the dagger across her skin. His hands remained steady as fat beads of hot blood formed on either cut. Calmly, Robbinn set the dagger back down and shook Oserys' hand, cut to cut, blood mingling.

He'd only ever read about blood pacts, but he knew they were a binding contract, running far deeper than a promise, he hoped he was doing it right. Without dropping her severe eye Robbinn fumbled in his pocket, pulling out two small vials. He opened them both one handed and squeezed Oserys' hand over the glass containers. Two drops of blood were placed in each, then sealed, attached to a chain, and finally their hands separat-

111

ed.

Robbinn held out one of the vials in his fist.

"Now it's a blood pact." He finished, firmly.

Oserys slowly, silently, took it from him and affixed it around her neck, and under her tunic.

"A blood pact indeed. You know what happens if we break these, don't you?" Oserys replied, slowly.

"Yes. Our blood spills, and we'll die a slow, painful death. Magic isn't a strong thing in the world, but blood pacts are," he spoke firmly, insisting he knew what he was doing. Amber eyes grew fierce as he stared at Oserys.

"I believe you. Although," she stood, then closed the gap between the two of them and spoke in a whisper. "If I were you, I'd find another way to prove your word than blood pacts when you're king. Better for close friends than diplomatic communications."

They both laughed a little, despite Robbinn feeling slightly agitated at the idea that she'd seen through him so easily.

"I should have you executed for cheek like that." He joked.

"Catch me if you can, prince!" she laughed back to him as she picked a book off the nearest shelf and sat to read it. Robbinn took her lead, quite pleased with the goings of the conversation: he fixed his own half of the blood pact around his neck, tucked it under his tunic, picked up a book, and settled on the floor to read without another word.

After their conversation and Robbinn's ill advised blood pact, the next few days went rather smoothly. Robbinn and Oserys had reached a new sort of understanding, and the bond they grew over their common ground was an uncommonly strong one. Despite riding out with his guest daily, Luciaan still hadn't told him when he was going to guide them to this 'special place' of his, which frustrated the prince as he wanted to go

112

and had a terrible habit of impatience when it came to his groom's promises.

Even more unnervingly, Falkonn still invited the two for breakfast every morning with him and Oleyyna; Robbinn suspected he was hoping to hear an engagement announcement before anybody else. *The old bastard will be sorely mistaken,* Robbinn thought to himself waspishly one morning as he and Oserys headed for breakfast. Of course he did plan to marry her, but that didn't mean he planned to announce it immediately, especially not to his father first.

Falkonn looked frail and ill; like he had lost weight and hadn't slept. The dark circles under his eyes were almost the colour of coal – perhaps this was what paranoia did to a man. He was in an oddly jovial mood this particular morning, pouring tea for his wife and imaginary guests like a child having a pretend tea party.

"Robbinn, my dear boy!" Falkonn called out excitedly as he set eyes on him. "Come, sit with me, I have something to ask you."

Oleyyna's eyes remained on her hands, folded in her lap. She looked extremely uncomfortable, sitting stiffly while her husband deteriorated beside her.

Eyeing his mother with concern, Robbinn sat beside his father – a man he had begun to recognise less and less.

"Robbinn, I wonder if you would consent to coming with me for a short ride out, just before lunch?" despite his odd behaviour, Falkonn's eyes flashed dangerously. Robbinn knew he had no room for negotiation.

"All right." He caught the way Falkonn's face flushed with rage at his tone. "Sorry, yes, Father. Shall I have Oserys' horse readied with—"

"No!" Falkonn snapped, slamming his fist down on the table, making two of its occupants flinch. "No, I want it to be just us. There is something I wish to speak with you about"

"I see. Then that's fine," said Robbinn, his voice quite level where his fathers was now strained.

Chapter Eleven

Shortly after breakfast a servant was sent down to warn Luciaan that the king wanted to ride out with the prince, promptly causing a widespread panic, as the yard was horrendously messy, as Luciaan would fill Robbinn in on later.

However by the time they arrived at the stable, it was spotless: each horse had been given a full groom, the corridors swept, each stable mucked out and neatened, every rug folded, uniforms on the stableboys cleaned, each bridle and headcollar in view was spotless, even the yard tools were clean as they hung on the walls. Luciaan was holding the captain, a tall, slightly stocky, muscly liver chestnut stallion with fiery eyes and a handsome roman nose, and a red headed stableboy held Solmyrer at the mounting block outside the barn. Ever the fidget, captain pawed at the ground in his excitement to move.

"Ah, Lucius is it?" Falkonn called, ignoring everything else around him, including tall, hot, Pereggnir about to enter, led by a small stableboy.

"Luciaan, Father." Robbinn hissed, finding a sharp edge to his voice when Luciaan was the subject.

"Right, I do apologise, Luciaan, I mean no offense!"

"None taken, Your Grace." Luciaan bowed low, his white hair falling forward onto his chest. Robbinn noticed that it had not been cut in a while, for it was growing to the middle of his ribs now; he even spotted a thin plait that he had put there with his own hands, evidently left in since it was placed.

Falkonn progressed as Pereggnir's hindquarters were retreating. He made the mistake of patting the touchy beast on the rump. Before anyone could register it, the stallion had kicked out, hard, and made connection with the king's thigh. Falkonn didn't even have time to yelp before Pereggnir's foot returned to the ground and he began to walk on.

The string of curses that followed were not the type to be repeated without one asking the gods for forgiveness. But, being the king, Falkonn had a pass.

"WHO'S HORSE IS THAT?" he bellowed, furious.

Luciaan gulped. "Mine, Your Grace."

"HOW MUCH DID IT COST YOU?" Falkonn's roar was so loud and unnerving that several pygmy dragons that were roosting in the barn flew off and many horses withdrew their heads into their stables.

"My home at the time, sir, all my money, and ten years of military service." Luciaan, however, Luciaan stood bravely in the face of the raging king, holding his eye. Luciaan was an uncommonly tall man who towered over most of the population, horses and humans alike. Falkonn was not exempt from this and normally that would bother him, but not this time. The man's size in both height and muscle combined with his bravery seemed to touch something in Falkonn's fury.

His voice lowered.

"More than I can afford to replace then, eh? Especially just for just a kick." He even chuckled. An unnervingly quick change, given his screaming moments earlier.

"I doubt anyone could replace him, Your Grace."

"You know, I like you. Luciaan, was it? What's your last name?" Falkonn demanded, staring up into Luciaan's eyes. Even from here Robbinn could see a certain steel to the usually so soft and inviting eyes of his lover. He knew Luciaan had a past, but ten years of military service? He certainly didn't know that.

"Ciniswood, Your Grace. Luciaan Ciniswood." Said Luciaan like a soldier repeating back orders. His feet were suddenly quite square, his shoulders too. Robbinn had never seen him use that kind of posture before. Perhaps he was a soldier, before he came to work here and he wasn't just lying to save his horse's neck.

"Ciniswood... and you say you served for ten years? How old are you?" Falkonn purred in a deadly calm voice.

"Thirty-one, Your Grace. I served from the age of eighteen." Once more Luciaan spoke like a soldier. Robbinn felt conflicted. On the one hand, the tone of his voice and watching him follow orders like that sparked a wonderful heat in his stomach, but on the other that meant that Luciaan's past was far more grizzly than he had ever thought to imagine. But then again, that scar on his face had to come from somewhere. Some part of Robbinn had long believed he had just been born with it, or been on the wrong side of something with wicked claws as a young boy – much the same as himself.

Even now as he tried to focus on Luciaan the memory forced itself to be centre stage – the enormous bird flashing its silver talons at his face, he was only four years old, he remembered calling for his mother to fix it, to kiss it better, but she couldn't because Falkonn had found him and screamed at him for crying about it.

"BOYS DO NOT CRY, ESPECIALLY NOT SONS OF MINE!" Falkonn had roared down at his trembling, bleeding little boy.

Robbinn shook his head as Falkonn and Luciaan finished talking, feeling as though he was wading through molasses; thankfully recovering before Falkonn noticed. Luciaan however, certainly did notice. Their eyes met for a moment, and he could see the concern flash in the icy blue and honey brown – Robbinn smiled softly behind Falkonn's back to let Luciaan know he was all right.

Before too long, father and son fell into step together on the backs of their capable horses. The air between them felt heavy and tense. When the king called you out for a ride alone, it was almost never good news. He was tiptoeing around something important that he didn't want to say. Were Robbinn more inclined to be sympathetic, or had he believed Falkonn worthy of his sympathy, (neither of which were true in this case), he would simply ask his father to say whatever was bothering him. However, Falkonn had taken a twenty-four yearlong mission to destroy the idea of his son's sympathy for him: something he had killed a very long time ago.

Falkonn fumbled with his words. Robbinn remained silent, drinking in his discomfort like a vampire draining his first meal in decades.

"I—" he tried to start, "I wanted to tell you something, son."

There was a very awkward pause that Robbinn thoroughly enjoyed.

"What is it, Father?" Finally he began to aid his father.

"I… er—" Falkonn muttered a curse under his breath. "Well… This is very difficult for me and I thought I'd have more time to prepare to tell you, but I've been told I don't."

Robbinn stared blankly and was planning to continue this game when all too abruptly he realised what Falkonn was talking about. He remembered listening at his parents' chamber door and hearing his mother beg him to warn their son that he was dying. Now here he was saying he didn't have as much time as he first thought…

Oh shit, Robbinn thought bitterly.

"Son. I'm—" Falkonn began, pausing to heave a deep sigh. "I'm dying. I will continue to rule, but you will be expected to do any travelling I would have done. I intend to rule until my last breath, but you will be my mouthpiece. You will have extra lessons starting tomorrow where I shall teach you everything I know, to prepare you to take the throne."

Once the first two words were out the rest spilled like a burst dam – uncontrolled and unexpected, continuing until there was nothing left. Robbinn stared, unable to find words to respond.

"Speak, boy! Don't just leave me with these words for fucks sake." Falkonn barked, prickling with what his son presumed was embarrassment or frustration, or some combination of both. He saw a deep red colour travel up his father's face.

"I... I don't know what to say, Father," Robbinn said, far more honestly than he had intended.

"Your mother wanted me to tell you sooner. I wish now that I'd listened to her. She's quite the woman, Oleyyna." Garbled Falkonn wistfully. Apparently just saying something was enough for him.

Robbinn couldn't remember much of the rest of his ride, it all passed in a sort of blur, something he found to be quite odd. He'd sort of had a heads up on this particular revelation, and the time to process it, so he didn't understand why he felt so blindsided by the information. Somewhere he reached out for what Luciaan would tell him.

"It's possible that it's such a daunting thing that instead of processing it your mind just buried it. Or decided it wasn't real." Luciaan's voice rang out in his head clear as day. He planned to go to him later about it, and would compare how close this prediction was.

Before he knew it, they arrived back at the yard and he was landing on his feet at Solmyrer's side and patting his neck before handing him off to a nearby stableboy.

Where could he go now? There was no way of seeing Luciaan until later on as the stables were far too busy, but he needed to speak with someone, or find some kind of comfort somewhere. Suddenly it all became clear! His library! That's where he had to go! To all of his storybooks and his cosy little corner with blankets and pillows and he'd ask Clauude for a pot of tea... Yes, that sounded lovely. And so he set off at a run before anyone could stop him, forcing his body to obey his command and carry him all the way up the stairs to his safe haven.

By the time he reached the corridor he was locked onto his target and seeing nothing else, hearing nothing else, and certainly not slowing down. Without wasting a second he threw open the heavy door as though it weighed nothing and strode inside—Where he saw... Oserys' back. Her dark skin, every muscle in her standing proud against it, contrasted by a pair of arms. Pale arms. And legs, hooked around her hips. Robbinn still hadn't realised quite what it was he had walked in on when Arriella's gasping came to an abrupt stop and Oserys turned to look at him.

"Fucking hell, Robbinn!" Oserys snarled without bite. "Do you ever knock?"

Robbinn gaped as he realised what had just happened. He had just interrupted them making love in his library. In his library!

"THIS IS MY LIBRARY! I DO NOT NEED TO KNOCK!" Robbinn yelled without realising how loud his voice was. But he was laughing as he hollered at her. Arriella had her head in her hands, her face bright red. Oserys turned around to face him and he abruptly remembered that she was in fact half

120

naked – her breasts were the first thing he noticed. Full and soft in appearance, sitting on pectoral muscles that even Luciaan, (whom Robbinn had once joked had bigger tits than most maidens), would be jealous of. Arriella, he saw, was of a far softer build, but that wasn't to say she was weak in the slightest, the woman had clearly been trained in some way.

Oserys laughed as Arriella hid her face, Robbinn casting his eye to the window dramatically. "Cover up then! I have to speak with you anyway, Oserys."

They didn't need telling twice. Quickly they were decently clothed and waiting to hear what the prince was going to say, but not before he settled in his windowsill with a book in his lap – just to hold, for the comfort. It was one of his favourites: about a world of pirates, fairies and lost children finding their way home before they are forgotten. He began to repeat what Falkonn had finally told him, watching their faces grow pale and shocked.

"Oserys, I'll be appointing you as my head guard, and of course asking you to be my wife. I think the arrangement shall benefit the both of us, and it's about time women were promoted in this court." He said firmly.

Oserys opened her mouth to reply when suddenly, a guard burst into Robbinn's library, leading a group of others. It was Aldredd. Robbinn's heart dropped like a stone to a riverbed. He scrambled to his feet, throwing his book aside in his rush.

"Falkonn has collapsed." Aldredd panted. "He doesn't have much time."

Robbinn, Oserys and their cloud of guards flew to the king's bedchambers like bats out of hell. Taking the stairs two, three – some of the tallest guards even four – at a time, all of them competing to get their first. Time seemed to slow, it felt as though they were attempting to run through treacle.

Robbinn threw the door open so hard that it slammed into the wall behind it and left a mark. His mother flinched at the crack of the door as she retreated from Falkonn's forehead – she seemed to have been kissing it. Her cheeks were red and her eyes puffy, her breaths coming sharply as she wiped her eyes, gesturing towards the king. As Robbinn's gaze shifted slowly to Falkonn, Oleyyna began to weep softly.

He looked thoroughly out of place on his ornate bed, covered in the finest of furs. He was pale, paler than he had been earlier. His cheeks were hollow, his skin oddly loose. Robbinn had never seen a man look so ill; the king appeared to have lost weight between the few minutes between their ride and now.

The once strong, imposing warrior now lay weak and pale, hardly able to lift his arms to greet his son. Robbinn surprised himself when he found a distinct lack of empathy for his father. Instead, something hot and bubbling reared its head as he crossed to sit with the dying man. He stared down into the cold, steel eyes of his father, finding a new kind of desperation in them that he had never before seen. Clutched tightly in his father's fist was the crown that would usually sit on his brow at any given moment; elegant, tall spines joined by a net of antlers, heavily encrusted with precious jewels – legend told that it took a decade to craft. Dry, cracked lips parted to struggle over words to the son he pushed away.

"Son." He croaked.

"Father?" Robbinn spoke with coldness. He held no sympathy for this man any longer. Staring down his nose he watched the realisation cross the face of his father.

"I'm sorry." it took him a few moments to force the words from his mouth, but once he had he relaxed back against his pillows. Robbinn laid his hand over his father's tense fist and leaned in over him. He came as close as possible and muttered in a horribly calm voice. Like the moment before lightning strike, when every being held its breath. He did not look at his father as he spoke. Falkonn did not deserve such a kindness.

"I am going to dance on your grave."

Steely eyes grew wide with shock, possibly with terror. He couldn't manage a response. Oleyyna grew desperate in her crying as she saw her husband's face change.

"What?" she demanded. "What did you say, Robbinn?"

Slowly and deliberately Robbinn dragged his gaze from the patch of pillow beside Falkonn's weak head to settle on his mother, making a point of moving his head before his eyes.

"What did you say?" Oleyyna grew impatient now, her demand turning far sharper than she would ever normally dare to use on her son.

"I said I forgave him." He lied pleasantly, turning his eyes back to Falkonn, this time meeting the weak, tired, sick looking steel of his father's. Distantly, Robbinn felt a feeble push under his hand as Falkonn tried to pull his own free. He pressed down harder with his. "I am going to marry Oserys Daeemori. I feel her personality shall compliment mine quite nicely. I will be putting wedding plans into motion momentarily."

Abruptly he felt a hand on his shoulder and a presence behind him. He didn't need to look to know it was Oserys. Yes, she was taking the role of wife to be like a duck to water.

"She shall also be appointed as my head guard, and so her father shall be invited to move into the castle with us until further notice." Robbinn finished, staring down into his father's eyes with disdain.

Oleyyna burst into tears as Robbinn stood, took his wife to be by the arm, and swept from the room. He continued a good distance down the corridor before he spoke to her again, all of his previous learning coming to lead his actions now.

123

"Oserys, I would like you to write to your father. Tell him the news, invite him to stay until our wedding and tell him he is welcome to live here with us from then." His orders were softly spoken, but commanding in tone.

"Will we live in this castle?" Oserys asked tentatively.

"To begin with, yes. I understand you have pets that prefer the North, don't you?" Robbinn slowly turned his eye to her. "We shall discuss it. Of course, until which time that we produce an heir, another topic to be explored another day," he added that part quite firmly before continuing, "We shall need to be seen together. After that point separate living may be our best option. There is much to think about and discuss, but for now, move everything you can here. We shall be wed in the Church of The Five in… let's say two months. We can always move it if need be."

"We can, indeed," Oserys replied absently.

"You can promote Arriella as you see fit, by the way."

From the corner of his eye he could see her posture raise just a little with what he hoped was glee.

Chapter Twelve

Over the next few weeks, Robbinn had little rest. On top of his new, further lessons from Falkonn, he had to plan his wedding, be seen with Oserys, carry out the wedding rituals, prepare for Oserys I's arrival, act as Falkonn's mouthpiece and somewhere in between find the time to eat, sleep and continue his normal lessons. He felt an awful rift of guilt start to open up in his stomach around twelve days into this new routine, for he hadn't been able to see Luciaan at all since his visit before the king's collapse and he had wanted to show him something special.

On the nineteenth day of the new regime, he finally broke down in his library into Oserys' strong shoulder. Night was just starting to break outside, and he had just finished his hectic, stressful day. Through tears he told her how guilty he felt, he had been able to tell the poor man anything, and by now he had no doubt heard of their engagement.

"I just don't know what to do, Oserys," Robbinn had blubbered, "I feel so guilty about it and I miss him so, so much."

Thankfully, Oserys had been remarkably kind, sitting on his windowsill and letting him lean on her in a hug, combing her fingers soothingly through his hair. Briefly he wondered just how angry his father might get with him for being so weak, but another squeeze from Oserys banished the thought from his head. Falkonn was growing weaker by the day, at this rate he certainly wasn't going to live long.

Not only did he have to think about his wedding, but his

coronation too. With highly likely only weeks in between. Gods, everything was starting to feel very real.

"Perhaps," Oserys' voice brought him back to the present, "you ought to delegate some tasks, and make time for him. For example, I could do some of our wedding preparations, and give you a list of how many creatures Father will be bringing, you could bring them to him and talk informally, too."

Robbinn paused for a moment, thinking deeply about her suggestion before leaning up and seizing her by the shoulders to kiss her on both cheeks.

"You my dear woman," he said, beaming at her, "are a genius."

"I have my moments," Oserys smirked.

They both jumped when a stone hit the window, drawing their attention outside. Robbinn scrambled to look at who or what cast it.

Robbinn couldn't believe his eyes, Oserys gaped down at the path, dimly lit by hanging oil lamps. There, swaying and stumbling, clutching a bottle in his hand, was Luciaan. His hair, usually intentionally dishevelled in appearance, was nothing short of a mess, sticking out at odd ends with pieces of straw sticking out. In fact, even from here it looked like he'd slept in a stable.

He was shouting up at the library window, "AM I GOOD ENOUGH FOR YOU NOW, ROBBINN?" He gestured down at his hips where the most peculiar of his appearance became quite apparent to the prince. The mad bastard was wearing a skirt. Robbinn glanced at Oserys, then stared back at Luciaan.

"Are you mad?" Robbinn hissed, leaning out of the window. "Don't move! I'm coming down!" And with that, he flew down out the stairs, through a hidden servant's door and sprinted full speed towards that great moron.

"What is wrong with you?" Robbinn demanded, seizing Luciaan by the shoulders and shaking him violently. Luciaan glared down at him before responding, but he couldn't seem to focus properly. He swayed worryingly, evidently far more drunk than Robbinn initially thought – he reeked of alcohol.

"You," Luciaan jabbed a finger at Robbinn's chest, his words slurred, "have been avoiding me, haven't you?"

Robbinn opened his mouth to reply, but Luciaan cut him off. "I know about your woman, was it really that bad of me?" his voice suddenly began to tremble as tears welled up in his eyes. Robbinn bit his lip – this was exactly what he was afraid of, the offer Luciaan had given was an immensely important, vulnerable one, and ignoring it would be like stabbing him. Which, he realised, is exactly what it seemed like to Luciaan.

"Shh, come inside. I have to explain." Robbinn hissed, steering his groom inside, up into the library he'd just sprinted out of. Oserys was waiting to shut and bolt the door behind them. Robbinn hardly noticed, pushing the drunken giant in, towards the desk.

Luciaan collapsed into Robbinn's chair and stared up at him, unfocused eyed filled with tears. Gods, this was hard to watch – to Robbinn the man was so strong and unshakable, he was like a brick wall, an immovable object: an idea he had found comfort and security in. He didn't know what to do now that his Luciaan was hurt, and by him no less.

"Luci—" He began, but faltered. He didn't know how to start as light blue and honey brown puppy eyes stared at him, desperate for reasoning. Suddenly it all very quickly came pouring out of his mouth at once. "The king is dying. The day after you asked me on that trip, there was a poisoning attempt and a couple of days after that he collapsed. People started coming to me for more. And I had to announce my engagement." At the mention of this, Luciaan winced. "Between us, it's only for appearances," he whispered, hoping to comfort the man.

Luciaan instantly brightened with intense hope, his gaze shifting to Oserys who smiled kindly at him.

"I'm actually a lesbian." Oserys murmured to him. "My handmaiden owns my heart and soul."

Luciaan straightened up, quickly recovering from his slump at this admission.

"I wanted to come and tell you, but Father started to give me more lessons, and now I've had to plan my coronation, think about his funeral and my wedding – I haven't had a second to come and see you." Robbinn continued gently.

"So... So you just didn't get the chance?" Luciaan asked slowly.

"I know how it seems that I ignored you on purpose, with such a special offer. I'm so, so sorry, Luci. I promise I didn't mean to." He reached out and placed his hands on either side of Luciaan's face, brushing tears from his cheeks and leaning forward to dot a small kiss on his forehead. Strangely he felt no guilt for this action, with his present company.

"S'pose I should explain this," Luciaan whimpered, gesturing to his lap, covered by a long skirt.

"You don't need to if you'd rather not," Robbinn said kindly. In truth he absolutely did want to know.

"I was crushed when you didn't come and see me. If I was brave enough, I'd have come and seen you. But I didn't want to risk upsetting you more," Luciaan rambled, evidently quite embarrassed about all of it now, "so I got drunk, about an hour ago I started. Thought you might like me again if I was more like your woman." Robbinn visibly resisted the urge to laugh. "I know I know, seems stupid now. You can laugh if you want."

"You didn't know the full of it, in some ways it makes

sense, especially because you're drunk," Robbinn said sooth-ingly, swallowing his laughter just to make him feel better.

"Offer still stands by the way. Maybe when you're mar-ried." Luciaan was still slurring his words, although he seemed to have a good idea of what he was saying.

"I'd still very much like to! I'm hoping to promote you, by the way. Head advisor for our cavalry, meaning we'll be in closer contact."

Luciaan's eyes snapped up towards him, wide and plead-ing.

"Really?" Luciaan asked, hesitantly.

"Yes. Things are getting quite tense in the kingdom, I need somebody I can trust at the head of my armies. Hence Oseerys I coming to live here, I intend to ask his permission to appoint his daughter my general." Robbinn explained calmly.

Oserys looked up at once, her eyes wide with excitement.

"Really? As well as your wife?" she asked hurriedly.

"Yes, things need to change. I trust nobody in my father's court, I must therefore create my own," Robbinn said firmly, taking Luciaan's hand. "Luci, your promotion should be hap-pening anytime in the next few weeks. I swear to you I will make this right."

Luciaan's spirits seem to have been suitably lifted by the time Oserys left to keep watch of the door. Robbinn wrapped his arms tightly around Luciaan, pressing a much-deserved kiss into his temple. He felt his tree trunk like arms around him in return, and squeezed his darling groom, apologizing once more.

"S'all right, I'm the one being silly and getting all jealous," Luciaan mumbled into Robbinn's shoulder.

"No, no, I understand. I would've been jealous too," Rob-binn said, pulling back to kiss Luciaan properly, brushing sil-very hair out of his eyes as he moved.

"Mm. I should get home, don't want to get you in trouble." Luciaan leaned back with a weak smile. He clearly didn't truly want to leave, but out of what seemed to be compassion and respect for his prince, was exercising extreme self-control in order to leave before being spotted.

"I'll send your promotion in writing, all right?" Robbinn asked, guiding him to his feet.

"All right. I hope it won't be too long before I can see you again." Luciaan smiled again before making his way home.

The next morning broke with an oddly strained feeling, although Robbinn felt the weight of boulders on his back. He was certain that sometime soon he'd be positively crippled by it, considering his ability to maintain his posture a miracle. He felt a flutter of sympathetic pain in his collarbone, as though his body was beginning to feel his metaphorical weight.

Today he planned to visit the Church of The Five and the high priests and priestesses that were to marry him and Oserys. She of course accompanied him. He had advised her that he planned to wear a common cloak over his clothes in order to avoid attention from his people and she had offered to wear some of her finest, that way he could pass as her servant, an idea Robbinn quite heartily accepted.

She met him by the stables with the warden stood quite proudly at her side, not needing to be held by his reins, wearing her full armour. Head to toe she wore it, gleaming black with green and silver accents and an intricate dragon curling its neck back to release its fire sculpted on her chest plate. There was a long, green cloak attached to her shoulders, similar to the one she wore upon her arrival. The helmet in her hands had a furrowed brow and a row of small, elegant spines over the head. In fact, the more he looked, the more spines he spotted – the set was clearly modelled after a dragon. Robbinn had heard tell that her father's too was inspired by dragons.

The prince, on the other hand, wore his favourite shabby, old, heavy, brown woollen cloak over the top of his clothes – muted grey and black tones, rather than his usual scarlets and golds – the hood up to partially obscure his face.

"Good gods, you look like more of a royal than I do on a good day," Robbinn said, aghast. "I ought to hand over my crown now!"

Oserys laughed, touching her horse's shoulder with her knuckle and he kneeled, allowing her an easier time mounting him.

"Remind me to ask you how you teach them that." Robbinn added, trying to keep the admiration out of his voice as he led Solmyrer to the mounting block, (who was wearing an old, mouldy bridle, an equally old bit, but his usual saddle, which was covered with an old, tattered piece of cloth), making sure to sling the cloak over the horse's hindquarters.

Together they looked every bit the noblewoman and servant they were aiming for as Robbinn took them down a disused path, 'to avoid the public eye as much as possible.'

The warden seemed to be rather a lot of horse beside his steady, sweet Solmyrer – he marches along with perfectly contained power. Robbinn had never seen such a willingly obedient horse. Thankfully the road was just as disused and overgrown as he remembered, he told her that rumours of werewolves had been spread around the area, so people were quite terrified of using that particular road.

"Inventive! People are still terrified of werewolves, are they?" Oserys asked lightly.

"Unfortunately, yes. It's ridiculous, honestly. They have access to the knowledge, and as far as I know persecuting them is against the law. And if it's not, I will certainly be making it so very fucking quickly once I'm in power," Robbinn replied, testily.

"You're feeling all right about that then, are you?"

"I'm surprising myself. Mother said she'll deal with his funeral, but I'd rather chuck the bastard off a cliff for the vultures," he said bitterly as Solmyrer tossed his head, annoyed by his sudden tension. Robbinn muttered an apology and patted his neck gently. This seemed to be acceptable, as his chestnut head lowered again into a more relaxed position.

"That's good, it would be awful to have even more on your shoulders. I reckon you'll make a brilliant king, omen or no. You'll win your kingdom over," Oserys said confidently. Robbinn wasn't sure where she got it from.

"I think war is going to break out the second the clammy old fucker's heart stops." He grumbled. "The mess he's made… I'm not sure it'll even wait until he dies to start unfurling."

"Really? What's he been doing?" Oserys asked, now quite concerned.

"Let's just say he's pissed off as many leaders as he can, as well as the trolls, centaurs, werewolves, the werebears and all their allies. It's like he's tried to start a war. I'll tell you more when we get back, it's not safe to keep going here."

"All right. I'd like to hear as much as you can tell me, though."

By now they had reached the capital city of Arkordouur, known as Ydmirr's Keep. It was densely populated by aristocrats, traders, debt collectors and an enormous quantity of peasants, living in what was essentially a labyrinth of warm houses, the paths and roads surprisingly varied in width – on some three carriages could easily pass side by side with some room for traders' stalls either side, but others a single pony would have trouble passing through.

Thankfully they only had to cross one or two of the wider paths where there were most people, much of their travelling could be done in narrow, quiet, paths. However, for those few wider paths, their disguise worked impeccably – she even put her helmet on for those moments, and a few people called over to her, prompting small waves. Evidently they all presumed her to be her father, but allowed her to pass without hinderance.

Finally the Church of The Five came into view – it was an enormous building almost resembling a castle with extra-long corridors and extremely tall ceilings all surrounding a circular tower where the five most accurate, smoke-coloured dragon marble statues of the gods stood.

That glorious building took Robbinn's breath away each and every time he saw it, and he strongly suspected that the feeling would never fade as he gazed up at it, stained glass windows catching the light wonderfully.

A few more tight turns on narrow roads later, they arrived outside the back door of the church and ducked inside once their horses were tied securely. Robbinn had of course sent a note ahead of them, telling the priests and priestesses when the pair would be arriving. Inside there was a central circle, corresponding with the tower above the statues of the gods standing in a half circle shape, where an altar stood proudly at the very centre, tall enough to have steps at the back, where priests would relay their gods' word. Hundreds of rows of pews cascaded down the length of the enormous room, easily enough to seat at least a thousand people.

At the front of the altar, before empty hall stood five people dressed in brightly coloured robes and similarly coloured tears painted on faces partially obscured by dark veils, waiting for them.

Three women and two men. Each god corresponded to a different colour, which corresponded to a different priest in turn. On the far left, parallel to Ydmirr's statue, stood a man dressed in deep, blood red – he was tall and broad, and the glimpse of his jaw that Robbinn caught was strong. Stood to the right of him was a slender, hourglass shaped woman with long, white hair that reminded him of Luciaan's, dressed head to toe in shimmering, rippling black, parallel to Pereggnir's statue – judging by what he could see, she was a young woman, despite what the colour of her hair might have indicated.

Beside her was another woman, this one tall and strong in her posture, looking similar to Oserys in her build, her robes were a glorious, shining gold colour. In contrast to the other two very pale people, she had very similar golden-brown skin to Oserys, and equally similar black hair. She stood parallel to the statue of Ydnias. Beside her was another man – he was the tallest of them all – with deep, dark navy blue-coloured robes and a tight jaw that reminded Robbinn uncomfortably of Falkonn in his prime; this man stood parallel to the statue of Ildyr. He didn't allow his eyes to linger on this man.

Finally, on the far right stood another woman, dressed in startling white, her red hair just visible cascading onto her chest – she was slender and of rather delicate build, standing parallel to Vyxena's statue.

In all honesty, this sight Robbinn found to be quite intimidating – the idea that he couldn't see any of their eyes unnerved him. He couldn't imagine what it would be like to be wed by them, nor crowned. Swallowing his nerves as he removed his shabby cloak and bowed his head, Robbinn spoke.

"Brothers, sisters," he muttered, and each one inclined their heads towards him.

"Prince Robbinn Falkonn Carbeu III," Ydmirr's priest said in a smooth, level voice that carried no emotion. "Welcome to the Church of The Five. We understand you're here to plan your wedding."

134

Chapter Thirteen

"Your Grace, have you decided which god you are planning to pledge to at your coronation?" Pereggnir's priestess asked slightly sharply.

Robbinn blinked, quite confused, they were here for his wedding, not his coronation. "I—er, no. I haven't."

He had of course thought about it, presently he was torn between Ydmirr and Ydnias, but had made no decisions just yet. Robbinn felt the priests and priestesses eyeing him uncomfortably.

"Vyxena tells me you will make a decision in due time. It is traditional that your wedding be led by the priest or priestess of your pledging, and their statue be visited first." The goddess of life's priestess spoke this time. Robbinn only just restrained himself from snarling at her for speaking of that Goddess – the one who had cursed him to this life and coaxed Falkonn into creating this mess that now he had to clean up.

"I see… Then, what preparations can be made in the meantime?" Robbinn asked, trying to recompose himself enough for polite conversation.

"Yes, the running of the event can be discussed now, and decorations," Ydmirr's priest said carefully. "As you are aware, there are a few usual, repeated traditions, being a celebratory feast between the joined families, traditionally following the ceremony. Exchanging of rings and of blood before the gods, and of course a binding of the hands and making of vows before your chosen god." The man didn't stop talking until he finished, and did not give Robbinn chance to interject.

He certainly didn't like this inflated sense of authority the priest gave off. After all, he was only chosen based on his appearance – much like their statues, priests and priestesses must be of similar enough appearance for the gods to use them. Granted, the process to anoint him a priest of Ydmirr was far longer and more arduous than simply being born. Although he did admit he held a small amount of respect for the man's parents, as they must have defended him quite fiercely, if not hidden him altogether, to protect him from superstitious infanticide.

"I see. And as for decorations? If I remember correctly, it is traditional that the bride wear her family's colours and add the colour of the family she marries into at the end, often in a necklace or extra veil?" Robbinn asked, he too continued without allowing the priest any chance to cut in before he glanced at serene Oserys.

"Yes, that is correct. My lady, what are your colours?" Ydmirr's priest asked as he turned to Oserys, who met his eye with her intense scarlet gaze.

"Emerald green, gold and silver," she replied coolly.

"Mine are black, scarlet and gold, which of course you would know," Robbinn said as the priest opened his mouth to speak, cutting him off quite firmly.

"I—erm, yes. I did know. Now you may wish to incorporate your chosen god's colour into the wedding decorations or your own jewellery too. Generally, candles, flowers, and drapes are the norm, coloured the same as the groom's family, and these are often changed during the vows to intertwine the new ones." The same priest spoke once more.

"Do we have to agree on a god?" Robbinn asked abruptly.

136

The priest stumbled slightly, evidently not expecting this particular line of questioning.

"N—No, no you don't need to," he stuttered, lowering his head. Robbinn thought he might be slightly intimidated as the conversation continued.

"I see. If we choose different gods, how does the ceremony differ?" Robbinn asked, his voice now a lazy drawl.

"Differ?" he repeated. It sounded as though only the groom's opinion would matter. "It wouldn't differ at all, Your Grace."

"Oh would it not?" Robbinn repeated, unimpressed. The priest before him squirmed under his intensely displeased gaze. "If nothing else, I pride myself on the promotion of the voices of women. If we disagree, I want there to be a difference. If that means repeating our vows or our marital blood pact." He leaned closer, hardening his gaze. "So be it." He ended in a low growl.

Robbinn felt a faint twinge of pleasure when he saw the priest squirm as though he was about to piss himself.

"Right, Your Grace." He turned, his voice trembling slightly and spoke to Oserys. "My lady, do you have a god in mind?"

"My personal connections are generally to Ydmirr and Ydnias," she turned to Robbinn, her expression unreadable in her calm, collected state – somehow, she looked as though she did this every day. "If you have similar inclinations that would be ideal."

"You are in luck. The god whom I am closest to is Ydmirr, although Ydnias is one of my closer considerations for my coronation." Of course, having to pick a god to watch over his rule was something Falkonn had told him, but this was truly the first he had heard of doing it for a wedding, too. "I would assume either of the two are suitable for our wedding," he eyed the five anxious priests and priestesses with severe intent, "regardless of

137

what silly superstition might say." He finished in a growl.

"I see. Then we ought to have further discussion, my dear." Oserys finished – evidently she had been previously prepared for what weddings actually meant. Somewhere deep within him, Robbinn was grateful for her serene, immovable calm which filled him with confidence. It excited him, in a strange, hungry way.

"Indeed. As for decorations and performance, I believe it would be prudent to follow every traditional method, unless Oserys has observed separate custom she would like to see implemented?" Robbinn felt his voice come out in a bored sort of drawl, his eyes moving lazily between Oserys and the group of increasingly nervous people.

"I do not, our usual customs are much the same as yours other than our brides tend to add the necklace themselves, to exaggerate the tone that it is her choice to join a family, rather than property whose ownership is being passed over." Her serene tone faltered slightly with an edge of bitterness.

The priests gulped. Robbinn nodded his agreement.

"Usually," Ildyr's priest spoke up in a deep, growling voice which shook slightly as the two fixed their gaze on him. "The Father of the groom is the one to present the new item. However," he continued quickly, "if it is your will, then tradition can of course be broken."

The man opened his mouth to speak more, but hesitated. Robbinn arched an eyebrow at him.

"Speak, man," he commanded simply. Seeing no way not to continue, the man wet his lips and continued on.

"It is only that we worry such controversial choices of the gods may lead to an uproar, and it—" he started, but Robbinn swiftly and cleanly interrupted him.

"It may be prudent to maintain all other good luck totems

and traditions, is that what you are saying?" Robbinn finished with a cold expression.

"I—erm—yes. It is." He stuttered.

"I do not care. In any case, I warn you that the king may be extraordinarily weak on the day. He may not be up to the task." Robbinn felt his lip curl. For all the stress Falkonn's illness was putting on him, he was still enjoying watching him suffer.

"I am aware of the king's condition. Vyxena tells me so." The priestess draped in stark white robes seemed to speak without thinking, for as Robbinn turned to stare coldly at her, he saw her throat tighten.

"Oh does she? Good, I shall know to leave you out of things in future, as I'm sure Vyxena tells you." Robbinn purred dangerously, sneering down his nose at the woman, once more enjoying the sight of her squirming uncomfortably.

She said nothing, and he turned away, satisfied that his message had been received quite clearly. The rest of their visit was dedicated to what types of flowers were to be used to decorate every hall and pew, what kind of gown Oserys planned to wear and of course in what colour. Eventually they turned off into a small, cramped room without the priests to consider their gods together.

"Who do you feel closest to?" Robbinn had asked, interested.

"Truthfully, Ydnias. She has appeared to me before now, in a time of need." Oserys admitted with an air of warmth in her voice.

"You look like her, too." Robbinn smiled.

"You think so? Father always said so." Oserys' warmth grew like a piece of kindling bursting into flames.

"Did he?" he asked, tilting his head slightly.

"Yes, he often joked that I carried her storms on my shoulders – I always thought it sweet of him." She beamed, more than happy to speak about this.

"Well, given the weather upon your arrival, I daresay he was right!" he gave a soft, airy chuckle.

"Go on then, which are you closest to?" Oserys prompted, moving the conversation where it mattered.

"Ydmirr. He appeared to me when I was still… erm, questioning myself. Not that I'm still entirely sure what he means. I'd like to choose him for our wedding. But, we can use both, if you'd prefer that."

"Hm… I think Ydmirr would be the better choice to prompt a strong foundation, given his marriage to Pereggnir is still going well. Ydnias can be irritable, I fear she may be too volatile to create the same," Oserys said calmly and rationally. Robbinn gaped, having wholly expected this issue to be their first disagreement, but here she was, gracefully agreeing with him. She laughed when she caught sight of his expression.

"You expected me to disagree?" she asked with a playful smile.

"I—well, yes! You have every reason to, and you absolutely can, if you aren't sure?" Robbinn offered tentatively.

"Well, I certainly appreciate that. However, I believe that Ydmirr is the more appropriate choice, given it's a wedding. From what I hear, he is still very happily married to Pereggnir and is a very attentive husband – this is something I hope to channel." Oserys seemed quite happy to explain her position. In a trend Robbinn sensed would not be broken anytime soon, he was amazed by Oserys as she smiled pleasantly, her eyes warming with it. He sighed quite contentedly, releasing tension from his body.

"Well, that makes things easy, doesn't it?" he chuckled, smiling at her.

"It does indeed! I think this marriage will work out for us very well indeed," she replied, a cunning edge taking off the pleasant edge to her smile. Robbinn quite abruptly remembered something and pulled out a small wooden box, covered with silken fabric and decorated with gold beading. He held it out to her.

"That reminds me, we ought to mark the engagement, don't you think?" Robbinn said, in quite a matter-of-fact tone as Oserys took the box from him and opened it to reveal a beautiful, albeit old, engagement ring. It was forged from the same metal as Falkonn's crown, a brilliant gold colour but about as hard as silver, wrapped like vines around an almost glowing black stone. Oserys' bright red eyes widened at the sight of it, removing it from the box and slipping it onto her finger.

"Robbinn—good lords it's beautiful!" she gasped, admiring the perfect fit.

"Passed down through my family, I do hope you treasure it." Robbinn gave a nod of approval, and without much further discussion he took his fiancée's hand in his own, fixed his face to look perfectly loving, and exited the room.

Planning the rest of the wedding was quite the breeze, and now all that was left was to arrange his clothes, the dress Oserys was to wear, and to await the day to arrive.

Oseerys senior arrived two days following this trip, and was settled into a wing near his daughter's. He too brought along his enormous black horse, named The Titan and a few servants, but rather differently from his daughter, he brought dragons with him - two Northern Greater Dragons that usually slept in volcanoes, but appeared to find the late autumn bite to the air quite like a hot summer breeze. They weren't quite the size of a palace, and Oseerys I had claimed them to be young, and to Robbinn's astonishment one of the dragons actually confirmed this, telling Robbinn she was only thirteen years of age and Greater Deathcallers didn't reach their full size until they were twenty.

The old warrior had greeted the prince with his two huge three headed dogs, the shape of some sort of sighthound like Luciaan's sweet Bonnie, but the first Robbinn met was brindle where she was greying and with thicker fur. Each head seemed to join seamlessly with the others, but it was quickly evident that each one had a different personality. The body of the dog was deep chested and mostly black, aside from a white stripe down his chest and most of his belly; the inside of each of his legs were all brindle, and the pattern travelled around each ankle and down to his toes like four pretty gloves. Each face was identical, the stripe from his chest coming up each neck where it faded into brindle all over his muzzle and spots which appeared as eyebrows, save for a thin white stripe down each nose.

Oseerys I told Robbinn his dog was named Bertinnus, and had looked around for another, growled and shouted for one called Errnest, when a second three headed dog, this one skinnier and pale blonde all over with three, very pretty faces with longer noses than his brother's, came bounding up to his master's side, wagging his whole hind end in his excitement.

No sooner had his horse been stabled and his dragons settled had Oseerys I strode up to meet the weak, sickly king; walking with just as much purpose and power as his daughter, two enormous three headed dogs at his heels where his cloak swirled – that strong, imposing stride something he had evidently passed down to her as well as his name. Robbinn had followed just out of sight and listened carefully at the door, hoping to hear something encouraging. He heard Oseerys I cross the room and growl at Errnest to keep his feet on the floor, then sit down.

"Take my hand." Croaked Falkonn, his sheets rustling as he moved. Robbinn heard their hands clap together in what was surely a firm grip.

"My old friend... You look like shit," Oserys muttered, laughing quietly. To Robbinn's shock, Falkonn laughed too – although it did sound more like a horse coughing than actual human laughter.

"I'm dying, 'Serys. I've made a fucking mess of this kingdom. The South and the West both now want more land free from my family's rule. Every major lord in both those areas and the south are pissed off because Robbinn didn't marry their daughters but has announced his announcement to Daddy's old friend. I'm supposed to give the centaurs their land back and I can't tell you how many letters I've had saying that the tax system is fucking bullshit." Falkonn had spoken very fast, as though afraid he'd lose his strength mid-sentence.

"Fuck me, Falkonn. When did all this start?" Oserys growled, though his tone was exasperated.

"Months ago. It's been a long time coming, my father took colony after colony. The biggest threat is the South and West colonies teaming up, from what I've heard – they're planning on taking a country between our main continent and their land mass, and they want more. They're being led by some fucking self-proclaimed King, Hardweaverr or something stupid like that. Some of my connections are even telling me the fucking pirate pests are planning on getting involved."

Suddenly there was a horrible snarling noise coming from what sounded like at least five out of six heads that had been slowly raising in volume over the last couple of moments. If he listened carefully he could hear the gnashing and snapping of teeth and the odd little bark, but it didn't seem to be fighting.

"BOYS." Oserys snapped, causing the noise to cease in-

143

stantaneously. Robbinn heard two tails beating against something solid. It sounded as though his three headed dogs had been playing.

"Sorry. They're morons. There's a king wanting to overthrow you, is there?" Oserys muttered apologetically. Robbinn had heard a lot of this before, but not quite in all this detail. He couldn't help feeling anger rising in him – just when was Falkonn going to tell him in true detail?

"Not me. They're apparently going to wait until I die and attack Robbinn. I think it would've happened regardless of who he married, but I'm glad it's your daughter, she can teach him a lot. I'd hoped you'd agree to take care of them and guide them if it does become war." Falkonn's voice had turned slightly pleading at the edge.

"I'd consider it an honour. I'm planning to name my daughter general to my armies, anyway. She'll be an asset for him in any case." Said Oserys, soothingly.

"I see. Robbinn's named a new head advisor for the cavalry. Our now ex head groom. Apparently, he was a soldier in his youth. I'm sure he'll be fine, with support." Falkonn sighed. Robbinn heard him lie back against his pillows.

"Just stay alive until his wedding, arsewipe." Oserys chuckled. Falkonn gave a weak laugh. There are very few people who would get away with calling King Falkonn VI an arsewipe – Robbinn felt he must have thoroughly earned such right, and felt a sudden surge of respect for the man blossom within him.

"I shall try," Falkonn replied, moments later. "But I can promise nothing."

Chapter Fourteen

Just over a month later, when winter had come into full force; castle and grounds blanketed in thick, white, gleaming snow, almost everyone was bundling up in cloak after cloak, even the horses were turned out with thick rugs on; the day of Robbinn's wedding came around.

Clauude as usual was dressing him, although it was not only him in the room. In his favourite armchair, withered, frail and almost grey in the face, sat Falkonn; the once proud, strong king looked an inch from death. At his arm stood one of his 'closest personal advisors', the head advisor of his cavalry to be exact, Luciaan Ciniswood.

Luciaan looked far, far too handsome in new uniform and on his new salary – head to toe in black, gold and scarlet, with a horse's head hand embroidered on the left of his chest. He had been rather enjoying keeping him close, and so far, any gossip was purely about the possibility of war. Even Falkonn seemed to harbour no suspicion. Or rather, if he did, he was keeping them to himself.

At Falkonn's other side, in Robbinn's second armchair, sat his mother; wearing a slightly dewy expression born of what appeared to be intense pride as she watched Clauude dress her dearest son for such an important day as his wedding.

As usual, Clauude dressed him quite gently but with appropriate haste – fastening each button and stud into place with well-practiced hands, affixing the silver Skreghle headed fastening for his cloak at his shoulder and finally placing his crown upon his head, handed to him by Falkonn himself.

Robbinn stepped before his full-length looking glass and examined himself carefully, his eyes meeting Luciaan's every so often. His black tunic was stiff, made of high-quality fabric, fastened in two long lines of gold buttons that started at his collar and ending at around his waist before they tucked into his smooth, black trousers which were piped down the outer seam with gold and laced at the back to fit perfectly. At his shoulder, fixed to the tunic by the skreghle head was a thick, calf length cloak, lined with a dazzlingly red fur inside, but black on the outside. Robbinn's crown was far more muted than his father's, with hardly half the jewels and less intricate, looking far less than six stags locking antlers and more like a wreath of thorns. Every inch of his clothing was lined with thick, warm, black fur to keep him warm – although it was so warm in his chambers that his cheeks started to flush a pale pink.

With great difficulty he pulled his eyes from Luciaan's through the mirror to examine himself, and finding everything in order, turned to present his appearance to his company.

"How do I look?" he asked his small audience.

"Oh Robbinn, my dear boy," Oleyyna half wailed, her emotions having swollen out of her chest as she stood up, clutching at her heart. "You look so handsome."

"I quite agree, Your Grace." Purred Luciaan, his eyes examining the ornate gold buttons down his chest, no doubt imagining what it would be like to remove.

"Yes, you're quite right, Oleyyna," Falkonn said with considerable effort.

"Any woman would be lucky to face you." Smiled Luciaan, to nods of agreement from the two beside him, for as usual lately, Oleyyna had started crying and was unable to speak – although she nodded fiercely at Luciaan's words as Falkonn grasped his arm, clearly as tightly as he could manage.

"You," he began, mustering yet more strength to speak, "you took the words right from my mouth, Ciniswood."

"Why thank you." Robbinn said pleasantly, taking in a deep, confident breath and casting his eye to the window. "Well then, I suppose we ought to go. Ciniswood, would you help Father to the carriage? If memory serves, you saw to the horses, did you not?"

"I did indeed, Your Grace," he replied, turning his head to the frail king. "It would be an honour to assist you, your majesty." Luciaan offered out a kind arm, and Falkonn begrudgingly wrapped his own around it to help himself to stand, pushing hard on the armrest to force his tired body to obey.

The journey through the castle was slow, owing to the extra time Falkonn had to take in order to stay on his feet, although it seemed Luciaan's strong arm provided more than ample help. As expected, the castle grounds were covered in thick, pearly white snow and there was a noticeable bite to the air where their breath fogged. Stood proudly not far from the grand doors was a large, black and gold carriage, attached to which stood six tall, fine, black, winged horses. Robbinn whipped around to Luciaan with an accusatory glare.

"Where on earth did you get these?" he demanded as Luciaan leered down at him but didn't speak. Oseerys I strode out from behind the carriage, his three headed dogs Bertinnus and Errnest at his heels, wearing a silver collar on each neck, every one decorated with a miniature hydra's head holding a circular ring in its mouth.

"They are a wedding present," he answered for the cornered advisor with a chuckle, "from me. My daughter is very fond of the beasts, and your cavalry advisor told me you quite

147

enjoy horses. Do you like them?"

Robbinn didn't answer immediately, instead he walked around the carriage, looking each horse over as they pawed at the ground, tossed their great heads and fluttering their massive wings. The harnesses they wore were ornately decorated, the three on the left side wore black and gold, the bridles forming an intricate web on their faces that was supplemented by gold leaf around their eyes and on their foreheads, the piping on the leather against their skin however was a deep, rich scarlet in colour – representing his family. The three on the right side wore harnesses of the same shape, but where the leather on the right was black, theirs was green, the piping silver but the metal decoration was the same gold, representing the Daeemori family.

Upon further inspection, Robbinn saw that their manes were plaited with red and green ribbons, intertwined within the hair—further representing the coming marriage. Not that he cared all that much about the decoration; he found it difficult to drag his eyes away from the horses' enormous, glossy wings. It looked as though if they were to take flight, they'd have at least a six-metre wingspan, easily more – each horse was almost as tall as Robbinn at the withers, with broad, muscular shoulders and thick necks to support their wings. He was utterly speechless, not even unicorns made him this breathless with the beauty.

"Pereggnir's tits..." Robbinn muttered under his breath, then upon remembering his company poorly disguised his words with a cough. "They're beautiful... I can't thank you enough, how much did they cost you? Surely being so rare they're expensive?"

The old warrior laughed, his dogs wagging their tails.

"No, not at all! We breed some of the only domesticated

ones on the planet, they tend to be a good source of our income as a settlement." He smiled, opening the door of the black and gold carriage to reveal a deep emerald-green velvet covering the cushions inside. "If I may, your majesty, Your Grace, we ought to get going or my daughter shall beat us there!"

"Good point, Daeemori. Come, Father." Robbinn gestured to the open door and Luciaan began to lead him towards it as half the kingdom's knights appeared on their horses, both soldier and mount wearing full armour, polished to the point of gleaming, ready to form an escort – Aldredd among them.

Once the king was settled into the carriage with the help of Oserys and Luciaan, the rest of his company followed, his wife sitting beside him. The journey was surprisingly pleasant, for Falkonn held his tongue – whether it was through grace or exhaustion Robbinn couldn't be sure – and the kingdom seemed to put aside its loathing of him for resembling Ydmirr and was celebrating the wedding with flowers thrown at the carriage and loud, excited cheering as the streets swarmed with people. In fact there were so many people out to celebrate that they formed a single mass, like a many headed monster, roaring its pleasure as they passed.

Upon reaching the church, barriers were put in place to prevent any members of the public interrupting the ceremony – but that wasn't to say the church was at all empty. Hundreds of Lords and Ladies took up the seats, apparently from all areas of the kingdom that weren't currently threatening war. But even as Robbinn passed, he was sure he saw a pirate sat near the middle, with who must have been his first mate.

The imposing building was indescribably beautiful. There was thin, wispy fabric of black, scarlet, silver, green and gold were draped from the highest ceilings, over each window, under the chandeliers – with enormous bunches of black, white, scarlet, blue and gold flowers, the last of which were painted, cascading down each wall from under every window and on the end of each pew. The statues of every god wore a crown of flowers in their associated colours on their inclined heads.

There was an entire orchestra in the crowd, one on the end of each pew ready to sing his bride down the isle to the altar circle where the five priests stood at the foot of their chosen god to welcome him. They closed in on him at once like a group of giant vultures, and guided him to a scarlet pillow before the altar, telling him to kneel on it. And there he waited for his bride as the group of priests stepped back again.

After what felt like ten minutes, music started to take over the excited chatter echoing in the massive building and the roar of the crowds building outside. It was slow and sweet music, announcing what was supposed to be the happiest moment of his life, and quite abruptly he felt his heart leap into his throat and sweat start to prickle down his back and against his brow. Unoccupied hands began to fidget, his old nervous gesture of picking at his fingernails started as his bride approached behind him. Robbinn's chest and throat felt tight with the anticipation of what was to come – he would once more make a blood pact to Oserys Daeemori II in mere moments.

Her approach was given away by the audible gasps of several people. She must have looked utterly beautiful.

Trying his hardest to ignore his pounding heart and to work his face into something presentable, Robbinn raised his head as Oserys knelt beside him. She wore the most beautiful green gown with silver accents, there were dragons embroidered in threads only just darker than the main fabric all over it, and there was a wyrm taking up the back panel of the dress. Her shoulders were covered with scale mail, which connected a sheer length of green fabric down the middle of her back to the floor with lengths of gold chain.

She wore a silver veil over her beautiful face and the intricate front of her bodice which was high necked and stiff, two trees embroidered up both sides of her chest, either side of a seam, the slender trunks fading into the wide band at her waist. Oserys' silky black hair was intricately braided into a circular shape at the back of her head, there were at least four of them, winding like snakes over her head. Two lengths were free, cascading like black rivers down her chest. She turned her head slightly to look at him with a smile. He did his best to return it.

"Dear families, friends, allies." Ydmirr's priest began, stepping forward to the altar, his arms outstretched. "We gather today to join two souls under the gods. Prince Robbinn Falkonn Carbeu, third of his name, heir to the throne of Arkordouur, and Oserys Thenea Daeemori the second kneel before the glorious five."

His hands lowered towards them.

"Please, rise with me and join us all in prayer over the couple." Robbinn and Oserys remained on their kneels as their guests rose and joined in with the priest in his prayer.

"All seeing, all hearing, all controlling five, we pray to you for your blessing.

To Vyxena we pray for long, painless lives.

To Ydnias we pray for clear skies to guide us.

To Ildyr we pray for mercy upon our sailors.

To Ydmirr we pray for peace in our existence,

To Pereggnir we pray for a kind, swift death.

To you divine five we pray."

The building fell silent with the grinding of stone. Four of the five statues of the gods had inclined their heads further and extended one arm each down to the two kneeling before them.

The gods were here, listening to everything. Robbinn and

Oserys had of course been warned that Pereggnir may not move her statue so that it would not have been a shock to them when four arms were outstretched instead of five.

"We humble mortals give thanks for those who have joined us today for such a joyous occasion." The priest descended into the usual sermon about the glory of the gods and revealed that the couple had chosen the name of Ydmirr to be married in, to a very much expected gasp of horror across the magnificent hall. Gracefully stepping over this interruption, the priest continued talking and invited one person from each pew to bring the row's offerings to the foot of each god's statue.

"The time comes for the exchanging of rings and of blood," Ydmirr's priest said, the others descending on Oserys and Robbinn once more, bending at the waist with their hands outstretched. The two of them copied.

Ydmirr's priest approached them with a small, red cushion in his hands, upon which sat a long, black, scarlet tipped dagger. The ceremonial dagger. With what he clearly thought was a reassuring smile, the man handed Robbinn the weapon, as they had rehearsed weeks earlier. As he had done months before, only this time with his heart racing, Robbinn draw the blade across his palm, sparing himself no depth as dark beads of blood were pulled up in its wake, then held it to Oserys, handle first this time. Bravely Oserys drew the blade across her own palm, she too spared herself no depth, and replaced the dagger on its pillow to be taken away.

Thick, hot blood pooled in the palms of their hands for a moment before they were joined, palm to palm, cut to cut, and finally their eyes met once again. Ydmirr's priest produced two vials, one decorated with a silver dragon, the other with a gold skreghle, and held the silver one under their hands. Two large drops of blood were caught in it before the priest switched them to place the same in the gold one. The vials were sealed and placed around their necks.

Finally, the priest produced a second crimson pillow from his robes which he took down to the king and Oseerys senior. Each produced a ring, and placed it upon the pillow before the priest returned to the bride and groom. Oserys' ring was placed on his daughter's finger first, a simple, gold one with a small dragon engraved on it. Falkonn's was placed on Robbinn's, clearly crafted with inspiration drawn from the two crowns, like a small, twisted antler.

"If you will follow me, we shall move on to vows and the binding of the hands before Ydmirr."

Together, still holding hands, Robbinn and Oserys stood and followed the crimson clad priest into Ydmirr's room, his statue turning its head to follow them as they walked.

The small, intimate room contained another pair of small cushions to kneel on, a window where more and more snow was building up, a small altar, and a second, human sized statue of Ydmirr, his sword drawn. With the now quite expected grinding sound of stone, Ydmirr's statue replaced his sword in its scabbard and looked at them, smiling.

"I am quite glad you have chosen me."

His priest gaped as the statue spoke, stalling momentarily as he steered Oserys and Robbinn towards the cushions. The latter smiled at the statue.

"You seemed the best option, I trust you." He said quietly.

"And you have the only marriage that we have been told of, and it has lasted longest." Oserys chimed in, quite happily as Ydmirr's statue laughed.

"That is quite true. We gods do not often guide your vows, but we do know them, and as I haven't been chosen in so very long, I shall do it. If, of course, you all find that agreeable?" the

153

statue asked, its eyes on the priest.

"Yes," he stammered, before composing himself, "yes, I see no reason why not. Would you like me to bind the hands for you?"

"No, no, I can do it. If you could just pass the ribbons to me." The statue stepped down from its plinth with a faint tap, like someone had dropped pebbles onto paved stone. It held out its hand for the emerald green and scarlet ribbons, which the priest placed in its stone palm.

"Oserys Thenea Daeemori, do you swear to protect and support Robbinn Falkonn Carbeu in his every endeavour?" The statue asked, beginning to wrap the green ribbon around their hands.

"I do." Oserys stared up at the moving statue with a determined expression.

"Do you swear that from now until your death that you will be his most trusted advisor, his closest friend, his wife?"

"I do." It passed the ribbon around their hands a second time.

"Do you accept him to be your husband, your friend, your human, with all of his flaws, and thus cherish him in mind, soul and body?"

"I do." The statue tied the ribbon and picked up the red one.

"Robbinn Falkonn Carbeu, do you swear to protect and support Oserys Thenea Daeemori in her every endeavour?" The statue's mild voice asked once more, beginning to bind their hands in once more with the red ribbon.

"I do."

"Do you swear that from now until your death that you will be her most trusted advisor, her closest friend, her husband?"

"I do." It made another loop with the ribbon around their

154

hands.

"Do you accept her to be your wife, your friend, your human, with all of her flaws, and thus cherish her in mind, soul and body?"

"I do." The statue tied the ribbon and held their joined hands in its own.

"Then I pronounce you husband and wife. Go forth, and finish your ceremony. I shall be watching." He winked, and slowly stepped back onto his plinth and reassumed his pose from earlier with the same grinding noise.

The priest, stunned into silence, followed. Upon resuming their positions, Falkonn stood with Oserys' assistance to hand her a necklace. The stone was black, the metal housing it gold, and the ribbon it sat on blood red. With her father's help, Oserys affixed it around her neck to a reproachful murmur from a few of their guests which was thankfully drowned out by the orchestra as they stood. Similar joyful music saw the now married couple back out to their carriage, which was to take them to their chosen honeymoon destination, a palace on the coast, a few hours outside Ydmirr's Keep.

Chapter Fifteen

No sooner had they left the carriage had a dragon landed on Robbinn's shoulder, bearing a message addressed to him on black parchment. It was Zekeyus, his dragon whom had not accompanied Robbinn and his wife to the coast. *Oh shit,* Robbinn thought scornfully, *more good news.* He removed the scroll from Zekeyus, thumbed it open irritably, and began to read. It took reading the letter three times for him to even register what it said.

'Dear Robbinn. Your father has passed away. Please come back at once, nowhere is safe any more. – Oleyyna.'

Oserys, helping Arriella out of the carriage, glanced at him. Luciaan, who he had brought with him instead of Clauude under the pretence of giving the latter a well-earned break, wandered over and placed a hand on his shoulder.

"What's wrong, Robbinn?" He asked quietly, pressing a kiss into his temple once he had checked the footman wasn't looking,

Robbinn's mouth went dry. His promise from months ago to dance on Falkonn's grave suddenly came crashing into his mind like spooked horses through a fence. He couldn't speak, and instead just handed him the letter to save the effort of speaking.

"Holy shit..." Luciaan muttered, reading the letter twice over. "What does she mean that nowhere is safe?"

"Did I ever explain to you everything that was going to

happen as soon as I became king?" Robbinn asked quietly.

"No. There wasn't time." Luciaan sounded nervous now.

"War," Robbinn replied thickly. "In short, anyway." He turned to look at his new wife. "Oserys. Come here please." Robbinn knew he must have looked extremely white in the face, because Oserys' eyes grew wide and nervous as she strode over to him.

"What's happened?" she asked urgently, her eyes flicking sharply between him and Luciaan.

"Father... hm. Pass her the note will you, Luci." Robbinn's eye had moved to fix firmly on the sky. Silently, Luciaan handed Oserys the letter. She took it and read it at least three times before looking up, going steadily paler. In fact, she looked as though she was about to vomit.

"Can everyone ride bareback?" She asked, quite abruptly. Robbinn stared blankly at her, not understanding why she had asked that specific question.

"Yes, why?" he replied, frowning.

"We'll take the winged horses, ride them back. It'll take half an hour at most, and nobody thinks to look in the sky, so we won't be seen," Oserys explained, her gaze landing on the footman as he wandered back out of the nearby woodland.

"Good idea, my lady," Luciaan said, taking charge of the situation and striding over to the carriage where the six winged horses still stood attached to it and spoke to the footman. Moments later he untied four horses and placed their harnesses inside, then led them over to the group.

"He says since the carriage is so light and these horses so strong, he can start taking the others back, but I said we'd send word to have it all retrieved," Luciaan explained coolly.

"You, my dear, are incredible." Robbinn beamed as Luciaan handed out the horses, one each for him, Robbinn, Oserys and Arriella.

Luciaan dutifully helped each of his companions onto their mounts which now only wore their bridles, before hoisting himself up gracefully onto the largest. Robbinn felt oddly secure on the back of his impressive steed as it tossed its head and pawed at the ground impatiently.

His legs sat just behind its wing joints at its shoulders, which in itself was a relatively normal position – however the shoulders of the winged horse were far, far broader than any normal one, with far a thicker neck and an almost absurd amount of muscle down its back. Once all of his companions were seated, he squeezed on and directed his horse towards the long stretch before the palace, between two points of a horse-shoe shaped clearing.

"Come on then, up," he muttered anxiously, clicking his tongue, and urging with his seat for canter which the horse burst into like cannon fire. It galloped at full speed towards the tree line, enormous wings outstretched, feeling the wind and as the wall of trees approached, the beast began to beat them. Finally, when Robbinn began to feel as though the horse was going to crash through to the trees, it sank back on its hindquarters and pushed off into the air as though jumping an enormous fence.

The moment he and his raven-coloured mount were in the air, he whipped his head around to look behind him where one, two and three more black, winged, masses joined him in the air. Luciaan's steed pulled forward to be beside Robbinn, its rider housing quite an excited expression – evidently he had done this before, much like Oserys, who when he glanced at her, looked quite serene, as though she were going for a nice, quiet canter through a field. Robbinn however, felt quite sick. The horse's body moved as though it was in an extremely floaty canter, which should have been familiar, comforting even, but somehow it made him feel worse. He didn't dare open his mouth for fear of vomiting over the horse's shoulder.

The enormous wings remained relatively still, changing angle to maintain its altitude, but the floaty canter movements eventually levelled out, which made him feel much less nauseous. After a little while he certainly began to see the appeal of travelling this way, but it would certainly take more getting used to. He still didn't dare to open his mouth, despite feeling better, and instead allowed Luciaan to lead the way back.

Far too soon, the horse's wings tilted down, and the group began to descend and Robbinn felt his stomach give a great lurch as he was suddenly pointing at the ground. This was nothing like jumping ditches on normal horses. This was far too fast and far too steep, and he shut his eyes for the remainder of landing, although he was very aware of the horse's legs starting to gallop in mid-air, and when it landed had to slow down into canter, then to trot, to walk and finally a halt.

Robbinn didn't open his eyes again until his horse's hooves had all returned to the floor and had stopped moving, and didn't get off until everyone else had landed too.

"Gods," Robbinn said, his voice trembling, "that will take some getting used to."

Oserys laughed at him as Luciaan took the horses over to the new head groom once Oserys and Arriella had dismounted, then raced back to Robbinn's side as he started for the doors.

Robbinn strode through the castle at great speed towards his parent's chambers as he attempted to compose himself. He knew he'd be coming to his dead father and mourning mother. He knew he was coming to take the crown from him and assume his throne as king. His heart pounded against his ribs as he reached the door and knocked.

Oleyyna opened it and wailed like a wounded dog, flinging

her arms around him, and dragging him into the room. Falkonn lay in his bed; his skin pale, his tight purple lips slightly open, his steely eyes only just closed. Robbinn stood there silently as his mother cried her heart out into him, staring at his father's corpse. The intricate crown still sat upon his brow.

Robbinn felt his arms close around his mother without his command, guiding her back into the room to allow him inside, still staring at Falkonn. He didn't know what to do about his mother's cries, nor the strangely lost expression on Aldredd's face, nor the distraught one on Oseerys senior's pale face. He also found it odd how numb he actually felt, instead of angry or scared or sad, even satisfied that the mad old fool had finally kicked the bucket. He simply felt… nothing.

"Aldredd," Robbinn said, finally, "I would like you to, for now, be the head of my personal guard. If you would like to, of course. I recognise that during such a devastating time for you it may be helpful to have work to do."

Aldredd gave a soft, choked sob.

"Thank you, Your Grace. That is very…" he trailed off, taking a deep breath, "very kind."

"And Oserys, I would like to make you a similar offer. I would like you to be a part of my advisory court. You're the only one I trust from my father's," Robbinn continued, turning to the distraught man.

"I'd consider it an honour, Your Grace. Thank you." He nodded, his shiny black hair falling into his face as he glanced at his daughter, who laid her hand on Robbinn's shoulder.

Finally, the prince turned his numb gaze to his mother, who still cried against him.

"Mother." His voice was as kind as he could muster. "Listen to me, Mother." He waited for her to fall quiet and look up at him.

"I'd like you too as a member of my court, in an advisory role. I'd like to keep you close. You know what Father did to this kingdom, I want you safe," he spoke firmly now, to ensure he was understood by the shaking, sniffling woman.

"Son," she started thickly, her lined face creasing further with her agony as she stared up at him with glassy eyes, "I too would consider it an honour."

"Good. Aldredd, see my mother to the tower, ask Ydmirr for guidance. I'll see to Father." Robbinn gently moved his mother's arms and guided her in Aldredd's direction, whom she clung to like a rock in a treacherous ocean as he led her out of the room.

Now it was Robbinn, the two Daeemoris, Arriella and Luciaan left in the room, but he felt perfectly comfortable around them all, and didn't send any of them away when he approached Falkonn's body, staring coldly into his waxy face.

"Look at you. You died a pathetic death, didn't you?" Nobody else made a sound. Robbinn reached down as though meaning to neaten Falkonn's hair, but instead removed the crown from his brow. His skin was still warm to the touch. He wasn't all that long dead. "I think this belongs to me now. I'm going to keep my promise, you know." He continued to speak as though nobody else was there.

"But I can continue this conversation at a later date, can't I?" Finally he looked up and met the bright red eyes opposite him of the first Daeemori, slightly lined around the edges. "Do you know what he was? What he did?"

"In his youth, he was a good ruler. Behind closed doors he was bloodthirsty. He craved war," Oserys replied, quietly.

"Do you know what he said to me?" Robbinn's eyes bored into Oserys'.

"I know what he said about you." The old warrior offered,

looking quite uncomfortable, speaking over the body of his dear friend.

"He told me that I was a disappointment more than he said my name. He once said that the only reason he didn't drown me as a baby was because I was an excuse to train his armies and collect more and more taxes from our starving kingdom. Your daughter speaks of you very highly. She trusts you. I trust her. My father trusted you. I did not trust my father." He tilted his head slightly, his voice cold. "Do you see my dilemma?"

"I do." He broke the now very uncomfortable eye contact, shifting his gaze to his daughter, then to Arriella who stood in the middle of the room, then to Luciaan who still stood at the door. He closed it quietly as Oseerys I found the words.

"I know of my daughter's sexuality. I urged her not to marry you, because I wanted her to be happy. I know her heart belongs to Arriella. I was going to come and stop her, in fact. But she told me about you. I have the secrets that could have the four of you executed. But I will not do it. I will not condemn my daughter to death. I trust her judgement, thus I trust you." He spoke very fast, but firmly. Robbinn remained quiet, simply surveying him for a moment as he thought.

"I see." Robbinn said slowly. He held the silence for just a little longer, broken only by a groaning noise made by one of Errnest's heads as he scratched it on the floor with his paws. "I want you to proceed with this information in mind. Check each and every member of my father's court, tell me if I can trust them. Ideally I'd like a representing lord or lady from each area that doesn't currently want to attack me when this news breaks. Do you understand me?"

"Yes, Your Grace." Oserys gave an understanding downward nod, his thick curtains of black hair falling in front of his face. "I shall see to it from today. Might I ask you a question?"

"You may." Robbinn's tone didn't lighten, despite his feelings towards the man sitting across from him.

"Would you like help with Falkonn's funeral proceedings?" his voice was kind and silky this time, Robbinn blinked.

"Yes. I should think so. Would you be so kind as to alert the healers and priests, they'll want to be performing rituals." He asked, finally looking away to examine the walls. In decoration they were very similar to his own – ornately decorated in black, gold and scarlet with various carvings on the wall – but it was more extravagant, the carvings more detailed and of higher quality. These of course, would soon be his chambers when his mother moved to the mourning wing, this bed he would share with the woman behind him.

"Yes, Your Grace. I'm sorry to see my old friend go, in some ways. But I must admit you seem to have a far more level head than him. I wish you good luck." With that, he stood and swept from the room, his dogs at his heels.

Despite feeling three pairs of eyes on him, Robbinn maintained the silence left by Oserys like the first delicate snowfall of the year that he didn't want to disturb as he stood and crossed to the wall, to examine the paint there, Falkonn's crown still clutched in his hand. His crown, now.

"Oserys." He turned his head just enough to see her. "I believe we ought to share this chamber for appearances. We unfortunately will not be taking our honeymoon, although I fear you may not be all that disappointed. My library and your current chambers are of course, still yours to use as you see fit." He gave a small, meaningful look between her and Arriella, who nodded enthusiastically.

"Luciaan, you'll be getting new chambers soon. I want you close to me at all times. Am I clear?" He didn't meet Luciaan's mismatched eyes until he asked his question.

"You are," Luciaan replied simply.

Robbinn turned once again to his father's looking glass, and stepped forward to examine his reflection. He was startled to see he didn't recognise his own expression, and horrified to see that Luciaan's expression was one of muted fear and alarm. Perhaps his love didn't recognise him, either. The thought was terrifying, almost as awful as being like Falkonn, still lying dead and uncovered in his bed.

"Oserys, Arriella, would you give us a moment?"

"Yes, of course. Come dear, we should see that the carriage is going to get back safely," Oserys said quickly, taking Arriella's hand and leading her out.

The door clicked shut behind them. Neither Robbinn nor Luciaan moved. The silence between them continued to stretch from tense to plain uncomfortable as each waited for the other to speak, eyes locked through the mirror.

"Tell me what's troubling you, my love." Said Robbinn, smoothly. Luciaan's eyes brightened immediately.

"Love?" he asked, hopefully.

"Yes, I think it's quite appropriate," Robbinn replied, frowning slightly. "Unless you don't like that?"

"No, no, I do. You've just," Luciaan paused to think. Robbinn remained quiet, quite aware that Luciaan's linguistic skills were not his strongest point. "You've never had a name for us before."

Robbinn blinked, quite bewildered by what came tumbling out of Luciaan's perfect mouth. After a couple of moments, he remembered. It felt like years ago, after he had crept out to the stables with him to make feverish, almost animalistic love that left him covered in the most wonderful bite marks and bruises, and upon asking Luciaan more about his past he had been met with a sheepish 'no.' Robbinn still regretted his handling of that

164

situation, but he had pressed him quite aggressively as to why he couldn't know. Luciaan's words still echoed in his mind like a scar that wouldn't heal:

"I mean more that it's been a while and you still don't have a name for this. Whatever we are. I like you a lot, Robbinn. But I've lived with being gay long enough to know my worth. At least some of it."

His voice had been hurt and strained, as though the very thought had caused him great pain.

"Yes. Have I not told you before?" Robbinn asked, puzzled.

"No, believe it or not," Luciaan chuckled, "I still haven't managed to develop mind reading abilities. Surely you remember my lack of ability causing me to get pissed and put a skirt on."

Finally, Robbinn's face cracked into a smile and a laugh followed. Luciaan looked quite relieved to see him laugh.

"Well then, I shall say it now." Robbinn sucked in a nervous breath, then met those kind, soft eyes of Luciaan's. "You own my heart and soul, nobody else ever will. You saw me for what I was in a far plainer way than anybody else ever has, or will, if I can help it. It's always been you; it's always going to be you."

Luciaan looked like he was about to cry, and he spoke in a slightly strained voice, as though he were trying to hold back his emotions. Robbinn hadn't anticipated this meaning quite so much to him.

"Robbinn, I mean it when I say for you, I would move heaven and earth. If you asked me to, I would bring mountains to their knees and bring you the heads of the gods. The thought of you brings me so much light, I have already used it to bring me home before now. I am dedicated to you, and you alone."

165

Luciaan watched him with fierceness and determination in his eyes that Robbinn had never before seen.

Still staring into Luciaan's eyes, Robbinn placed the crown in his hands onto his head.

"Then with you at my side, I will crush this war."

Chapter Sixteen

When the evening before Falkonn's burial finally arrived, he had been lying in the middle of the church where Robbinn had been married for five days. On each day a separate ritual was performed, one for each god, to prepare the king for his journey to the afterlife.

Robbinn had remained in the church with his mother for the entire time, assisting in the daily washing and dressing of the body; he made a point of being cool and collected in public view, refusing to show weakness to his people – he wanted to be a beacon of strength and serenity for his mourning kingdom.

This approach seemed to have worked, as the few times he had been seen by his subjects they all seemed to be comforted by his stony strength, and none had pissed on him from an upstairs window just yet.

Luciaan pulled him aside on the night before Falkonn's final journey for a short conversation while Oserys spoke to a few members of the public, assuring them that the new king had full control over the final funeral procession.

"Robbinn, I wonder if you'd like to see that thing I told you about ages ago? I know there's not much time, but I think it's important for you to see before your coronation." Asked Luciaan quietly, leaning in to whisper in his ear as though conveying a secret message.

"Yeah, okay," Robbinn replied quickly, desperate for a change of scene. "Is it still all right if Oserys comes?"

"Yes, of course. Just come quickly, I have horses waiting at the back." Luciaan swept away to the back of the church and Robbinn saw him sling a thick, shabby, dark coloured cloak over his shoulders and pull the hood up. Robbinn hurried over to his wife and placed a hand on her shoulder from behind as he too leaned in close to mutter into her ear as she finished talking to the old, distraught couple.

"Come with me quickly, we need to go now, it's important," he muttered hastily. Oserys didn't need telling twice, as she met him beside Luciaan who handed them both shabby old cloaks, hoods up to hide their faces.

Luciaan took the lead once they were settled on inconspicuous horses, all three of them a similar dirty, muddy bay colour – they moved very quickly, cantering through winding streets to come out at the end to find a small, overgrown old temple of the five. They must have been several miles away, in the middle of a thick forest, the journey having taken around a quarter of an hour.

Robbinn frowned, quite perplexed as to why Luciaan had brought them from a church to a temple of all things, and felt the distinct annoyance at wasted time begin to rise up in his chest, but he swallowed it carefully.

"What are we doing here?" He asked as he dismounted his puffing horse and tied it up outside.

"You'll see soon, I promise it's important." Luciaan too dismounted, tied up his horse, then lit a torch. "I told you that I'd been okay with who I am for a long time. There's a reason for that, which hopefully you're about to find out. Depends who's out to play." He smiled, then led Robbinn and Oserys towards the old, crumbling temple.

He stumbled into the old temple. Old but evidently not unloved… He gazed up at the statue that his subjects prayed to, so often that there were groves from their knees worn into the stone beneath it as Luciaan walked around it, lighting candles.

Finally, his eyes settled on the dragon marble that depicted the gods. There was one for each of them, arranged in a line which was odd, as Robbinn was used to seeing them in a semi-circle. As always, the gods of war and death were intertwined, the details of this often varied church to church – the elegant one where his father lay only had them holding hands but here they were embracing, Ydmirr staring up into Pereggnir's eyes, their lips almost touching.

Scripture told them that the two were husband and wife, but a man and a woman were not those whom he laid eyes on. The shorter of the two was Ydmirr, he was easy to recognise – lit by the orange and yellow of candles was that familiar, strong, lean form littered with scars from his battles. His head tilted up to meet the lips of the other, who must be Pereggnir. This depiction looked startlingly similar to Luciaan... Tall and long haired and unfairly handsome. Before Robbinn had the chance to look for long, Pereggnir began to move with the familiar sound of grinding stone. Slowly the statue moved away from his husband and stepped down, waiting for him to do the same and holding a hand outstretched to help him down, which he took with a smile.

Floored, all the prince could do was stare, mouth agape, his eyes wide as everything he had ever understood about the gods came crashing down around his ears.

"Hello there, dear child," said Pereggnir, his voice deep and smooth – just like Luciaan's.

"I—you're... You're supposed to be—" stammered Robbinn.

"A woman?" He laughed good naturedly. "Unfortunately not. That is a mistranslation which has irritated me for centu-

169

ries. As I'm sure you know, us gods cannot inhabit a vessel unless it is similar enough to us in appearance."

"That's—that's why you never visit? Because our statues are wrong?" Suddenly what Ydmirr had told him months ago made sense. *There is nothing wrong with you.* The realisation must have been obvious, it seemed to prompt Pereggnir's hand on his shoulder.

"I need you to take the information you have now and fix things. Correct my statues for me, and I shall owe you a debt."

Robbinn stared, his thoughts tripping over one another in their efforts to come out first. What would this mean for the kingdom? For his marriage? For future young boys and girls who would grow up to be gay like him? And Pereggnir was offering him a deal. There was war about to break, the threat of it hung in the air even now, as the upcoming funeral rose tensions even further.

"A debt? What kind of debt?" Robbinn asked, slowly. "I'll do it regardless, you ought to be your true self." He added slightly hastily, sensing how he may have come across.

"Anything you ask of me," Pereggnir replied kindly as his husband leaned in to add to the conversation.

"Or of me, since you were wed under my name." Ydmirr smiled, bowing his head slightly.

"There is war on the horizon. As we speak the Southern and Western nations rally against the throne, they're approaching fast with the help of the pirates. I would like the assurance that we are going to win it, if that's something you can give me," Robbinn asked, finally.

There was a moment of silence that stretched on agonizingly long, tense moments.

"We can give you this. But we will never do it again, as this opportunity may never be presented again," Pereggnir said finally, glancing at his husband. "However, we can only grant you the request that your war will be won, not a perfect ending to it. We can only sway the odds so much. I can't guarantee that you won't suffer great losses, but you will remain on the throne and victorious."

"Then we have a deal. I'll have it seen to immediately," Robbinn said firmly, nodding his head.

"Thank you," Robbinn glanced between their faces, "this guidance is incredibly important to me. Especially you, Ydmirr. Your patience has been more than I deserve."

Robbinn turned to leave, muttering to Oserys that she was more than welcome to have her own discussions with the two, as she had seemed lost for words in a way that he had never seen in her before, no doubt she was thinking about what this revelation would mean for her and Arriella, and possibly their marriage.

It was dark by the time they returned to the church, and this time Robbinn road fastest and hardest through the winding streets, his horse skidding so fast to a halt that sparks flew from its shoes – but he didn't wait to see it tied, he thrust the reins into Luciaan's hands before he had chance to dismount himself, and ran full pelt into the church.

Thankfully it was quite empty besides the priests.

"You," he demanded, striding up to Pereggnir's priestess, "have you ever truly been contacted by Pereggnir?"

She gulped, looking around to her fellows nervously before she replied, "No."

"Do you know why that is?" Robbinn pressed her furiously.

"We aren't certain. We always assumed she was busy," she replied slowly, possibly wondering where he was going with this.

"Pereggnir is known for not visiting, no? Go and get me your oldest scriptures. Now." Robbinn commanded silkily. The priestess didn't need telling twice – she sprinted off out of sight and returned a few minutes later with an old book that had evidently been repaired numerous times.

"Check the writing around Pereggnir," he commanded, watching her open the book carefully and slowly turn to the first few pieces about the God of Death.

"Can you read this, Your Grace?" she muttered, quite anxiously.

"Some. Mother has taught me many different languages in preparation for my rule," Robbinn explained, his eyes scanning the pages for any mention of it being tampered with, or the original pronouns.

And then, quite suddenly, there it sat. In an ancient runic language, sat the symbol for 'him'. Granted, it was very similar to the one for 'her', and the ones for 'he' and 'she' were only a small angle and a small dot's difference – easy to chalk up to handwriting or discolouration of the page.

"There. That quite clearly refers to Pereggnir as a 'him'. Look, next to Ydmirr. And that," he squinted, leaning closer to find a small, inconspicuous piece of parchment pasted on, with the rune for 'wife' scrawled on top in a slightly different colour, "has been tampered with. Look, all of you."

The priests huddled in close as he carefully peeled it off and there, easily recognisable, even if it was slightly beaten up now, was the rune for 'husband'.

"Pereggnir is not a goddess, but a god." There was an audible gasp around the group as Oserys walked in to join them.

"How did you know about this?" Pereggnir's priestess demanded angrily.

"I have just spoken to him," Robbinn replied, simply.

172

There was a stunned moment of silence that quickly grew into disbelief, and even faster into anger. Anger which Robbinn could understand from the priestess whose world he had just torn down – she had after all, dedicated her entire life to this cause, to the worship of the gods, and now here was the king coming in to tell her it was all for naught.

One of them opened his mouth to protest, but Oserys cut him off before he could make a sound.

"I spoke with him too, and I daresay we're not the only ones," she said dangerously.

"I want the statues replaced with male ones as soon as you can. If you seek proof, ask my cavalry advisor, Luciaan to take you out to the temple. It is imperative that these statues be replaced as soon as possible, do you all understand?" Robbinn said firmly and quickly, looking around the group of priests, who all nodded ferociously.

"Good. For now I shall retire for the night, I hope you are successful." Robbinn nodded to them all, turned, and swept away.

The next morning, Robbinn felt strangely subdued as Claude dressed him in black, heavy clothes saved for funeral processions. Hoards of people were gathered outside the church, behind the army and the cavalry, and every servant in the castle had been dressed up and come down to assist the procession.

When Robbinn looked out of the window he saw an ocean of black, with the odd flash of red or gold as though the sun was shining on it, even though the sun was quite hidden today. Each and every member of the household cavalry was in attendance as well as every foot soldier, general, captain and advisory member of Falkonn's army, all of them mounted on fine, strong horses which were dressed up with their war drapes. There was a line of high-ranking officers at the front of the formation and a line of knights at the back – each of them looking like a small, black, armoured dragon as they stood.

At the very back of the group stood the hearse carriage, pulled by the same six, winged horses that had pulled Robbinn at his wedding, this time waiting for Falkonn's sarcophagus to be loaded in the back of it.

Luciaan was down there too, holding Solmyrer and the captain either side of his own Pereggnir, waiting for Robbinn to join them. But first he had to assist in the performing of the final rituals before the journey could begin.

When he made his way to the main room of the church where four of five gods were looking down, hands outstretched to the large, white marble sarcophagus that contained Falkonn's body lay open.

The priests held out special bottles of fragrant oils, one per god to be placed on Falkonn's skin while the priests prayed.

"Today, we prepare Falkonn Caarvide Carbeu for his final journey to Pereggnir's arms. We place oil of poppies over his eyes, in the hopes that she will guide his way."

Robbinn placed a drop of oil on his father's closed eyelids, and placed the bottle back.

"We place lily oil over the heart, in the hopes that Ydmirr will strengthen his spirit."

Robbinn placed a drop over Falkonn's heart, and replaced the bottle.

"We place algae oil over the feet, so that he may pass Ildyr's domain freely."

Robbinn dutifully placed a drop on each foot, and replaced the bottle.

"We place rhododendron oil on the hands, to ask Ydnias to protect him."

Once more, Robbinn followed his orders, placing a drop of

174

the oil on each hand, his eyes not leaving the corpse.

"Finally, we place lavender oil in the forehead, to ask Vyxena for final guidance in his last journey."

At last Robbin placed a drop of lavender oil on his father's forehead, keeping his cold gaze upon his pale, taught skin.

Silently, the priests moved away to pick up the lid of the sarcophagus – it was carved from the same white marble as the rest of it, only with Falkonn's image sculpted into it. It was nothing short of magnificent, as though Falkonn himself had been cast into stone, lying back with a peaceful expression that Robbinn had never seen before and in his mind looked slightly odd on his face, his hands folded across his chest, crown on his head which was propped against a pillow.

It was lowered onto the lower part, slotting into place with a loud clunk. The marble was sealed with a gold coloured glue of some sort, Falkonn's old personal guard were invited to enter. When the group of eight – the only name he knew being Aldredd – picked up the sarcophagus, they shook with its weight like eight trees shaking under the force of a storm, and Robbinn noticed that the panels on the outside were decorated too, segmented into a total of ten, (one at the front and back, four on each side), each carved to tell a scene. His birth, his father's funeral, his wedding, his coronation, his ten-year anniversary on the throne, the birth of his son, his twenty-year jubilee on the throne, his first triumph in war, his death showing his wife sobbing, and his arrival to the afterlife were all carved from a panel each. It must have taken years to carve in such glorious detail.

Robbinn was not given the time to contemplate this, as the priests had begun to walk very slowly out of the doors, into the wailing, blubbering crowd who were kept at bay by the few soldiers not in formation. Oserys waited for him beside Oleyyna, both on horseback; Oserys on the warden, and Oleyyna on her great chestnut mare affectionately known as Peggy, both horses draped in rugs of royal colours, even their breastplates shining with gold. Both women wore traditional clothing of mourning, head to toe in fine black clothing with skreghle head broaches holding their knee length cloaks around their shoulders in the snow as bystanders threw so many flowers it began to feel like there was a storm rolling in by the way they blocked out the lights.

Robbinn too wore traditional mourning clothing, his tunic, coat, trousers, and cloak were all black, aside from his belt, which was gold, and Falkonn's antler like crown sat upon his head. He took the moment of mounting his horse and leaning down to check the girth strap to fix his face into something stony and miserable as snow began to fall.

Before very long passed, Falkonn's sarcophagus was loaded into the carriage, and the priests too mounted horses, the procession began; the priests leading everyone.

It took hours to march through the streets back to the castle to the sound of drums, wailing and blubbering, snow falling thick and fast from the very start and continuing for the entire journey, to the point that there was almost a foot of it on the hearse's roof.

When they finally arrived at the castle the snow was growing into near blizzard conditions, and the group of guards taking Falkonn's sarcophagus down to the crypts all shook at the knees the whole way down. The procession of soldiers, knights and nobles stopped and situated themselves in a line as Robbinn, Oleyyna, and Oserys descended the stairs after the priests and personal guard.

The crypt was not somewhere Robbinn particularly enjoyed visiting – in honesty he found it unsettlingly creepy. Each and every deceased member of his family had been laid to rest here, all marked by a second statue in their likeness, and a marble nameplate. They were also incredibly active – very few of them had moved on and it wasn't uncommon to see them clawing their way out of their sarcophagus to scream and cry at the living visiting them.

The same was true now, there were the gaunt, skeletally thin, shadowy, transparent faces poking out from the lids of most of the marble sarcophagi, watching them place Falkonn in with them while they wailed wordlessly.

As such, the placing of Falkonn's body in the crypt was slightly rushed to say the least – everyone wanted to be out of that place as soon as possible to escape the screaming ghosts.

Chapter Seventeen

The crowd that had accumulated outside the castle walls dissipated relatively quickly, as the snow only got worse, and people decided they would rather retreat into their warm, insulated homes than be outside freezing half to death – many of them simply dropped some flowers and left. Robbinn found he couldn't blame them, for as soon as he had the chance, he too had retreated into the warmth, his particular warmth being that of Luciaan's arms, in his bed surrounded by furs and candles.

He tipped his head back into Luciaan's shoulder, finally able to be alone with him and completely unwilling to waste even a second of it. He was completely filled with the scent and presence Luciaan carried – something he had always found great comfort in, whether he had been there in person or not.

"Thank you, Luciaan," Robbinn said quite abruptly, and the fingers tracing soft, absentminded circles into his stomach stopped.

"What for?" Luciaan asked, confusion obvious in his voice.

"Everything," Robbinn replied, sleepy and stupid from the oily candles spewing thick, sweet scents into the room. Luciaan gave a small, nervous sounding laugh.

"What specifically?"

"Taking me to that temple, for one. For treating me like a person, and thinking about me. I still remember when we rode out together for the first time on Clyde and you'd already done my stirrups for me," said Robbinn, dreamily remembering that warm feeling in his chest when he realised. He shifted his gaze up to find Luciaan's eyes. "Do you remember?"

"'Course I do. I did it hoping you'd spot it." He was relaxed again now, understanding that Robbinn was just feeling soft and slow, not feeling anything he should be worried about. "I'm glad you did."

"I started watching you turning horses out months before we actually met, you know." Robbinn murmured, turning his face further into Luciaan's neck, inhaling the scent of his sweat with a great deal of glee.

"I know, I saw you." Luciaan pulled him further into his side, his hand reaching his prince's hair to stroke it softly. The sensation almost made Robbinn purr. "How else would I have come to the stupid conclusion that you were seeing Oserys?"

Robbinn chuckled, the dots slowly connecting.

"This could very well be our last night of peace, you know." He said after a moment. Luciaan went slightly rigid.

"I can feel it. It's like the moment before lightning strike, there's a moment when everyone and everything knows what's going to happen, the crows know that soon they'll be fat and happy, telling their grandchildren about that day. I've seen it before, felt it." Luciaan's voice was quiet and hollow, his eyes unfocussed and his grip far less soft.

Robbinn didn't speak, just willed him to continue in his mind – as though Luciaan could read it. After a quiet moment, Luciaan drew breath to speak again.

"I was only a teenager when I joined the army for the first time, in the Western Continent. The training was hard, but there was nothing to prepare us for the reality of war. Even then it wasn't considered to be 'bad'. I'll never forget it. The morning when it first started, everything was silent, but in a strange way. Like everything knew what would happen. I wasn't lucky

179

enough to be given a tent, I slept against Preg." 'Preg' Robbinn presumed was a nickname for his horse, Pereggnir. He didn't speak, just listened to the tale that Luciaan was so reluctant to tell him a few months ago. "I had a sword, a shield, and some leather armour. Preg had more, full steel. I was more expendable than him. If a soldier died but a fully trained, brave horse like him lived, there was always more men. I remember mounting up, checking my girth, gathering his reins, and joining formation. After that it kind of turned into a blur. I couldn't tell you how many people I killed that day. We took the city back by the evening, killed women and children to do it. I remember setting light to the pile of corpses. The stench of human burning... Fuck, it was awful. Next battle I was given armour too. Each following I climbed rank simply for surviving." He paused, Robbinn watched his pupils dilate again as his eyes returned to him.

"I swore when I left that I wasn't ever going to go back into war. I couldn't do it again, the killing, the cruelty, the filth, but for you, if you asked me, I would."

Robbinn flushed bright pink at his finishing statement as though he were a young maid being flirted with for the first time.

"Would you swear to it?" He asked quietly, staring up into his eyes.

"Yes," Luciaan replied eagerly, fumbling to seize Robbinn's hand. "I would. You need only ask, and I will come."

"I shall treasure this promise then." Robbinn found Luciaan's hand first and grabbed it, squeezing it firmly to prove himself. "I will not let it go to waste."

Luciaan leaned over to kiss his forehead gently and mutter into his hair.

"I trust you, my king."

"Oh that sounds strange, doesn't it?" Robbinn giggled, feeling rather like a little girl. "I'm not used to being king yet, Luci."

Luciaan chuckled softly, brushing hairs out of Robbinn's pretty amber eyes.

"It feels weird to say. You've always been prince, haven't you? Next thing to plan is your coronation, isn't it?" Luciaan asked quietly.

"Yes, it is. I've got no idea what to do with it. Maybe a celebratory ball, I've never exactly danced with you and I'd very much like to," Robbinn's voice was dreamy, as though his head was up in the clouds.

"You'll be horrified to know I don't know how to dance!" Luciaan laughed a little louder this time as Robbinn gasped in his correctly predicted horror, only just cut off with a giggle. He put a hand to his forehead theatrically, as though he would surely faint at the very thought.

"Then I shall teach you!" Robbinn exclaimed, abruptly twisting around in Luciaan's arms to straddle his hips, arms held aloft to punctuate his promise. "I'll teach you to dance, so that we can do it during my coronation."

Luciaan's laugh lingered like ripples on the surface of a lake as he gazed up at his lover, hands holding his hips in place.

"You shouldn't have a problem learning, you already have an excellent sense of rhythm." Robbinn purred, his hands travelling up Luciaan's chest to the lacing holding his tunic together at the front. As much as Robbinn adored Luciaan's more rugged look as a head groom, nobody could deny how handsome the man was in the fine, expensive clothes his new pay let him afford.

With expert tailoring, his enormous, muscular form was easily extenuated with well-placed seams and adjustable cinch-

181

ing with a medium collar to show off his long neck and lead seamlessly into the strips of muscle forming his shoulders.

Luciaan smirked up at him, evidently quite flattered by the complement that had already been kicked from his mind in favour of admiring his perfect body.

With a quick bite to his lip, Robbinn leaned down to steal a kiss from Luciaan's surprisingly soft lips – it didn't matter how many times he had kissed them, he was quite certain the pleasant surprise would never get old.

He felt Luciaan's huge hand leave his hip and rest against his face, leading him in closer as his other hand slunk up under his tunic, seeking out skin to touch. Luciaan kissed him deeper and slower, his hands starting to wander, leaving his face to pull his tunic out of the way to touch him more – which absolutely wasn't to say Robbinn wasn't too pushing fabric out of his path to Luciaan's skin. He enjoyed the power Luciaan was giving him, allowing him to set the pace and timing, allowing him to be the one to draw sharp, pleased breaths from Luciaan rather than the other way around.

Robbinn rocked and ground his hips into Luciaan with soft tenderness as he shed his own tunic and untied his dear groom's beneath him. Heat pooled in his gut as he stopped to take off his trousers – despite the overwhelming urge to tear them off, he made a good show of doing it slowly.

"Consider this your first dancing lesson, Luci," Robbinn muttered breathlessly, climbing back into Luciaan's lap. "Despite leading the waltz, you must be aware of only what your partner is doing and feeling. Do you understand, Luci?"

With a slightly tense sigh at the pressure, Luciaan tipped his head back but didn't reply; his brow remained furrowed, and his eyes screwed shut, a slight flush of red heating his cheeks and just about starting to reach his collarbones.

182

"Answer me, darling," demanded Robbinn in a silky voice.

"I understand." His eyes finally opened again to meet Robbinn's, framed pretty, white lashes. Luciaan smiled adoringly up at him. "Teach me more, love."

Robbinn didn't need to be told twice as he reached over Luciaan for the bottle of oil kept on the headboard and pushed it into Luciaan's enormous, sculpted, long fingered hands. It was immediately uncorked and a little of it poured onto waiting hands where it stayed, warming to body temperature before it was smoothly rubbed into Robbinn's skin. Slowly up and down Robbinn's slender, toned back Luciaan's hands pressed in just enough to be felt, making his muscles relax under the gentle pressure.

Robbinn could already hardly think, and he was supposed to be in charge this time, but Luciaan didn't seem to mind taking the lead – usually he'd change positions, but this time he left Robbinn where he'd put himself, slowly working his gentle massage from the middle of Robbinn's back downward towards his hips where finger shaped bruises from their last few encounters still sat proudly blue and purple against Robbinn's pale skin.

Luciaan's touch edged off to be even softly over the bruises, presumably anticipating the sore spots, but Robbinn grabbed his hands and pressed them harder into the bruising, biting his lip between a soft mutter: "I like the sting."

At the sight of Luciaan's grin, Robbinn promptly lost himself to the throws of passion: his body acted of its own accord to seek out what felt like hot, delicious heaven. All he heard was his own gasping whines and Luciaan's groans through gritted teeth as their hips moved without direction for the remainder of the evening. Robbinn remembered it was gentle and loving, filled with softness akin to that of feathers – he couldn't imagine anything more perfect for the day.

Robbinn awoke the next day in Luciaan's adoring embrace as light filtered in from the window with the tapping of Zekeyus' nose on the window. Taking a small length of fur around his slender waist, Robbinn padded over to open the window and allow the little creature inside.

He clicked and trilled affectionately as he hopped in and shook his leg in Robbinn's direction where a letter was attached. Without much thought as to who on earth got hold of his dragon, Robbinn took the letter from him and unfurled it – it was hastily scribbled onto a scrap of parchment that had been torn from a larger piece, there were blotches of ink on it and whoever had written it seemed to have broken a quill.

'Robbinn,

Meet me at your father's study immediately. Do not be seen if you can avoid it. This is urgent.

Aldredd.'

Robbinn frowned down at it, reading the thing twice over again as he walked back to his bed and perched on it, reaching out to shake Luciaan into the conscious world without taking his eyes off the note.

"Luci." Finally Robbinn dragged his eyes from the parchment to look at Luciaan as he grumbled his displeasure at being disturbed. "Luci!"

"Mmnh…" Robbinn jabbed him in the ribs. "OW—Robbinn! Dirty tricks…" He sat up and stretched his arms over his head, still very sleepy. Until, however, he spotted the look on Robbinn's face. "What is it?"

Robbinn thrust the note at him without a word. Luciaan took it and read it.

"Aldredd? What's he asking you that for? Wonder what he wants…" He trailed off, getting out of bed and pulling Rob-

184

binn's clothes for the day from his grand wardrobe. "S'pose you ought to get dressed then."

"Yeah. Father's study is upstairs. It won't take me long to get dressed." Luciaan wrapped his arms around Robbinn from behind and pressed a kiss into his neck.

"I can help you, if you like," Luciaan muttered, offering his tunic out to him.

"Please, darling." Robbinn smiled, feeling his cheeks heat up.

As promised, it didn't take him long to dress and sneak up to his father's old study where Aldredd was waiting for him, fully armoured, wearing a look of worry written on his face.

"Your Grace, thank you for humouring me. I apologise for the way I invited you here, Zekeyus was the safest way to make sure nobody would intercept the message," Aldredd muttered, pacing around the old desk.

"Intercept? Safest?" Robbinn blinked in confusion. "What are you talking about? And please, call me Robbinn."

"There is a spy in our midst." Aldredd replied simply.

"What?" Demanded Robbinn, his tone sharpening. "Who? How do you know?"

"Your father had been threatened with war for months before his passing, as I'm sure you know. But they knew he was dying. There is an uprising in the Western territories, some false king is trying to emerge. His name is Hermontt Hardweaverr. He has 'freed' several colonies on his way towards the continent."

Robbinn muttered the surname under his breath. He knew that name from somewhere, but he couldn't quite put his finger on it.

"Hardweaverr... Wait a moment. A Hardweaverr was executed at that ball, wasn't there?"

"You made the connection much faster than Falkonn. Huxell and Hermontt are twin brothers. The uprising was already starting, assassinating Falkonn would have been the downfall of this kingdom, but they didn't count on the presence of the Daeemoris that night," Aldredd explained patiently but with urgency.

"I can't imagine the execution helped the tension at all," Robbinn said bitterly.

"I think you're absolutely right. I don't know who the spy is, but I believe it to be one of the serving staff. There are hints in these letters, threatening Falkonn and I think you should read them." Aldredd stepped behind the desk and opened a drawer to pull out stacks and stacks of letters and place them on top for Robbinn to see.

"How long has this been happening?" Robbinn asked slowly, making his way to the chair as Aldredd stepped out of his way.

"Years, easily," Aldredd answered quickly – Robbinn presumed he'd wanted to tell him for a good while.

"And why is this the first I'm hearing of it?" His amber eyes were cast down at the letters as he sat, and looked for the oldest one to read first.

"Falkonn forbade me from telling anyone. You, specifically," muttered Aldredd, keeping his voice low so as to keep Robbinn's distraction to a minimum.

"Did he say why?" He asked idly.

"The same reason he kept his illness from you for so long. He didn't think you were ready to handle it," Aldredd replied, again quite simply.

"How do you know that? Mother said nobody but her was told." Robbinn demanded, sharply turning his gaze on the formidable man beside him.

"You were never the only Carbeu man with secrets, Rob-binn," he said with a hint of mischief in his eyes.

"What's that supposed to mean?"

"I'm not at liberty to tell. Your father and I kept things for each other – I won't allow his death to stop that." Aldredd lowered his head, dropping Robbinn's eye. "I'm sorry."

"You're a loyal man. Unless these secrets are of a distasteful nature, of course. In which case you would simply be a slimy little bastard who deserves nothing but death. When you're ready, I would like to know what your secret is, so that I too may keep it. In return I shall give you one of mine." Robbinn's command came coolly but dangerously – as though Aldredd had no choice in the matter. "I would like to verify your trustworthiness, especially given that there is a spy."

"You suspect me?" Aldredd asked, looking up sharply in his astonishment.

"No. But I would like to trust you, and I do not want to misplace it. Do you see my issue?" Robbinn asked pointedly.

"I do." Aldredd bit his lip and steeled his face as though preparing for a battle. "In that case, I shall tell you what Falkonn kept hidden for me, for so many years."

Chapter Eighteen

Without another word, Aldredd shut and bolted the study door, causing Robbinn's stomach to lurch and his throat to tighten. It was all he could do not to outwardly show his worry at being shut in a room with a formidable warrior, after demanding proof of loyalty.

"The secret your father kept for me pertained to my birth. More specifically what I was born as. Of course, you asked for proof too." Aldredd said, slowly turning around again. Robbinn's palms started to sweat.

"I also said when you're ready." Robbinn said curtly.

"I'm as ready as I'll ever be. I didn't exactly decide to tell Falkonn, he sort of just found out." He paused, taking a breath as Robbinn stared at him.

"I wasn't born as Aldredd," the man finally muttered. "I was Allcina to my loving mother. Vyxena had blessed her with a girl."

"What?" Robbinn still stared, mouth hanging open, struck into silence by the revelation. "There's no way!"

"There is. I am what is known as a Marked One. Do you know what that means?" Aldredd asked, suddenly talking very fast.

"I've heard the term, never a definition," Robbinn mumbled.

"Vyxena has given me the wrong body for my mind. I was born as a woman, but I am a man. That is the secret Falkonn kept for me." Aldredd finished, his head hung in what appeared to be shame.

"I see. I had asked you to prove your claim, but I will not ask about this. I believe you," Robbinn said, finality in his voice. "I believe I also promised you a secret in return."

"You did, Your Grace. But please don't think you must, I am but a soldier in all of this where you are king," Aldredd replied, keeping his head low.

"Head up, man!" Robbinn spoke so sharply that Aldredd flinched, then stared at him incredulously. "If I am correct and what I'm seeing is shame, then you must be rid of it! In any way you can, eradicate it." Aldredd's face lit up with what looked very much like relief at his words.

"Your Grace—that is more than I deserve."

"No it is not. You are not the only one of us Vyxena has cursed. I'm..." he tried to say it but the words caught in his throat. He'd never said it out loud before. Thankfully Aldredd was patient, and simply waited quietly for him to continue. Robbinn took a deep breath and proceeded slowly. "I'm gay. Now that you know I want you to keep it as closely as you do your own, if not more so. Protect it with your life, and I will protect yours with mine."

Robbinn stuck out his hand to Aldredd, who looked at it for half a second, then took it firmly in his own which was rough and calloused where Robbinn's was soft and smooth, then shook it firmly.

"I will, sir."

"Then we have an agreement." Their eyes met for a few focused moments, and broke with a mutual nod. "You have my trust, and I have yours. Tell me at what point in these letters did you conclude there was a spy?"

"Here, when they were aware of Oserys Daeemori's visit

189

before it was announced," Aldredd said, urgency returning to his voice as he retrieved a letter and handed it to him.

"I see. When was this?" Robbinn turned it over in his hands, then held it to the light to begin reading. The slanted, swirling hand read:

'Dear Falkonn,

I have heard tell that your son has finally made a decision. Congratulations, I'm sure he will make Oserys Daeemori II very happy, much to everyone's surprise. In other news, I have secured allies in the pirates and their beasts! Isn't that lovely? Expect them on your shores when Robbinn is king.

Yours,

Hermontt Hardweaverr, the New King'

"This was sent the day after you told your parents about Oserys' visit." Aldredd clarified as Robbinn's eyes scanned the page.

"It has to be one of the serving staff, it was only them and us present at that point." Robbinn's brow furrowed as his mind raced to form a plan, ideas running into, over and under each other to be first out like spooked horses escaping a pen. "All right, here is my plan. You mention very specific, false, leads to each member of staff. It must be different for each person, and you will write it down. Do it sporadically, so that no pattern can be discerned. It has to be something that, if it were true, a spy would want to take to his superior."

"And if they take the bait, since it's all different, we'll know who it is. That's a better plan than Falkonn had, I have to say," muttered Aldredd, nodding.

"Exactly. I want you and only you to do it, take all the time you need to be certain. I'm planning my coronation, but I do believe I ought to consort with these bothersome pirates first," Robbinn said, finality evident in his tone.

Over the next week, Robbinn sent out what was quite frankly a ridiculous number of dragons to the known pirate legends, asking them to meet him on the white sand coast of Ildyr's Keep, the largest of at least seventy coastal cities on the Arkordouur continent, at the end of the week.

During this week, he was also rushing to plan a coronation under a concealed threat of war, and that absolutely would not stop him from hosting a ball. Not even Hermontt Hardweaverr would stop him stealing a dance with the love of his life before this war broke out, and he was certain his darling wife would feel the same about her own great love.

As he sat in his library, writing out invitations to noblemen and women, it occurred to him that he ought to check on the progress of changing Pereggnir's statues to be accurate – so he pushed aside his current invitation, pulled out a new piece of parchment, and scribbled out a rushed letter:

'Dear Priests and Priestesses,

I hope this letter finds your church well. I would like to know how my latest instruction regarding Pereggnir's statue has been carried out. Please update me via a replying dragon – however if I receive nothing for two days, on the third I shall visit you myself.

Yours,

King Robbinn Carbeu'

He couldn't think of anything stranger than signing off a letter as king as he wrote and sealed the letter, but by the time he had attached it to Zekeyus, he had realised how appropriate it truly was and banished his strange feeling about it by the time the little dragon had taken flight. When he had returned to his invitations, he had decided the title rather suited him.

A few hours into his horribly dull work, Robbinn was surprised when Zekeyus returned.

"Back already?" he muttered, letting him in with a soft smile as the beast hopped in through the window and perched on his shoulder, being rewarded with a small piece of cured meat from the pot on Robbinn's desk.

As expected, Zekeyus had returned with a response from the church. Robbinn laid it out flat on his desk, and began to read the equally short letter.

'Dear King Robbinn,

We have had all of Pereggnir's statues replaced, and have found that he is far more active. We offer our thanks, and have taken the liberty of having another statue made for your tower. Would it be agreeable if our associates deliver it and replace the incorrect one tomorrow?

With Faith of the Five,

Your priests.'

Robbinn smiled a little at the start of the letter, where it referred to him as King. He certainly thought power suited him quite well indeed. Before writing a response, Robbinn stood up to climb a tower that he hadn't climbed since his suitor's ball, where Oserys had cut Huxell Hardweaverr's throat before the gods, where Ydmirr first appeared to him – it felt like a lifetime ago.

With Zekeyus still perched on his shoulder, Robbinn found himself surrounded by his five gods, facing Ydmirr – the formidable god of war. He cleared his throat as he approached the statue before addressing it in what he hoped was a serene tone.

"Ydmirr?" he looked curiously at the statue as it blinked just once, very slowly, and turned its head. Thankfully, its handsome features broke into a smile.

"Robbinn! How are you getting on with this king business?" the statue asked jovially as he stepped down lightly from

192

his plinth. Zekeyus squawked in alarm and flew off.

"Quite well! In fact I have just received word that the church has finished replacing your husband's statues! I sought you out on this fine afternoon to ask if this was true?" Robbinn smiled too, rather encouraged by Ydmirr's mood.

"It is indeed! He is utterly delighted to be able to visit his people once again, he even appeared quite animatedly in the giant one, I do regret that you weren't there to see it!" The statue laughed with the memory, and Robbin smiled all the brighter.

"I was planning to have his statue replaced up here too. And now that he has been appeased, I would like to be able to speak with him discretely." These words seemed to seize the statue's attention from the entertaining memory.

"Oh?" It asked, almost sharply. "Why might that be?"

"I was contemplating naming him my god at my coronation. My original consideration was Ydnias, but now that Pereggnir has returned I am conflicted." Robbinn replied coolly, hoping to hide slight anxiety at Ydmirr's tone.

"Choose Ydnias. She may be difficult to appease, but in choosing me for your wedding, Pereggnir too will guard you, especially since you have helped him return to himself," said the statue, firmly.

"I see. Any tips for convincing her to speak to me?" Robbinn asked hopefully. Somewhere behind him came the sound of grinding stone, and a faint tap as a statue stepped down from its plinth. Robbinn turned at a voice he didn't recognise.

"Good afternoon, King Robbinn," Ydnias' statue said, standing there tall and strong like Oserys.

"Good afternoon," Robbinn replied slowly, trying hard to remain polite despite feeling as though he was about to burst with the excitement, "I hope you are well?"

"Indeed, I am. Your wife has spoken to me at length about you and your services to us gods. I would consider it a privilege to be your sworn god. Ydmirr tells me there will soon be need of him, is this true?" It spoke with a certain edge of authority, its arms folded over its chest.

"It is indeed. I am in fact going to parley with pirates soon, I wondered if I might ask for your guidance?"

"Indeed you may. I believe it may be useful to offer them money and some free reign over the oceans," Ydnias said after a moment's thought.

"I quite agree. I don't know what the other side is offering, but I want mine to be better." Robbinn mused, his arms folding over his chest.

"I believe Pereggnir has offered you victory in return for his statues being returned? Why not tell them that?" the statue turned to Ydmirr's, which had turned to stare away from the conversation. "If he is permitted to do so?"

"I shall find out, just a moment." The statue's life vanished for a few seconds, then returned like an invisible giant breathed life into it again. "You must not speak explicitly of your deal, but using his name as a threat would be relatively normal, and you are at perfect liberty to do so if you wish."

"So I am permitted to say, for example, 'The gods are on my side, I suggest you do the same', I would not be in breach of our deal?" Robbinn asked, his brow furrowed in thought.

"Yes, that is correct. As long as you do not say 'I made a deal with Pereggnir' or something similar your agreement will be intact." Ydmirr's statue nodded with its words. Robbinn's gaze turned to Ydnias' statue.

"Would you be able to back me up during this interaction? I am not asking you to appear, I want it to be dismissible as co-incidence, but pirates being pirates are a superstitious people, aren't they?" He asked slowly.

"Yes," Ydnias looked at him slyly through the statue, as though she were very much interested in what he had in mind, "what are you suggesting?"

"A light storm," Robbinn said simply, "I would like it if you could create a strike of lightning, close enough for us to hear the thunder when I make the threat. Feel free to strike one of their ships, or their monsters."

"I like that idea." Robbinn watched the statue's eyes widen with excitement. "I like you, I will do this if you name me your god."

"In that case we have a deal. I'd like you to tell me if there is anything I can do for you in terms of statues or changes to offerings and the like, and I'll do my best to meet any request that you send to me. That is a promise." He spoke with a smooth finality which felt slightly strange in his mouth, with his voice.

Robbinn descended the tower with his head held high, a satisfied feeling in his soul, and Zekeyus returned to his shoulder for the journey back to his library – evidently he had simply flitted away to perch in a nearby tree until the statues stopped moving. As he walked back down, he formulated a mental list of people to bring with him to negotiate with the pirates – it had to be only his most trusted fellows.

On his journey, he passed Clauude whom he instructed to tell Aldredd to meet him in his library as soon as he had time. Clauude hurried off to complete his orders, and Robbinn was left alone in the black and gold hallways once more. For a reason he couldn't put his finger on, the castle felt strangely empty and cold, as though he had not a friend to his name besides the lizard on his shoulder. Robbinn decided to pay it no mind with a deliberate mental push that he punctuated with a real one as he reached his library door and pressed it open.

He always found it hard to feel alone when surrounded by books, the ghosts of stories he had sought comfort from time and time again finding themselves new purpose in their thousands of combined identities filling the empty, silent space. For a moment, Robbinn simply stood there, picturing his favourite characters milling around the space together, exchanging their tales as written in the thousands of pages. Before he could lose himself too wholly in his imagination, Robbinn was joined by Aldredd, who quickly shut the door behind him.

"Aldredd, thank you for seeing me so quickly. I have a message for you," Robbinn commanded with a touch of urgency to his tone, just enough for Aldredd to hear.

"You have my full attention, Your Grace," Aldredd replied, meeting his king's gaze.

"I have decided who I am taking with me to speak to the pirates this week. I want you to see to it that they are all adequately prepared," Robbinn said firmly, looking to Aldredd for the affirming nod to continue. "First, the obvious: my wife, and her handmaiden. You, secondly. My mother, and Luciaan. I will take nobody else, and I want nobody else to know. Do you understand me?"

"Yes, Your Grace." Aldredd nodded again, visibly formulating his plan.

"Have you made any progress on you-know-what?" Robbin asked, carefully.

"Yes, but I am no closer to an answer. I have worked through roughly half thus far and nothing." Robbinn felt his shoulders sag slightly at the news as it left Aldredd's mouth.

"All right... I won't be taking anyone else with us, just on the off chance it's one of them," Robbinn confirmed, although in truth he couldn't imagine a world where Clauude of all people or any of his other personal staff were in contact with the greatest enemy to the crown.

"That's a good plan, my lord. I shall continue when we come back – the coast is almost two day's ride away. I shall see to it that we are ready to leave by the evening," Aldredd replied, his hand on the doorknob.

"Good, I would like to go as soon as possible, but quietly. See to it that we may leave in the dark. I don't want the public to get wind of this until it is over, if at all possible," Robbinn added, with finality in his voice.

"Yes, Your Grace. I will return to you when everything is ready." Aldredd bowed low, and left the room. Robbinn took in a deep breath as the door clicked shut. He felt as though he were being pulled in a thousand directions, and exhausted because of it. There was nothing he wanted more than a quiet evening with Luciaan, curled up with him by the fire in the cabin that used to be his home before his promotion warranted personal chambers in the castle.

"Bloody hell, why does everything have to be so shit?" Robbinn muttered darkly to himself.

Chapter Nineteen

"You're taking me to see the pirates? Why?" Luciaan asked, his expression bewildered as Robbinn and his other chosen company joined him hours later in the cold, snowy, dark courtyard to leave.

"Because I trust you, Luciaan," Robbinn said for the third time, irritation starting to gnaw at the edge of his voice.

"Yeah, I get that, but what am I supposed to do to help you with this?" Luciaan demanded as he sprung up onto Pereggnir's back – a name which now seemed to suit a stallion far more, and his owner too – as agitation began to also show in him.

"Stand there and look terrifying, I've had your armour packed so put that on when we get there. We're trying to convince them not to go against us. You represent my cavalry, Aldredd my foot soldiers, my swordsmen, and my wife my archers. Oserys dear, would you speak to me over here for a moment?" his attention switched so quickly and sharply that he saw Luciaan blink stupidly in his shock.

Oserys looked up from her conversation immediately and made her way to follow Robbinn a few paces away.

"Yes?" She asked when they were out of earshot of everyone else.

"I want you to send a message to your father. Tell him to bring a dragon or two, just in case things go poorly. Am I understood?" His voice was quiet in an attempt to keep it from being carried. Daeemori I had left weeks ago to carry out his task of testing Robbinn's advisors on the back of his dragon but had told Robbinn to ask through his daughter if he needed help.

"Do you think things will go poorly?" Oserys asked, nodding her head impatiently.

"They're pirates, they are quite unpredictable. I'd just like my bases to be covered." Robbinn answered simply as he began to shiver.

"I see. I'll have it done, it won't take them long to meet us." Oserys replied, seemingly untouched by the cold.

Fucking Northerners, Robbinn thought to himself darkly.

"Good. Come, we need to get on the road or we'll miss the rendezvous." With that, Robbinn turned back towards Solmyrer to mount up and move his small group to the road.

"We'll travel as a group. Is everyone ready?" He asked once his company was settled on horseback, to a small chorus of nods and mutters in response. "Good, I warn you that we may encounter bandits of any kind, and various beasts. If such is the case I instruct you all to use necessary force to protect yourselves. Am I clear?" Once more, his company nodded and muttered their affirmation, and Robbinn turned Solmyrer against the wind that was beginning to pick up at an alarming rate towards a path through the woodland, and his group fell into step around him.

Luciaan found himself at Robbinn's side for most of the night, and upon feeling no need to break the quiet between the two, he simply said nothing. Just listened together to their horse's feet and saddles, to the wind in the trees dislodging snow resting on thousands of branches hundreds of feet above them. Robbinn too felt comfortable listening to his surroundings and smelling the damp earthiness below his horse's feet with the last edges of Luciaan's scent being blown towards him, and thus said nothing. They simply shared the quiet together as

Oserys and Arriella behind them muttered to one another.

Aldredd came to lead the group beside Oleyyna, and brought them to an old outpost he knew well to rest the horses as the opalescent moon began to sink behind the trees and orange morning light began to paint the sky above.

"We'll rest here for a few hours. I've had it scouted, it should be safe, but I'll still keep watch." Aldredd informed the group as he dismounted his horse, a gentle chestnut gelding named Tankard, and unsaddled him. His company followed suit, and as Oleyyna led the others inside, Luciaan hung back. Robbinn could hear their voices through the closed door as Arriella and Oserys lit a fire in an old, disused grate. He strained to listen, but couldn't make out any words, only tones – which were serious, but not unfriendly.

Choosing for the moment to ignore the hushed conversation, Robbinn chose to explore the tiny building now that the fire was beginning to heat it. It took him only nine paces to get from one end of the lower floor to the other, which when one had spent his entire life living in a place where it took more than twenty to reach the other side of his chambers, felt remarkably cramped. Robbinn soon spied a staircase on the wall opposite the door, but when he went to climb it, saw that the floor it led to had been sealed. He swiftly arrived at the conclusion that he was stuck with five other people in this tiny space. Just as this thought reached him, the wooden door opened again and Luciaan stepped inside.

"Aldredd and I will be taking turns keeping watch every so often. We're meeting a friend at a tavern in the evening to sleep tomorrow night, so we need to leave here around mid-morning and ride fast. Is that all right with everyone?" Luciaan said authoritatively, glancing around his nodding company as Oserys began to help Oleyyna with her bedroll.

"Good. This is the most dangerous stop, the rest are relatively safe. But that doesn't mean we can let down our guard – if you took a weapon with you, keep it close." He continued, sharing meaningful looks with Oserys and Arriella.

"It'll be cold enough to kill you in here if you're too far from the fire or each other – stay close by and stay warm," Oserys said gravely as she set out her own bedroll just a few inches away from Oleyyna's and indicated that Arriella's should be close too. Nobody dared question the woman of the North – legend told that the cold up there was enough to freeze people so solidly that their very soul would be trapped, and they'd be stuck in an icy prison forevermore.

Robbinn settled between Luciaan and Arriella to sleep as best as he could, wearing the same clothes from the day and his spare cloak over his back – Oserys was right, even by the fire it was freezing. He thought briefly about poor Solmyrer stood outside with a cloak over his back, but he too had five others to keep him warm, so he consoled himself with the idea that he'd be fine with that and his thick winter fur.

At some point during his rest, Robbinn felt Luciaan get up and leave, rousing Robbinn from his sleep until his heat was replaced by who he presumed was Aldredd, and the king slept on. Before he knew it, Robbinn was being thrust into the waking world once more, this time abruptly with a flurry of shouts and the sounds of swords clashing. He leapt to his feet without realising what he was doing, blinking bleary sleep from his eyes to make them adjust to the commotion happening around him.

There were too many people in the outpost, a voice Robbin didn't recognise; but Robbinn couldn't see what was going on until everything stopped just as suddenly as it started, and Luciaan was holding a man almost as big as he was from behind, holding a dagger to the intruder's throat.

"What the fuck—Someone tell me what's going on right this second!" Roared Robbinn, his hands starting to shake with the shock of being woken up like this.

"This bastard tried to kill you and take all your money, Robbinn." Snarled Luciaan, although his aggression was directed at the squirming, grunting man in his grip. He had blue eyes, short, dark brown hair, and chiselled features with a strange, circular scar on his cheek – but Robbinn was far more interested in Luciaan's voice, for he had never heard him take a tone like this before. However, what didn't escape his notice was how this would be thief was built like an ox and clearly as strong, but Luciaan was holding him like he was nothing.

"How do you know that, Ciniswood?" Robbinn demanded coldly. Luciaan opened his mouth to respond, but was spoken over by the man writhing in his arms.

"I admitted it! You Carbeu cunts have been stealing from the common people for decades!" The man hissed, even spitting at Robbinn's feet. Robbinn arched a brow.

"I believe I asked my advisor, not the scum he is restraining." His coldness seemed to surprise Luciaan and Aldredd judging by their expressions. "Regardless, since you have admitted to your attempted crimes, you ought to be properly punished." Robbinn paused to swallow thickly. He had never condemned a man to death before. He felt his mother's eyes on him and saw his wife's gaze directed at him too, and felt that this was the time. After a moment to steel himself, Robbinn drew breath to speak again over the man's voice, which had quickly descended into pathetic blubbering and wailing.

"With all the gods as my witnesses, Assailant," Robbinn's amber eyes met Luciaan's with new ice as he repeated the words his father had spoken before, "using Luciaan Ciniswood's hand as my own, I sentence you to die." He nodded at

Luciaan. Quick as a flash, Luciaan drew the dagger across the unnamed man's throat, ear to ear, spraying hot blood everywhere and rendering his voice to a horrible gurgling noise as his body tried to breathe through a severed airway. Robbinn watched him die, forced himself to watch the steaming blood-stain grow, the pain on his face, the desperate gurgling for what felt like hours as the man died, but it must only have been a few moments. Silent, Robbinn turned away from the man once certain he was dead.

"Shall we move on?" He asked, directing his gaze at Aldredd, who wore a rather impressed expression.

"Yes, and quickly. Luciaan and I will saddle the horses if you'd all pack up," Aldredd replied. "Shall we just leave him here?"

"Yes. As a warning, if you like." Robbinn shrugged passively as he began to pack up his bed roll, then help his mother with hers. Upon seeing him move, his company began to do the same and pack up the camp. Aldredd and Luciaan slipped out again to saddle all the horses for the next leg of their journey.

Before the corpse went cold, Robbinn and his group had mounted their horses again and were sharing out bread to each other with Aldredd in the lead. The pace they took this time was far faster once breakfast was finished, long stretches of gallops over barren, snowy path after barren, snowy path supplemented by walking breaks. Thankfully, being war horses, their mounts were all very fit, and took the hard journey in stride as long legs ate up the miles.

As fleeting daylight began to fade, their final walk stretch brought the group over a small hill to the tavern Luciaan had mentioned the previous evening. It was a tall, slightly top heavy building with yellow candles lit in every window and a small group of pygmy dragons roosting against each other on the thatched roof. There was a rather pleasant wave of rumbling sound coming from it, voices singing and laughing floating on the wind with the smell of mead and hearty food towards the cloaked, cold, tired group. Robbinn almost thought he'd imagined it; for it was surely too good to be true. Together the group dismounted and walked the last forty or so paces on the ground to give the horses some well-earned rest before they were put in small but cosy stables at the back of the building. Once untacked, Solmyrer immediately took to lying down and rolling in his thick, warm straw bedding and settled down to snooze until his evening feed was given to him. Robbinn was assured that he would be given a warm feed tonight, too.

With that assurance, the group made their way around the building to duck inside for hot food for themselves. Inside the tavern was what could only be described as pure joy – the small space was packed with customers shoulder to shoulder, laughing and joking and singing together in drunken stupor. The enchanting aroma of food and wine that had carried on the air earlier near enough lift them off their feet, inviting them inside as they took off their thick, heavy cloaks and shut the door firmly behind them.

Aldredd warned Robbinn to keep his head down, which he wasn't used to, but tried to do anyway as he trusted his guard deeply. His group was greeted at the bar by a wizened man with golden, russet brown skin amplified by the warm light of the candles and lanterns around him, heating up his dark eyes as he smiled invitingly.

"Hello there, travellers!" He had a sweet, nutty sounding voice with a strange accent that felt like a welcoming flash of sun on a cold day, but lowered to a whisper when he continued. "Would you be the group I was forewarned about?"

Aldredd marched up to the bar and laid his arm on it, showing the man a scrap of parchment. "Yes, that would be us. I asked for three rooms, food and drink, if you still have the space?"

"Of course! You're in rooms one to three; you can either sit here for your meals or go upstairs, I don't mind. It really depends on how low a profile you're looking to maintain." The man looked from face to face, waiting for an answer.

"I think it would be nice to stay down here, if we have our backs to the door we'll be difficult to recognise." Robbinn offered quietly, fiddling with his slightly unkempt chestnut curls to lie further over his tired face.

"I think being down here would do us some good, everyone seems pretty happy." Luciaan added, to a small murmur of agreement echoing around his company.

"Then it's settled! What can I get for you all on this fine evening?" The barkeeper asked jovially, pushing a strand of his long black hair out of his face. Robbinn noticed his little finger had been cleaved from his hand in the past, a gnarled scar being all that remained. Aldredd answered first.

"Anything you have that's hot and filling, the same for any drinks for me." Luciaan beside him nodded his agreement. Robbinn, unsure what to ask for, decided to follow in what Luciaan decided on.

"Whatever he's having," the unanointed king muttered sullenly.

"Mulled wine for the three of us please, and I think we'll all agree on food – whatever you have that's hot and filling." Oserys spoke for the women beside her, and the kind faced man nodded.

"I have just the thing." He smiled and turned away to prepare the large order as merry laughter and drunken singing filled the place of his voice. Luciaan smiled warmly at the sight

205

of so many people all together – Robbin was certain there were werewolves, hags, vampires and crosses of the lot mingled with all the humans, at least three bounty hunters, a group of what were certainly pirates, highwaymen and knights alike in the crowd. Where Robbinn expected them to be at each other's throats, they were all pressed up against one another, beaming and singing over their great tankards of strong ale and mead a song that all and none of them seemed to know but followed the same tune.

It didn't take long for the barkeeper to return with three tankards of hot, spiced apple cider for the three men, and equally large cups of mulled wine for the women as they had requested. The sweet, fruity scent alone made Robbinn swell with warmth as it seemed to wrap his whole body in an invisible blanket before he'd even taken a sip of it, something which brought a broad smile to his face. In unison the six weary travellers thanked the man as he turned back towards the kitchen. Oserys turned in her seat with a smile to watch the rest of the tavern's patrons sing to one another, slopping ale over one another but where Robbinn expected rage to break out, instead they burst into joyous laughter and continued their song.

Some of them, Robbinn noticed, were singing about Oserys I, his father-in-law. And the more he listened, the more he heard new tales of the legendary warrior's battles about how he used his good looks and silver tongue to escape sphynxes; swung his sword at many beasts and took their heads on the back of his saddle. Somewhere in these songs it was said that his mount, The Titan, the great black steed with fire in his eyes that Robbinn had once met, was much more than just a horse – this particular song told of how the man had outwitted a demon and stolen its powers and soul to bestow upon his horse, to extend such a perfect, obedient, brave stallion's life. Bewildered, Robbinn looked at his wife for some confirmation. She met his eye, and tapped the side of her nose with a wink. Robbinn found himself raising his brow at her in his intrigue.

Before he could start a conversation however, the tavern's owner returned with an assistant and six bowls of identical contents to place before each customer.

"This is something my mother always made for me growing up, she called it 'beast's stew', here served with mashed potatoes and bread. I hope you all enjoy it." He smiled and backed off, leaving them all to enjoy the glorious, steaming hot food. The second it hit Robbinn's tongue, he felt a sense of delight wash over him – the food he ate was usually refined and near enough cold by the time it was served, and he always found it to be hardly worth eating at all, but this was something else entirely. He could feel it warming his insides, filling him from his very core and bloody hell, he was starving. Robbinn ate like it was the first food he'd had in weeks, trying his best to savour every bite, making sure not to forget about his cider in the process. The combination filled him with such joy and satisfaction that he became suddenly quite sleepy.

Luciaan, however, seemed to be keeping up remarkably well with his surroundings, even now Robbinn assumed he too was full and warm – those blue and brown eyes of his were sharp as he watched, even tapping his hand on the bar in time with those who had at some point begun clapping. Robbinn watched as a bard with sleek, white-blonde hair, pretty blue eyes and a sneer that betrayed the tone of his song stood up on a table, carrying a lute as he played drunkenly a song of a lady of such beauty that she must surely be a fallen goddess to his adoring fans.

It became clear about three verses in that he was singing of the second Oserys, it was only when he reached the description of her eyes and skill in battle had Robbinn realised – this bard sang on and on about how he had watched her fight men far larger than herself, ride horses that many of the bravest men wouldn't have dared to climb on, and command dragons far more terrible than those her father could ever hope to.

Eventually, the group at the bar dispersed slightly, close enough that they could still see each other, but far enough to no longer be connected. Luciaan and Aldredd took to drinking and clapping and slamming their fists on the table as Arriella took to dancing with her new company and Oserys leaned on a wall, her drink in hand as she watched for any threat to her love. Oleyyna found new life in the midst of men far too drunk to recognise her, and stupid enough to pay her any attention at all – Robbinn hadn't seen her smile like this since his father became ill.

Robbinn himself however, remained at the bar, keeping his head down but watching his fellows have fun. That bard had certainly caught his interest – there was surely no way a man could be so inconceivably handsome with such an enchanting voice to match. He was still stood up on the table singing, almost glowing under the attention of his audience as he kept his eyes on the mysterious man still sitting at the bar known as Robbinn. As he kept watching, he noticed there was something slightly off about the way this man moved; it was as though he were floating in some strange liquid that suspended none but him.

Although it wasn't long before his curiosity was answered, as Robbinn listened to the words of his song, he learned this man was half siren! That explained everything from the way he moved to his incredible voice, but it certainly did not explain why there was a man behind the bard standing up and swinging his fist at *Luciaan*.

Chapter Twenty

It all happened very fast – happy singing turned to angry shouting as the drunk pirate's fist connected loudly with Luciaan's jaw. He was thrown with the force of it, but stood again with the look of a man getting ready to throw a return hardly a second later. The bard turned on him as quickly as the crowd, quick as a flash as jeering filled their ears his song switched to something far more jagged and angry, stamping his foot on the table as other banged their fists on tables.

As Aldredd flew to his feet to defend Luciaan, the crowd began to cheer and clap to the faster beat so kindly provided by the bard's feet; the other pirates rose too, and before anyone could really see what happened, the entire bar floor was in a full-on brawl. The bard playing angry lute hopped from table to table as punches were thrown and shouting rose – eventually he landed on the bar in front of Robbinn, who didn't acknowledge him immediately.

Instead, he tuned to the kind faced owner of the tavern who was watching this happen, quite clearly amused by the sight, and placed his lute on the bar beside Robbinn.

"Are you not going to step in?" Robbinn asked, more than a little alarm in his voice as beside him the bard climbed down into the empty seat beside him, flicking his long hair over his shoulder.

"No. It's more fun and less hassle to just bet on the outcome." Answered the friendly man, passing the bard another drink and asking who started it.

"Redbeard over there." Drawled the bard, pointing at him as he accepted his drink. "Do you see him? Being held down and pummelled by that great bear of a man?"

Robbinn and the barman craned their necks in unison to see, as promised, the pirate that swung on Luciaan being held down and repeatedly punched by the very man he tried to attack.

"My my—what a mistake that turned out to be." Said the bard through a curled lip as the fight continued. Behind him the barman grumbled as he produced a handful of fat, gold coins and handed them over to the bard, who took them from him with hardly suppressed glee.

"Thank you. I did tell you it'd be him." He purred over his shoulder.

"Shut it, Luxx." Growled the friendly barman before the half siren's attention shifted to Robbinn.

"So, your majesty," Luxx began coolly, "what are you doing here of all places?"

Robbinn stared at him for a moment, feeling a mix of terror and rage at his intended disguise being ripped from him unceremoniously.

"Travelling." It had only taken Robbinn a moment to decide on a calm, almost ethereal approach, so he responded as though he were just talking about the weather. "I wanted a quaint little visit to the coast with my wife."

"But you brought the head of your cavalry with you?" Luxx asked, equally as nonchalantly. Robbinn cursed internally.

"You recognise him?" Robbinn asked, far more curtly. This time Luxx was the one to look as though he had slipped up – his eyes widened minutely as the sharper question hit his ears.

"I do." He sounded as though he was astounded by the idea that Robbinn didn't seem to know. "That man is *The Tapper of Mabin*."

The sounds of the brawl around him faded in Robbinn's ears as this man told him something utterly world shattering.

"What?" Robbinn's brow furrowed as he watched Luciaan fighting off about six pirates at once with impressive ease. He knew Luciaan had a military past, sure, but a title like that? He hadn't heard any of that. "Tell me more, why the tapper of all things? Is that why that pirate attacked him?"

"Probably, yes." Luxx took a slow, measured sip of his drink. "The Tapper of Mabin was a vicious soldier. He would've been a knight, if he'd sworn to King Falkonn. Legend has it he wouldn't speak, but he'd tap his sword or gloves on a wall or his shield to let his victim know they were going to die. The tapper had no sympathy for women nor children, it was only animals that seemed to evade his butchery. He was so violent that if soldiers heard his tapping, they'd turn tail and run. I heard it that some generals would have him gallop past the opposition as he tapped away and the other side would surrender immediately."

"I've never heard of him," Robbinn muttered, his lips cold with shock, but something in the back of his mind cheered at another little piece of leverage he had just been given. "How do you know its him? Was his face obvious?"

"I met him. I wrote his songs. He is death personified." Luxx replied, shaking his head.

"Are you certain that's him?" Robbinn pressed him as Luciaan finally threw the last of his assailants through a table and caught his eye, at which point Robbinn jerked his head towards the stairs, his message of 'bed. Now.' Quite obvious. Luciaan dragged himself towards his room.

"Positive. I was one of the few people that ever saw his face, and he approached me. Just mention it to him, you'll see." Luxx mused, returning to pleasantness.

"Hm. All right then, one more thing. I'd like to maintain contact with you, Luxx. My dragons should be able to find you if there is something they can scent you with – do you have something like that?" Robbinn asked, glancing around the still brawling room in search of his wife, his mother and Arriella – he couldn't see any of them, and presumed they too had gone to bed.

"Yes, I always keep something like that on my person," Luxx sounded almost nervous as he dug out a scrap of fabric from his pocket and handed it over, "might I ask why?"

"I liked your singing, and I have a coronation to plan," Robbinn said nonchalantly as he placed the fabric in a pouch on his belt and turned to the barkeeper. "And you, sir, shall be paid handsomely for this stay, I thank you greatly for it."

With that, Robbinn stood and crossed carefully between brawling tavern visitors and ascended the stairs to his bedroom.

It wasn't hard to guess where Luciaan was – where Oserys and Arriella had shut the door behind them; a very drunk and presumably more than a little dazed Luciaan has left it open, kicked off his boots and collapsed onto the bed. Robbinn rolled his eyes and checked nobody was watching before he darted inside and shut the door firmly behind him, bolting it for good measure. He was furious with the idea of his Luciaan hiding something like this from him. He briefly considered not letting any of it into his tone, instead caring for his drunk, bruised lover and addressing it later.

"Did you have a good time down there, *Tapper of Mabin*?" The consideration didn't last long. Robbinn spat his words like venom at Luciaan's back and watched them hit him like cold water. He flipped over as though jabbed with a hot poker, looking as though Robbinn had just slapped him.

"What are you on about?" Luciaan demanded defensively, furrowing his brow, and wincing as his bruised face creased painfully.

"I think you know exactly what I'm talking about," Robbinn said icily, although he felt sympathy rising as his poor Luciaan was clearly in some degree of pain. He sighed, dropping his head. "I don't like it when you lie to me, Luci."

"Oh piss off, it's for your safety that I didn't tell anyone!" Luciaan snarled, glaring harshly at him now.

"Was it now? Why don't you explain that to me while I sort out the mess you've made of yourself?" Robbinn snarled and continued on before he could stop himself as he stalked closer. "Not only are you a killer, but one so vile, so vicious and with such little mercy that entire battlefields would clear at the very sound of you!"

"Yeah, and I shed that armour YEARS ago! I was hardly a man, started at seventeen, when I got that name I was maybe twenty at most. Hardly a man at all, drunk on the power a sword gave me. Robbinn, I made *enemies* doing that shit." Luciaan spat.

"Why didn't you tell me?" Robbinn demanded.

"To protect you. Nobody knows, your father didn't even know. Maybe three people knew my face. That bard from today, I met with him once. I bet he told you, didn't he?" Luciaan added waspishly before he continued his answer. "I left because I was going to get my mother killed just by association. You know what happens when you're the most feared killer in the entirety of a border? You die, Robbinn. Gangs of people in the streets, braying for my head, threatening to kill those I knew, too. I had a friend slash my face, caked my hair in mud, painted

213

my horse and disappeared overnight."

Robbinn was stunned into silence by this rant. Despite everything in him wanting to be angry with him, Robbinn found himself feeling sympathy – it had to have been a heavy burden to bear, and he really did seem to regret his actions. Robbinn closed his amber eyes and took a deep, calming breath through his nose.

"I am choosing to believe you. Be under no illusion, Luciaan, that I feel utterly betrayed by y—" He began, but was interrupted.

"Don't do that." Luciaan snapped.

"Don't do what?" Robbinn asked, glaring.

"You're doing the stupid fucking king voice." He rubbed his eyes and hissed sharply at the pain from the bruises covering half his face.

"King voice?" Robbinn scoffed.

"Yeah, you do it when you're organising shit or you're uncertain of something, you take a breath and puff your chest out and you speak with this extra 'I'm better than you' tone." His voice turned mocking and he pulled out some rather spectacular air quotes. "You may as well start saying we." Luciaan blurted out frustratedly, as though he couldn't stop himself from saying it.

"You can tell?" Robbinn asked, suddenly quite unable and unwilling to hold onto his laughter as he felt a laugh start to rise in his throat.

"Of-fucking-course, I can tell! I don't think other people can though which is fucking insane," Luciaan stopped his ranting quite abruptly to stare at Robbinn, who had now lost his resolve and started to giggle. "What the hell are you laughing at?"

"You, dumbass. Because you know me so fucking well."

Robbinn beamed at him, realising all over again how much he loved this ridiculous man who was now beginning to smile. "I'm sorry, I shouldn't have been so quick to anger, you didn't deserve that. I want to be able to trust you, Luci. This is just a lot to take in." Robbinn bit his lip – now that he'd calmed down, he knew exactly what he wanted to ask. But gods, he didn't want to kill that smile so fast.

"What is it?" Luciaan asked slightly anxiously, his brow knitting together softly. Robbinn knew in his very soul that he couldn't hesitate any longer.

"This could be useful. Are you willing to come out of retirement? Not just yet, of course?" he asked tentatively, meeting Luciaan's gaze again. There was silence for a moment as Luciaan's sharp eyes burrowed into his until finally he muttered a response with darkened.

"I swore I would never do it again. That armour would never again touch me. But for you… For you my love, I would kill every man woman and child in the path of your victory."

Robbinn took Luciaan's hand and pressed it into his own chest, over his heart and held it there gently.

"Our victory." Robbinn's confidence grew like a barn fire as he closed the gap between them and kissed his love to seal his promise. "Now," he muttered into Luciaan's lips, "I think we ought to get some sleep. Tomorrow there'll be pirates to deal with."

The following morning passed over the tavern silently, with each and every patron sleeping soundly from a night of brawling and intense drinking; it would have been difficult to expect any of them to rise early. However, amongst the earliest to wake were Robbinn and his mother, who had likely had the least to drink the previous evening.

When he woke beside Luciaan, he felt his stomach beginning to knot with his anxiety, and more than once found his hands picking at his fingernails without his knowledge nor command to do so – thus he took to shoving them into his pockets at any given moment to hide his tell.

Downstairs he found his mother sitting alone at a table beside a window, a wooden bowl before her, and a cup of something hot beside it. Oleyyna liked tea just as much as her son did.

"Good morning, Mother," Robbinn said quietly, trying not to disturb her too abruptly. She turned and smiled at him regardless.

"Good morning, dear boy. Would you care to join me? I can see you're nervous," Oleyyna said kindly, nodding to the seat opposite her.

"You never fail to see right through me, Mother," Robbinn sighed, taking the seat gratefully.

"I understand, of course. This is your first instance of true negotiation; you're bound to be a bit unsettled – it's completely normal." She spoke softly and soothingly to her fretting son over the table, as though she were sending him for his first dancing lesson all over again. "Your father was just the same, although he was having kittens about it the night before, I think you've dealt with it all far better than him. You're more level-headed than he was, I like to think you've inherited my temperament."

"You think so?" Robbinn asked hopefully, finding himself well comforted by his mother's words.

"I do. I think you have turned out rather well – you have all the markers of a successful leader, my boy." She nodded her head with such grace that she almost looked like something out of a storybook.

"Thank you, Mother, that means more than I can say."

Robbinn's smile faded. "When we arrive today, I'd like you to remain at a safe distance from the pirate legends – they're unpredictable people as I'm sure you know. I'd also like it if you remained quiet, you're one of the people I would like to keep most safe. Do you think you can do that for me?"

"If you think it is best, I shall do it." She took on a wise expression as she agreed, then returned to her breakfast as conversation lightened. Robbinn didn't ask her for advice, or her opinion on the pirate negotiations. He didn't want to burden his mother with such nasty things, so instead he spoke of his wife to her, and she left him with advice on how to be a good husband, which sent and unexpected pang of guilt into his gut. He still remembered their conversation from what felt like a lifetime ago, when she had asked if he was gay. She was right of course, but the memory caused the guilt to quickly fester into anger that he swallowed like a bitter medicine.

Eventually the rest of the party came downstairs, Aldredd bringing a scrap of news:

"The pirate legends have arrived. We ought to go now." Robbinn and Oleyyna stood up at once, the latter racing upstairs to inject urgency into the hungover women.

"Luciaan, Aldredd, come help me saddle the horses, quickly!" he commanded as he pulled his cloak over his shoulders and pulled his hood up as he braced against the cold outside. His guard didn't need to be told twice, for the two men were at his side within seconds. The six horses were saddled once more and their riders had assembled. Robbinn called back briefly to give the tavern owner all the money on his person, and assured him that more would come as he thanked the man for his hospitality and sprinted back out where his companions had mounted their horses.

Solmyrer understandably didn't seem all that happy to see

him after such demanding work over the day and night before, but Robbinn hadn't the time to reassure him as he all but leapt onto his back. Aldredd took the lead and proceeded in gallop towards the coast, his horse flattening his ears and throwing his legs out without protest, something that seemed to urge Solmyrer to keep up.

Luckily there wasn't much travel left to do as from the roof of the tavern, the coast where at least forty ships had arrived at the docks was perfectly visible – as were the pirates disembarking. Robbinn could hardly feel the wind biting his face as Solmyrer raced his company down, as the numb feeling in his hands was quickly turning to pain despite the fact that he had put gloves on. He heard six sets of hooves striking the ground, the huffing snorts of the horses at the exertion, and his companions near gasping for breath over the sharp cold, which was worsened as the air grew saltier with the nearing ocean.

Beside Robbinn, where his face wasn't bruised and swollen, Luciaan's skin grew redder as he was blasted with more and more cold air, but he wasn't alone in this, Oleyyna and Arriella looked the same, Oserys to a lesser degree. For a moment Robbinn couldn't think at all, his heart simply pounded over anything that came to mind and he found himself watching Solmyrer's breath fog like a dragon spewing smoke.

He wasn't allowed such luxury for long, however, for before he knew what was happening, Aldredd slowed the group, and as they cantered onto the white sand beach where the inches of snow had relaxed into a mere dusting, and forty pirate legends stood, watching them approach.

Chapter Twenty-One

Robbinn could smell the pirates before he saw any of their faces, the stench of unwashed men mixed horribly rum and a vast array of scented oils intended to disguise the other two. Fumbling to untie his crown from Solmyrer's saddle as he moved forward to meet them, Robbinn felt his nose wrinkle, but did his best to relax his face. He took a breath and pushed his chest out as with Oserys at his side, both of them flanked by Luciaan and Aldredd, he approached the pirate legends.

"Gentlemen!" He called from Solmyrer's back, his crown sitting firmly on his head. "Welcome to Ildyr's Keep! I do hope your journey was pleasant?"

One of the pirates stepped forward, nominated to act as speaker for the rest. He was a dark-skinned man from years at sea under harsh sun, his skin leathery with his tan, covered in scars, his hair and beard long, black and unkempt, even from his distance, Robbinn could see his gold teeth flash as he smiled and swayed dangerously on his feet.

"For some of us." He slurred his words quite severely. "Others didn't think it was even worth coming." There was a ripple of agreement through at least a third of the pirate legends.

"I would like to thank each of you for coming to meet with me, regardless of previous affiliations or preconceptions." Robbinn said, pulling his face into a smile. If he was ever doing a 'king voice', it would be now.

"Aye. As we understand it, you have something to offer us

in return for our loyalty to you?" the leading pirate asked, with a murmur of excitement at the idea behind him.

"I do, yes. But with it, a warning." Robbinn held the pirate's brown eyes as the already clouded sky began to grow darker and an enormous shadow passed overhead. "Which would you like to hear first?"

The pirate sharply retreated as his fellows gasped behind him. His head turned to listen to others mutter into his ear before he responded.

"Your offer, first." His slurred words had begun to tremble with what looked like growing fear.

"Money, to each of you. Enough for your entire crews to have a handsome share each, free reign over the oceans, and the possibility of being first to see employment as the guardians to my aforementioned oceans." Robbinn purred, looking down his nose at the group of uncomfortable pirates as another colossal shadow passed overhead, this time accompanied by a deep rumbling sound.

"As for the warning, listen well when I tell you this: the gods are on my side, I suggest you do the same." At that moment, there was an almighty clap of thunder, and a bolt of lightning struck the surface of the ocean and seconds later a giant, squid-like monster floated to the surface, dead.

The pirates all but squealed like young girls, huddling together as close as they could get. Robbinn paused as a black Northern Greater Dragon landed behind him with the charred monster hanging from its jaws and Oserys Daeemori I on its back, taking up easily half the beach and whitening the faces of every pirate the king faced.

"What will it be, men?" He asked, trying to keep the excitement out of his voice.

"Might... Might we have time to discuss, your majesty?"

220

the nominated one stuttered.

"Of course. You need not answer as one. Those of you who wish to join me, stand by my side. Those who don't, this will be my only show of mercy – return to your ships," he replied amiably, as though discussing something as mundane as the weather.

Before any further words could be exchanged, the pirates broke into a vicious fight over what the majority were planning to do – in something as simple as a difference of opinion, alliances had been severed, wedges had been pushed between friends. This of course meant to cut down any man who tried to go to the 'wrong' side. Feeling his heart in his throat, Robbinn forced himself to remain quiet as he saw flashes of silver and red, heard the shouts, smelled the blood as it was spilled. It didn't take long for the fight to settle again, with about a third of the pirates lying dead in the sand, the rest splitting up to the sides they had picked.

Robbinn saw that he had the majority of the pirate's allegiance and allowed himself a small sneer despite his racing heart, before addressing his new allies.

"Thank you all for making such a good decision. I would like you to all situate yourselves along the coast, with messaging systems active to alert me to any of Hermontt Hardweaverr's ships. Do any of you know when he is planning to storm the continent?" Robbinn asked, urgency finding an edge in his voice.

A greying, balding, short, round pirate stepped forward, his tunic stained with the blood of his fellows stepped forward to offer a reply.

"As soon as he can. In the coming weeks, Your Grace, sir," he offered anxiously, his head remaining bowed as he refused to meet the king's eye.

"I see. Thank you, that information is most helpful. You will be expected to protect the coasts, any ships of Hardweaverr's that you see are to be apprehended with any and all force you deem necessary. Am I clear, men?" He didn't wait for the murmur of the affirmative before turning to look up at his father-in-law.

"Lord Daeemori," he called, voice raised enough to carry. The dragon Oseerys I was riding hunkered down on its front legs to bring his master down to eye level with Robbinn. "I'd like to speak with you regarding your armies soon. Do you have enough riders to situate a dragon at every major coastal city?"

"Easily. Mostly Deathcallers, is that right?" He directed the question to his dragon, who answered in a low, gravelly voice as it spat the remains of the sea monster from its mouth.

"Yes. Many mature ones, some easily old enough to take on fleets." It blew out a great jet of flame at the remaining tentacles of the beast, causing the air to be filled with the nauseating stench of burnt squid as the skin blistered and bubbled.

"I'd like you to do so, if you would help to distribute the pirates too, that would be most appreciated." Robbinn directed his command to both the man and his dragon, both of whom nodded their heads in understanding. "Good. My dear, Oserys, would you like to be the main point of contact, given that he is your father?"

"Yes, I'd be delighted darling." She acted every bit the adoring wife as she spoke and made eye contact with her father.

"Good. I shall be travelling back to the main castle, in that case. If any of you have any worries, I would like to hear about it – do not undervalue letters to me." He directed his words now to the pirates that cowered under the dragon's shadow. "I value each and every one of you as an ally, I will reiterate that if you have any worries or questions, I would like you to write to me.

Do you all understand?" He looked around for reassured nodding in the faces of the pirates, which he was quite glad to find. "Good."

The returning journey was made without Oserys and Arriella, nor did the same sense of urgency follow them, although that isn't to say there was no haste. Robbinn, Aldredd, Luciaan and Oleyyna returned at a smart march, and made a short call at the tavern for the bard Luxx. With a sigh of relief, Robbinn approached him quite eagerly and was greeted by a sneer down his long nose, and a bored drawl.

"Hello again. You're back so soon?" He asked over tuning his lute.

"Yes, I remember asking for a point of contact, but I would like to extend an invitation now. If you have a horse and are willing to come, I have some work for you pertaining to my coronation." Robbinn replied pleasantly, watching Luxx's eyes widen minutely with a great deal of satisfaction. "Given the... er, state of things, celebrations are being kept to a minimum. I think your singing could really help increase morale in high courts."

"It would be an honour, Your Grace." His sneer turned to a half smile. Evidently his bored drawl was simply his normal way of speaking. Robbinn could deal with that since the music he could produce was so heavenly. After all, it was interactions like these which would begin to set him apart from the kings before him, especially Falkonn.

"Good, we will be waiting for you outside." Robbinn smiled graciously and swept from the building to mount Solmyrer once more, who had warmed up considerably from his foul mood that morning when he had been given a carrot as an apology. Robbinn patted his horse's neck gratefully as he settled in for what he hoped was a short wait for Luxx.

Thankfully, before too soon passed, the handsome bard appeared around the corner sat lightly on a tall, fine grey horse. Luxx wore a long, thick cloak which covered the horse's hindquarters to keep them warm.

"Luxx, this is Luciaan Ciniswood," he pointed out the tall man on the equally tall horse, "the queen Mother, Oleyyna," he pointed her out too, "and Aldredd Haardwing."

Each of them nodded at one another politely, and fell into step as one group. Robbinn took to quiet contemplation as his companions chatted, Luxx mostly looking for anything he wasn't supposed to know. Pretending Luciaan and Luxx didn't know each other was an intentional move on Robbinn's part to protect the both of them in case the tapper had made an enemy in Aldredd.

By the time the sun was beginning to set, the group came to another tavern to spend the night in – this one wasn't nearly as welcoming nor as full as the previous one. There was a tense feeling in the air, and Luciaan had settled into a very poor mood once the horses were shut away to bed. His face was still bruised, although the cold air did seem to have helped the angry swelling, but his eyes were dark and tired – Robbinn thought nobody in their right mind would cross him tonight.

Thankfully, only one very stupid man decided to do so, once the group had taken a table together and had bowls of food before them – not as good as the previous night's, nor what he had for breakfast that morning, but not bad – and were simply trying to sit and enjoy it when the drunken fool appeared.

"Evenin' all!" The tall, slender man leered, his eyes on Oleyyna's hooded form. Her lips were pressed tightly together, and her brow furrowed. "Good gods, you're all a bit miserable, eh?"

"Fuck. Off," Luciaan growled, his already poor temper being tested by the second.

"Ooh, not very friendly are we?" Mocked the man, sticking his head out and putting his hands on his hips. Aldredd tightened his grip on his cup.

"Leave us be, or I will make you." Luciaan's glare grew fiercer, yet still the man kept going, leaning in a bit further, still looking at Oleyyna.

"Give us a smile, love." Quick as a flash, Luciaan stood up and threw a punch right at the man's throat. Before he could collapse into choking, gagging sounds, Luciaan had sat back down and returned to his meal, ignoring the man trying to breathe through his spasming windpipe.

The few people who had turned to watch quickly turned away and the group was left to their peace. In silence they ate, booked rooms and retired to bed, Oleyyna with Aldredd, Robbinn with Luciaan and Luxx alone. For a while, Robbinn rested quietly beside Luciaan, nervous to say anything to him for fear of triggering an angry response. He didn't know why Luciaan was angry in the first place, and hoped to all the gods that it wasn't at him.

Eventually he worked up the courage to gently touch the back of Luciaan's hand with his knuckles. He listened to Luciaan's breath catch in his throat at that small, soft touch and felt his rigid body starting to relax beside him, and took it as a sign to pursue the contact. Robbinn moved to lace his fingers with Luciaan's and squeeze gently, which resulted in a considerable amount of tension leaving his body with a small sigh. After a moment, Robbinn's squeeze was returned – a small attempt at reassurance, no doubt. It worked. Before there was room for words, Robbinn turned his head to look at the man lying beside him, all bruised and tired, just to admire the handsome face he

225

fell for. What he could see of it, anyway. He couldn't help but smile as their eyes met once more, and he saw Luciaan smile back as he turned to reach his free hand over to softly brush chestnut curls out of Robbinn's eyes.

"How would you like a dancing lesson? A real one this time," Robbinn asked quietly, finally breaking the silence. It didn't matter if Luciaan said yes or no in that moment. He just wanted to see that smile stay on his face. Thankfully, he huffed a laugh and nodded his head before he shifted to stand.

"I'd love one," he held out a hand to Robbinn, his smile still lingering.

"All right," Robbinn practically flew out of bed to take Luciaan's hand, "first you put your right hand on my shoulder, under my arm."

"Okay." Luciaan's brow pinched slightly as he made himself concentrate and understand what Robbinn was telling him, "Like this?"

"Yes, like that. And your left arm is positioned like mine, but you hold my hand." Robbinn held his elbow up to shoulder height, hand still grasping Luciaan's who copied him perfectly.

"And this?" Luciaan flicked his head to toss a strand of hair from his face – a gesture he always used when he had both hands busy, even if he could free one easily. Robbinn had always presumed he had learned to do this from his experience with horses, but knowing what he did now it was likely something else. He didn't dwell on it.

"Perfect! Now, positioning is the easy part. Actually moving is more difficult." Robbinn's lip twitched into a small smile. "We'll take it slowly, okay?"

"Okay." Luciaan nodded, his concentrated face looking as though he had been given a very exciting challenge.

"Take a step forward with your left foot only." Luciaan obeyed, and Robbinn stepped back with his right.

226

"Very good, now step forward and to the right with your right foot." Luciaan did as he was told quite easily, but silent in his focus and staring down at his feet. Robbinn stepped sideways to the left, mirroring his lead.

"Excellent! Next bring your left foot to your right." Robbinn once more watched Luciaan do as he was instructed, and moved his own right foot to beside his left.

"You're good at this. We're halfway through the movements now." Luciaan looked up to grin at him, but quickly returned his determined gaze to his feet. "Ready to keep going?"

Luciaan nodded silently but not without enthusiasm.

"Good. Step back with your right foot." He followed without hesitation, and Robbinn stepped forward with his left. "Well done! Step back and sideways to the left with the left foot."

Luciaan hesitated for a moment to think about what he was doing, but when he did move, he did so correctly, and Robbinn mirrored with his right foot moving forward.

"Excellent! Lastly bring your right foot next to your left foot." Robbinn beamed as Luciaan followed his direction and he moved his own left foot back to beside his right. "And that's all the basic steps, we repeat those as we move about the room."

Luciaan looked up and grinned at him again, clearly very pleased with himself for getting it right.

"Really? Can we practice that a bit then?" He asked, with a hopeful edge to his voice.

"I'd be delighted to!" Robbinn looked up into his eyes and found his entire being filled with warmth and joy just at the sight of him so proud of himself. His heart felt as though it was going to burst when Luciaan pulled him into his arms, tipped his weight back and leaned over to kiss him.

"Thank you for teaching me, darling." Luciaan smirked, their faces hardly an inch apart. Good gods, Robbinn could listen to Luciaan call him that for days on end.

"If this is what teaching gets me, I wonder what practicing would do?" Robbinn asked, his tone not as sultry as he had intended.

"Anything you want and more, darling."

With that, the two of them danced well into the night – as poor a decision as it may have been for the next day's travel, but neither cared in that moment. It did at some point occur to Robbinn that Luciaan's foul mood could have been caused by more than simply being exhausted from such hard travel. He had a particularly vicious streak of jealousy kept hidden deep within his personality, even Robbinn had only encountered it the once and it had resulted in Luciaan drunk out of his mind, wearing a dress, and roaring up at his library window. Secretly, given his usual response to disagreement was to talk about it, Robbinn thought his poor mood was rooted in jealousy, and thus let the issue rest undisturbed.

With a flurry of yawns from human and horse alike the next morning, the very last leg of the journey was taken, at a much faster pace once home was within their sights. The castle was pleasantly warm and inviting when they arrived, the sun beginning to sink behind the towers and turrets. Solmyrer and Pereggnir paused and called out loudly to the stables as they approached, and were greeted with a great crescendo of returning calls, one from each of the hundreds of horses in their stalls for the night. Beside Robbinn, Luciaan smiled at the sound – one he must be more than used to over his time as head groom. Nothing made that man smile like horses could, no person could ever hope to compete – something Robbinn had long made his peace with, and had decided he rather enjoyed. The sight of Luciaan's happiness made his own heart swell with warmth and a smile spread across his face, content to enjoy his glee.

Once the grateful horses had been taken off to their stables, the weary group could enter the castle, Robbinn asking a passing servant to show Luxx to a guest wing before he finally had his own bed in sight once again. He decided to skip his evening meal and dive straight into it – the moment his head hit the pillow, Robbinn was asleep.

Chapter Twenty-Two

Over the next couple of days, there was a definite sense of urgency about the castle, much the same as it had been when Robbinn had his last suitor's ball – there were servants bustling to and fro, rushing to decorate and clean in time for the Coronation and subsequent celebratory ball. Robbinn tried his best to stay out of the way. In truth, he had little time to do so anyway, as he laid the last plans for his coronation itself. He knew that Oserys had taken some of the planning to help relieve some of his stress, but he had expressed that he wanted his coronation would itself to be a rather small affair, with the ball as his main celebration. With the threat of war on the horizon, Robbinn didn't want to have anything more for fear of being interrupted.

It was only a few days away by the time he returned home, and by the time preparations were being finalized it was the night before. Robbinn had decided to have a hot bath drawn with divine oils and rose petals in it, and told Luciaan to join him through the hidden servant's entrance.

Once the doors were locked with just the two of them inside, Robbinn didn't hesitate to strip his clothes off to step into the hot water, catching a glimpse of Luciaan's expression as he watched, and found a mixture of adoration, love, excitement and strangely, bewilderment in his face. Robbinn chuckled softly as he stepped down into the large, tiled tub.

"What's that look for?" he asked, rousing Luciaan from his trance with a start.

"Huh? Oh, I'm just—er," Luciaan stopped and took a breath, presumably to gather his thoughts. "You're just so beautiful. And you picked me of all people, I'm just happy that you did."

Robbinn's cheeks began to burn, bright red with the sweet words pouring from Luciaan's lips, a part of him Robbinn suddenly felt the overwhelming urge to kiss.

"Get in, you great buffoon." He smiled, splashing the warm water at him playfully, to a wonderful, rippling laugh from his target – he did it again, just in the hopes of hearing that laugh again, and was luckily rewarded as Luciaan pulled his tunic off over his head, his muscles contracting with the force of his laughter. He seized a handful of petals and thew them in Robbinn's direction, who threw up his hands to protect himself with a grin.

"I'm coming, I'm coming. Give me a second." Luciaan smirked, apparently trying his hardest not to make a filthy joke, but he didn't need to as Robbinn was already laughing and blushing all over again as Luciaan waded over to meet him.

"Filthy king. How can your people be expected to respect you when you can't even listen to your own words without blushing like a maid?" Luciaan teased as he wrapped Robbinn in his arms, leaning down to press a kiss into his neck where he knew Robbinn to be ticklish, purely to make him giggle.

"You're an ass, you know that?" Robbinn laughed, enjoying the feeling of weightlessness his lover's arms gave him in tandem with the water.

"I know, but you love me really." Luciaan grinned his stupid, lovesick puppy grin at him, and Robbinn felt his heart melt.

"I do." Robbinn touched his forehead to Luciaan's softly. "I really do. I'd do anything for you, Luci."

"I'd do anything for you, too. I love you, Robbinn. I'm

231

glad you're more comfortable with us."

Robbinn thought about pressing Luciaan for more about his history. About the Tapper of Mabin. But he didn't say anything, he just enjoyed this closeness, this loving, comfortable conversation amidst the steamy water, the scent of roses and muted sounds from outside the bolted door.

"Can I ask you something, Robbinn?" His voice was slightly concerned.

"You can ask me anything you like, dear. Doesn't mean I'll answer." Robbinn's smile faded slightly, the laugh that accompanied his words more nervous.

"Who told you? That I was the tapper?" Luciaan asked quietly. Robbinn didn't reply immediately. He simply stayed there in silence as he contemplated his reply.

"The bard. The half siren one," he said slowly.

"Luxx? The one you invited here?" Luciaan asked, an edge of urgency creeping into his voice.

"Yes, why?" Robbinn was quickly feeling his stomach tighten, but Luciaan's body was relaxing again, despite his urgent tone.

"I showed only one bard my face, and it was him. That's fine, I haven't seen him since I jumped ship. I was worried he'd told someone else." Robbinn released a breath he hadn't realised he'd been holding as these words left Luciaan's mouth.

"Good gods, you can't scare me like that, Luci!" Yowled Robbinn, swatting Luciaan's shoulder as he started laughing again.

"I'm sorry! I thought he'd done something stupid is all, Luxx is a trustworthy man. I knew he was," Luciaan chuckled. Robbinn was subtly bitter about the idea of Luciaan knowing far more about the world than he did, but reminded himself that this was precisely the reason he chose to promote him to an ad-

232

visory role in the first place.

"It was still unfair to scare me like that." He pouted theatrically at Luciaan, who laughed a little more at him.

"You scared me! Someone else recognising me could have been disastrous. I'll tell you more about it soon. I don't want to ruin this moment." For the second time in just a few moments, Robbinn's heart melted in his chest as something so ridiculously sweet came tumbling out of Luciaan's mouth.

"Don't feel rushed. Tell me when you're ready – if you're ever ready – and I'll listen. I promoted you for a reason, Luci, and it wasn't just because I love you. I trust you," Robbinn said, feeling the sincerity was quite necessary.

"Thank you. I found the armour again, it's where I left it. If you have need of the tapper, he will make a return. I mean it." He tapped his finger against Robbinn's shoulder to punctuate his sentiment, making him shiver.

"I believe you. I don't know if we can win this without him. I hope so. You may need to learn to ride dragons, you know." Robbinn huffed a laugh at the absurdity of the idea despite feeling his stomach twist into knots at the idea of his coronation being tomorrow, and possibly followed almost immediately by war. His opposition was working his way towards the continent as he had this conversation 'liberating nations from Carbeu tyranny' as it had been recently called, according to Luxx.

"Imagine me on a fuckin' dragon! Weird thought, isn't it?" Luciaan smiled reassuringly at him as the world around Robbinn began to fade at the edges. "Robbinn? Are you all right?"

"Hm? Oh, yes. I'm just nervous, is all." Robbinn smiled weakly.

"I know. Would you like me to take it away for you?" Luciaan asked, running his hands over Robbinn's tired back, pressing his thumbs in just enough for the pressure to be felt.

"Yes please," Robbinn mumbled. And that was all it took, all the prompt Luciaan needed to work stiffness and soreness out of his muscles with his big, gentle hands. Robbinn found that he was never quite as at peace with the world as when Luciaan massaged him like this, for the tenderness of his touch banished most of his thoughts altogether, aside from the bliss of a relaxed body. The rest of his evening passed in quite the haze, a mixture of anxiety creeping back in and the afterglow of Luciaan taking such care of him.

By the time he was roused the next morning by Clauude, he had achieved only a little of the sleep he needed to accept his crown that day and dance into the night later on. He was silent as Clauude dressed him in his fine, expensive ceremonial robes of deep scarlet, with a white fur cloak around his shoulders which had a deer's skull on each shoulder, attached to one another by a thick chain, and his grandfather's sword at his hip in a gold scabbard.

He knew very little of the ritual he was to perform, but what he did know to expect was painful. Supposedly there was to be a 'blood crown' placed upon his head by the priest or statue of the god he had chosen to be anointed to.

Robbinn trudged through feet of snow to his overlarge, gold carriage, pulled by six enormous white horses, each one painted gold around its eyes and shoulders, shifting their weight from foot to foot in their impatience to move. None were to accompany him in his travel, so Oserys, his mother and a small collection of nobles waited at the Church of The Five for him to arrive and begin the ceremony.

When he arrived, Robbinn heard Luxx leading a small group of choir boys in aethereal music that seeped into the halls like an enticing scent, leading the new king to his place before

234

the now rather familiar altar. This time the church was decorated with nothing more than a few sparse banners bearing the Carbeu family crest. He could see all the way up to the supporting beams in the roof, carved with symbols he didn't understand and painted gold. As directed by the priests, Robbinn knelt before the altar.

"Friends. Family. Allies." Began the priests in flat, emotionless unison. "We gather to witness the anointing of King Robbinn Falkonn Carbeu, third of his name, to the throne of Arkordouur. Here, today, he will take his oath to rule with justice and security as directed by his chosen god. Today we anoint our new leader and pray for peace."

There was a murmur of agreement between the small audience as the priests turned to surround him from behind, each laying a hand on his shoulders and back, facing the statues.

"Call forth the god you have named, with strength and certainty," muttered the priests, together once more. Robbinn took a deep, shaky breath and hoped none could hear it before he spoke.

"Ydnias, I call you forward." He looked up at her statue, in the middle of the five as it raised its head to look at him. Robbinn felt four out of five hands leave his shoulders, and heard the priests step back, as the statue opened its mouth to speak.

"You, Robbinn Falkonn Carbeu, have called me forward to confirm your oath." It said, surveying the king with a calm, cool gaze. "Is the Sovereign willing to take the oath?"

"I am willing," Robbinn replied with feigned certainty as he stared up into the tall statue's eyes.

"Do you swear to govern the people of your kingdom of Arkordouur, its continent and colonies with justice, freedom and security?"

"I swear it," as he spoke, the remaining four priests togeth-

235

er picked up a golden crown of thorns and placed it gently upon his brow. He felt his heart pounding against his ribs.

"Do you swear to follow my guidance as your chosen god, and that of your appointed advisors?"

"I swear it." He felt the priests press the crown painfully into his skin. He tried his best not to wince.

"Do you swear that to the best of your ability you will protect, serve, and rule your people with mercy and severity where necessary, for the duration of your life, or until abdication to a suitable heir?"

"I swear it." This time he felt the sharp spikes dig further into his skin as hot beads of blood began to form as the priests gave a further push.

"Will you swear to the gods, my fellows, your undying fidelity? Will you swear to use our names responsibly? Will you swear to maintain the position of our church during your reign?"

"All of this I swear to do." The priests gave one final push, this time firmer than the others, and Robbinn felt the thorns shred his skin. His hands trembled against his knees.

"Come forth, so that you may be anointed." The statue gestured to a pillow on the floor at its feet. Robbinn stood, and made his way to kneel before her, his head bent, crown of golden thorns still dug into his scalp. A small droplet of blood fell from his forehead onto the floor as the priests surrounded him once again and began to mutter prayers to their chosen god. All but Ydnias' priestess, who appeared in front of him, with a bottle of Rhododendron oil in her hand. Without removing the crown, she dropped oil onto where the thorns had cut him.

"Using my priestess' hand as my own, I anoint you king of Arkordouur." The priestess mixed the blood on his face with the oil and drew out a small rune on his forehead. "Stand and sign your oath in blood."

Silence reigned in the room as Robbinn turned around to the altar, where a book lay with Falkonn's oath on the left page, and his own on the right. Ydnias' priestess presented him with the ceremonial dagger, as it was given to him at his wedding which suddenly felt very long ago, presented on a red cushion. Beside the book lay a long, black feather, tipped with gold that shone green when the light caught it: a skreghle feather quill. Ydnias' priestess directed him to cut into the palm of his hand then pass the dagger to her, and when he did so was surprised to see that she too drew the blade across her palm, then held it over his, allowing the blood to pool together before he was told to sign.

"These things I have promised today I shall perform and keep, lest I be smote where I stand by the Almighty Five." He spoke loudly and clearly as he dipped the quill into the blood in his hand to sign his name.

"Go forth, King Robbinn Falkonn Carbeu III, and rule on with dignity and integrity," the statue said with finality as it moved back to its original position with the rumbling grinding of stone.

With that, the small company gathered in the church stood to applaud Robbinn as he walked through the church a King, fat beads of blood still rolling down his face like tears, and returned to his carriage, to take him home again but without the usual procession through the streets for celebration, as Robbinn felt the idea may attract unwanted attention from the rising 'king'.

This return was followed closely by the noblemen and women listed to attend his ball. Robbinn had no intention of changing his clothes for this, or of removing his golden crown of thorns and the blood it had drawn.

As soon as the guests gathered in the castle ballroom, Robbinn took to stand before them as yet more snow piled up in the windows and the light outside began to fade. Now king, it was his job to speak before them, his dutiful wife at his side.

"Friends, I gather you all here to celebrate my coronation, to my first event as your king. I invite you all to partake in a meal with me, my equals, and proceed to dancing. It is my upmost pleasure to entertain all of you this evening, and I do hope that you all have an enjoyable time." He smiled graciously despite internally kicking himself for delivering such a poor introduction. "I would like to hand over to my darling mother, as she has far more experience than I at this sort of thing." There was a ripple of laughter as he sat at the familiar long table although in an unfamiliar spot, and Oleyyna rose.

"I think that was rather well done, for your first introductory speech, believe me when I say my late husband's was much, much worse. I unfortunately won't be disrespect his memory for your entertainment, but I will not be stopping anybody who was in attendance that night from repeating it." She laughed softly, casting her eyes out to familiar faces. "I have no doubt that Robbinn will improve in leaps and bounds. I have every faith in him, I hope you all do too."

With that, she too returned to her seat and considerably warmer company. Soft chatter filled the crowded room as castle staff served a rather different menu to the last ball hosted there, a far more rustic, and in Robbinn's view, more enjoyable than he had otherwise had. He had been careful to select dishes that weren't too heavy to dance on later, but nothing like the boring, simplistic 'elegant' food he had been used to as a child. Robbinn was delighted to see his guests enjoying these choices quite animatedly, as though it was something utterly groundbreaking to them all – his father-in-law, Oseerys senior, even nodded towards him with a proud smile.

Before too long, Robbinn stood once more with his wife on his arm, a glass of sweet wine in his hand, and a smile on his lips to address his guests and bring them to dance.

"Come my friends, allies, join my darling wife and I in some dancing! This is, after all, a celebration, however modest it may be." He nodded towards the orchestra waiting in the back of the ballroom, led by Luxx and his enchanting lute, at which point they began to play beautiful music. Robbinn took up his gentle grip on Oserys, holding her hand with what he hoped was a very convincing look of the truest adoration, and whisked her to the middle of the dance floor. From the corner of his eye as he spun and stepped this way and that, he spotted Luciaan watching him with an only slightly sullen expression on his face, but decided to ignore that for the moment as he danced with his wife. Before much longer passed, the floor began to fill with chatter and ladies' great skirts, the music floating beautifully in between and men squeezing into whatever room was left to dance with their king.

In all, Robbinn found it to be quite enjoyable, and evidently he had spent a good while dancing, as by the time he next glanced out of the windows, it was pitch black outside. Finally, as the music was picking up and his company forgetting he was there, Robbinn took his opportunity to sneak away and pull Luciaan into a quiet, hidden little room just behind the wall the orchestra was playing against. They didn't need to speak to one another to know what to do.

Luciaan led him onto the small floorspace and placed his hands around Robbinn in the position he had clearly been secretly practicing, and beamed down at him like he was the luckiest man in the world as they began the dance Robbinn had taught him almost a week ago. Thankfully, none of his guests had yet registered his absence, leaving him and his true love to dance away in peace. That is, until the door opened, and they jumped apart like startled cats, only to be met by the friendly faces of Oserys and Arriella apparently also looking for privacy.

"Sorry! We're just looking for somewhere to dance," Oserys muttered, looking as though she were about to back out again.

"No, no, come in. That's exactly what we were just doing, if you don't mind sharing with us, I'm sure Luci won't mind?" Robbinn looked up at Luciaan again, who smiled.

"I don't mind." He breathed dreamily.

"Neither do we," Arriella replied, shutting the door and placing a nearby chair behind it as she spoke. With that, the four of them fell into a comfortable quiet as any need for conversation was smothered quite nicely by the music creeping back in as Luciaan and Oserys whisked their partners around the room. Robbinn had never felt more at peace than he did in the arms of his love, beside the woman whom he could call his best friend, in a mutual embrace of comfort and understanding, an agreement to support one another as they had sealed in blood, what felt like years ago.

At some point Robbinn and Oserys had returned to the party in the next room to dismiss the ball, and thank those in attendance and disappear once they had climbed back into their ornate carriages back into the arms of Luciaan and Arriella, to dance well into the night, even after the music had long been silenced, and the candles hanging in chandeliers and candelabras had melted into nothingness.

Chapter Twenty-Three

Robbinn awoke the next morning to the most troubling news he had ever received, delivered to him by Aldredd. It was a simple scroll that had arrived not long before he had been roused from his sleep, written in simple handwriting, with a steady hand, as though Hardweaverr was writing to an old friend

'Dear King Robbinn,

Congratulations on your coronation. Enjoy it while you can, won't you? I'm coming to take it from you. I will be arriving on your shores very soon, do look out for the remaining pirates.

With the utmost disrespect,

Hermontt Hardweaverr, the New King'

Robbinn read it once, twice three times over. He was still rereading when Aldredd added the rest of it verbally.

"He's been spotted a while off the West Coast, he's closest to Mabin. We estimate that he'll reach us in three days. Oseerys senior is taking his dragon to prepare to defend—what would you have us do?"

Robbinn looked at him quite blankly for a moment before responding.

"Ready my army. We will be setting up camp a little off Mabin's border, there's open land around there, just in case the bastard changes course. Have Mabin and the other closest cities evacuated for now. Send my men there immediately, I will meet them soon. Am I clear?" Robbinn said, slowly and clearly, but

241

with a firm tone. Aldredd nodded immediately.

"Yes, Your Grace."

"I will be with you all momentarily, but make haste, I sense we do not have all that long. Evacuate first, my citizens must be protected while our army is not there." Robbinn added as Aldredd made for the door. Aldredd called over his shoulder that he understood as he sprinted back out.

Robbinn made for Luciaan's quarters immediately and banged on the door almost desperately until the tired man opened it.

"Mm?" He grumbled, half asleep.

"Get your armour, now. War is upon us, there isn't much time." These words woke Luciaan like a slap to the face.

"On it, I'll meet you at the stables." He gave a small, rushed nod with a very serious expression before sprinting out, down the hall. Robbinn wasted no time in racing to find Oserys, who had retired with Arriella. He knocked on her door feverishly, and was answered quickly.

"Don your armour. Find your dragons, we make for the coast now, our allies are setting up a camp just outside Mabin. War is upon us." Robbinn hissed, trying not to be heard as there was still a spy in their midst. Thankfully, Oserys nodded her understanding.

"I'll be with you at the gates momentarily," she said with a grave edge to her voice, already edging away from the door.

"Good." He didn't manage anything else before he was making for his mother's chambers to wake her and tell her of the dangers arising. Oleyyna wasn't difficult to find, she had taken to frequenting Falkonn's favourite places in the castle, this time he found her on the balcony that led off one of the long windows in his library.

"Mother?" Robbinn called, with urgency and command in

242

his voice that made his mother jump and turn around with tears in her eyes.

"Oh—Oh, Robbinn dear, what is it?" She asked tentatively as she stepped back inside.

"War is upon us, and although I will not stop you from coming with me, I must ask you to stay safe. I will need someone to watch over the kingdom while I lead." Robbinn spoke very fast, with unpractised words and watched the colour drain from his mother's face.

"What? You don't mean to say you're planning to fight, are you?" She demanded, crossing the short distance between them in the blink of an eye and grabbing his arms to shake him.

"Of course, I am. This crown belongs to me, I plan to defend it." Robbinn kicked himself for saying it like that. He should've said something about a good king leading his army instead of wanting to keep his crown.

Oleyyna stared up into his eyes for a moment, her brow furrowed and her hands shaking against his arms.

"You're leading your army onto the field of battle yourself instead of hiding from it, as many others would have done." Robbinn felt her hand reach his face and brush her thumb against his cheek softly. "You are not a boy any more. I cannot shield you the way I want to. You were born to be a king. And... And I'm proud you're already proving to be a good one. I will accompany you there, to your camp. Every battle needs a witness." Oleyyna finished determinedly.

"Then come quickly, we have three days at the maximum. The army is assembling as we speak, find some armour Mother. Stay safe, that's all that matters if you're coming. We're meeting at the gates as soon as possible." He stepped back to escape his mother's grip and leave, but she held him there for a moment longer.

243

"When you came in, just now, you reminded me of your father. The young man he used to be, when he and I were first married, but you seem to have a far more level head than he did. Make him proud. Make me proud." His skin crawled at her words, and he muttered something about there being no time for wasted words as he tugged himself away to run down to his personal armoury, a couple of doors down from his chambers.

Robbinn threw open the door to reveal his armour, mounted on the stand just inside. Similarly to Oserys', his armour was mainly a gleaming black colour, but where hers held green and silver accents, his held gold and scarlet ones. On his chest plate was an intricately sculpted Skreghle, its wings extended to take flight, its furious red eye represented by a beautiful garnet, the tips of its flight feathers were painted gold, at the points of his armour the metal was shaped to resemble feathers, and his helmet was pointed, moulded after a furious bird's head with a crown of antlers on its head. Like Oserys' armour, the more Robbinn looked, the more he could see – only his armour was modelled after a Dreaded Skreghle.

When he commissioned it, Robbinn had asked specifically for it to be made in a way that it could be put on without the help of a servant or squire, based on a strange feeling he had about the idea of needing help to don his armour quickly and having to rely on another. This difference he was rather glad of as he hastily threw on every piece in the way he had been taught as a boy. Once fully armoured, he opened a glass case containing his grandfather's sword and its gold scabbard and took it with him on his hurried passage down to the stables, where he would retrieve his horse.

Solmyrer was quiet and subdued as Robbinn saddled and armoured him in his stable. He was calm when Robbinn mounted him and ducked under the barn, the scarlet cloak attached to his rider's shoulders thrown over his hindquarters. Robbinn thought he must know something was going to happen – it was said that horses would always be some of the first to know of disaster.

Robbinn made to meet his wife, his mother and his general by the gates in the thick snow, by which point Solmyrer was acting every bit the calm, collected war horse, but waited before he saw them to find Luciaan, The Tapper of Mabin.

He found the silent, hulking figure around the stables and felt his stomach twist in an odd feeling of fear. Fear he thought was completely illogical, he knew the face under that helmet. The black, smooth helmet that seemed to churn and leak pure shadow, even in such bright light. He knew the eyes behind the pitch-black slits that stared blankly at him were the most beautiful eyes he had ever seen. But still, he felt unnerved. Unlike his own armour, Luciaan's did not seem to be modelled after any kind of animal nor any monster known to the bestiary. It was simply unnerving in a way he couldn't place, perhaps it was too black, too sharp, too still – he couldn't put his finger on it for a few moments, until finally it came to him. Bones. The ridges and dips of the armour, the fastenings, all of it looked like bones covered with metal. He leaned back to look at the helmet in more horrible detail and saw it to be modelled after a human skull, not a monster.

His eye fell to Luciaan's chest plate – there was no decoration, only a single stripe of silver down the middle, but there wasn't a single scratch on it, indicating he had never taken a hit while wearing this armour. Robbinn looked lower, to his belt and shield, where his long sword was held in its black scabbard, a dagger just in front of it, the former seeming to whisper in the silence between them.

"I want to protect your identity. When you wear this armour I will address you as tapper, or something along those lines." Robbinn stumbled on his words slightly as his voice trembled.

Luciaan laughed softly, his comforting voice slithering out from that helmet like a snake. "Are you frightened of me, little Robbinn?"

Robbinn felt a chill race down his spine at the silky, dangerous tone of his voice, but he refused to answer and turned his horse around to head for the gates.

"You *are* scared! I don't blame you, you'd join ranks of thousands of men that are afraid of me." He laughed again, louder this time as Pereggnir jogged under him to meet Robbinn's side. He knew Luciaan was only teasing, but it still irritated him regardless. "Are you going to run when I start tapping, too?"

Before he could even remotely register what he was doing, white hot anger flashed in his chest and he whipped around to spit at Luciaan.

"You know, for a man who is supposedly so ashamed of this name, you're in remarkably high spirits to be wearing it again."

He knew he'd crossed a line the second the words came out of his mouth, and wished he could take them back out of the air, he didn't need to see Luciaan's face to know he had already gone too far.

"Luci, I'm sorry." He started, but Luciaan cut him off sharply.

"*Don't you Luci me.*" Snarled Luciaan, slowing his horse to make Robbinn pull ahead of him, and returned to the hulking, brooding silence that had frightened him before.

Robbinn cursed himself as he led the way to the gates at a canter as his previous urgency returned. At the sight of Luciaan-

246

or more accurately, the Tapper of Mabin – behind him, there was a hiss of recognition and a sense of tension in the air as the vast majority of his company resisted the urge to turn tail and run.

He even saw Oserys move her horse slightly in front of Arriella's to protect her. Stood before him were the leaders of every part of his army, and a few small clusters of soldiers, most of them mounted, a few in waggons. Aldredd represented his foot soldiers and swordsmen, Oserys his archers and her father's dragons, and Luciaan his cavalry. To those gathered, Luciaan was absent and Robbinn waited to speak until he had formulated the necessary lie to cover his tracks.

"My friends. Today I lead you all to what may be your early graves. There is a man attempting to lay claim to this kingdom, he has taken over various countries already and is quickly approaching this continent. I am leading you to head him off. He may surrender at the sight of our strength. He may not. This may be an all-out war, this may be a battle, this may be the crushing of an attempted revolution with an iron fist – regardless, history is watching us." He glanced around at his company, looking as many soldiers as he could in the eye. "This man has been threatening us with war for years. As you know, many of our men have already been sent to begin setting up camps and rest stops for the rest of us and to evacuate Mabin, Luciaan has gone ahead to scout locations. Now you may all recognise this man," he turned to look at Luciaan, standing just a few steps behind him, silent and brooding, "as the Tapper of Mabin. He is an ally of our kingdom. There isn't time for questions, we must head for the city itself now."

With that, he urged for halt to canter, and took the lead on a well-known road, his wife joining one side, and his beast joining the other. Aldredd commanded the remaining soldiers to follow at the fastest pace they could maintain. They travelled as a group, like one enormous monster, scrambling across the continent, its many legs eating up the miles like it was nothing. This time instead of stopping overnight, they dismounted their horses and walked alongside them until light broke once more and they rode on. There simply wasn't the time to be resting their horses past a walk and small grazing during the night.

Robbinn felt sick and nervous the entire time, his fingers were numb and cold in his gloves as he rode and walked, he felt his mind running away from him like a spooked horse, but kept it all under a functional level. Luciaan was angry with him, and he couldn't speak to him about his feelings while he was the tapper even if he wasn't. Robbinn felt alone in a way he hadn't felt since first looking out of that damned window and seeing his stupid groom being so ridiculously handsome. Even surrounded by friends and family as he was, he felt so very alone.

Thankfully, his numb silence seemed to be taken as bravery in his march to what could so easily be death. Robbinn could only hope his army was far bigger than Hermontt's.

During the second day of travel a carrier dragon appeared and landed on Robbinn's shoulder, a scroll attached to its leg. He pulled back just enough to read it, allowing Aldredd to take the lead as he unfurled it. The handwriting he recognised to be Oserys I's, only rushed and slightly shaky.

'Robbinn,

Camp has been established, the enemy is still days off, I have dragons watching. Mabin and its surrounding cities have been evacuated, the men are resting. I think their winds have dropped, we likely still have three days before he reaches us.

Oseerys I'

Robbinn released a breath he hadn't realised he was holding and urged Solmyrer on to come level with Aldredd.

"The wind has changed; we still have time to get to them," he muttered the moment he was close enough, watching Aldredd visibly relax.

"Good. We should meet the camp tonight if we stop and walk the horses again. We seem to have an advantage, thank the gods." Aldredd glanced up with his thanks, a fleeting prayer. Robbinn knew he had been promised victory, but this surely wasn't that debt beginning to be repaid. It was surely just a stroke of luck. Regardless, he rode on and voiced none of this concern.

Aldredd kept glancing nervously at Luciaan, as though he was terrified that he'd suddenly attack without mercy nor remorse like he had done so many times before, although what surprised Robbinn was Aldredd's lack of question. He didn't ask him anything about the fact that the Tapper of Mabin, a ruthless, sadistic killer that had faded into legend was riding to meet his army alongside his king, like any other ally.

"Aldredd, when we arrive, I want you to send word to the rest of my allies, ask them to be on their guard, ready to send over soldiers. Just in case," Robbinn said, with an idle tone of command.

"Of course," Aldredd stumbled on his words momentarily, "of course, Your Grace. I'll have it done."

Luckily, the rest of the journey passed quietly, without interruption of any kind. Robbinn knew that the treesnares would be coming out of their hibernation soon; hideous monsters that took the shape of trees and snatched up unsuspecting passers-by to slowly and painfully make them a part of it. They had of course been exterminated in the area surrounding the castle, making them safe for the casual hacking and conditioning of horses, but the same couldn't be said for the entire continent – they were too still and far too slippery for an entire land mass to kill off. It would be safe to assume that any would-be bandits were trying hard to avoid the beasts at all costs.

Fortunately, they not only couldn't pluck a man off a speeding horse, they wouldn't attack one with company either, and went dormant at night, making Robbinn and his men quite safe as they dismounted at dusk. Once more they walked and grazed their horses during the final stretch to the army's camp. The first giveaway was smoke rising from many hundreds of fires and the mouths of dragons, the latter Robbinn saw as he climbed to the top of the valley his army was stationed in.

Quietly there came a sea of tents and a wave of chatter, the odd call of a horse, and a wall of scents including smoke, sweat, charred meats and horse up to meet them like a dog called to heel. Strangely, this was quite a cosy, comfortable atmosphere, but by no means an unwelcome one – Robbinn felt the men around him relax instinctively, and lead their horses down the bank at a far faster pace than they had climbed it.

Before Robbinn could even address Oseerys I as he strode up to meet them, the men he had brought began to whisper about the tapper being the man at his side, and tension rose like a pulled bowstring.

Robbinn internally cursed himself.

Chapter Twenty-Four

"Before you all get too carried away in rumour and suspicion," Robbinn began in a loud voice, with a hard enough tone to squash the whispering around him, "yes, it is true that I have with me the Tapper of Mabin. However, much like the master of dragons beside me and his daughter, my wife, the tapper is an ally of ours. You needn't fear his blade and if I find out any of you are conspiring against him, or gods forbid attack him, I will treat it as treason. Am I clear?" There was a ripple of the affirmative. "Good."

With that, he walked on towards his tent, flanked by Luciaan and the Daeemoris. Thankfully his men seemed to take his promise quite seriously, and let him leave without hinderance as he muttered to Oseerys I for updated news. In what was surely another stroke of luck, Hermontt had been seen furiously pacing his ship, apparently stuck a day's sail away from the coast.

"Good, that gives us a fair amount of time to prepare," Robbinn muttered, leading Solmyrer to be settled outside his tent. "The men that have travelled with me need to rest, as do their horses. How is everyone here?"

"Well rested, ready for a battle. They're almost itching to fight, the dragons too," Oseerys I replied, speaking half to Robbinn and half to his daughter.

"Good. I want everyone at their fiercest when we head him off," Robbinn replied as his father-in-law pointed Luciaan to his tent, just next to Robbinn's. "You needn't worry about him, either, but I want him close to me. Assemble the men tomorrow morning, I want to speak to them. Am I understood?"

"Yes, Your Grace." Oseerys bowed his head as Robbinn and his daughter exchanged a short glance.

"Good, in that case I leave you to your duties. For now, we must rest," Robbinn added, ducking into his tent.

However, he didn't stay there. He was still thinking about Luciaan, about the awful, sticky guilt beginning to pool in his gut as the memory of his fierce, disgusting words forced its way back into the forefront of his mind.

'You know, for a man who is supposedly so ashamed of this name, you're in remarkably high spirits to be wearing it again.'

He couldn't believe that he'd allowed those words to come out of his mouth, when Luciaan was very clearly feeling so vulnerable to be doing something he had abandoned so long ago and was likely frightened about doing again, Robbinn abruptly remembered him saying that being such a feared soldier meant people wanted his head.

"Gods, how could I be such a fucking asshole?" Robbinn muttered to himself as he slunk out of his tent once stripped of his armour, and crept towards Luciaan's, covered in a long, black cloak to hide himself in the darkness. There was a small shuffle inside, presumably Luciaan moving.

"Luciaan?" He whispered at the edge of the tent, listening for the movement that had betrayed his whereabouts moments ago. Then there was a pause, just long enough for Robbinn to think Luciaan wasn't going to speak at all. But then came his voice. Rough and angry, but his.

"What do you want?"

"To apologise." He heard an irritated growl.

"I don't need your apology."

"But do you want it?" Robbinn heard as Luciaan drew breath to respond, but his response didn't come. After a moment, he nudged the conversation, softly. "Do you?"

"Kind of. I'll listen, at least."

Robbinn released a breath he hadn't realised he was holding, and with it an enormous weight he hadn't noticed he'd been carrying. He sat down with his back to the waxed canvas and crossed his legs to speak.

"Thank you. You don't have to forgive me – I don't expect you to. What I said to you was cruel and unnecessary, and vicious in a way that I didn't have any right to tell you." He heard Luciaan shift, then felt his back lean against his own. "I have no idea what it was like for you, I have never done anything like it, and I could never hope to understand. Everything I have ever done I have been bred and prepared for, that is a luxury I have presumed you to have far too many times. From the bottom of my soul, Luciaan, I am sorry for saying that."

"You should know by now that words mean very little to me. It is actions I value. But I'll admit, that did make me feel a bit better. So I'm going to thank you for apologising, but I won't forgive you yet."

Robbinn felt his cheeks heating up in embarrassment, feeling as though he was owed forgiveness somehow, he admitted he was wrong and apologised for it, but quickly reminded himself that he had been taught on numerous occasions by his mother that apologising was not transactional. It was a lesson he had in honesty struggled with quite a bit as a young boy.

"Okay. Thank you for listening to me – I don't like upsetting you, Luci. You mean far too much to me, you're far too precious."

"Stop trying to melt me, bastard." He laughed and swatted the fabric between them around where Robbinn's shoulder was.

253

Oh gods that laugh could cure the world of all its ills given the chance. "Go on you, get to bed."

"You can't give the king orders! And I will go to bed, but not because you told me to." Robbinn pouted at the sky as he made to stand up. "And you should go because I said so."

He heard that wonderful, perfect laugh again as Luciaan stood up inside. He may not be forgiven, but he was happy that Luciaan was laughing with him again.

"All right, I'll go to bed. I'm bloody tired. Goodnight, darling." Robbinn felt his heart flip on itself as Luciaan bade him goodnight.

"Goodnight, my love."

Satisfied by this conversation and with his promise to do better, Robbinn returned to his tent, and with it his bed. With the weight of guilt lessened quite considerably, he fell asleep the moment his head hit the pillow. He had somewhat expected such an uncomfortable bed to hinder his sleep, but such a long ride had taken everything out of him, and he woke early the next morning feeling the most well rested he had in months.

It didn't take him long to dress and leave to address his army, muttering a soft apology to Solmyrer as he mounted his grumpy horse once more, even promising it would be for just a short ride this time. On his left, Luciaan rode up in silence, wearing his armour once more and adopting the Tapper of Mabin once again. Robbinn smiled at him, holding his helmet under his arm in favour of wearing his crown. Luciaan inclined his head slightly, staring right at him through the slits in his helmet.

As requested, Oseerys had assembled the men in the stretch of meadows Mabin used for farming that may soon be a battlefield. They had been arranged into six blocks of men, two rows of three, their bodies and faces mingling into oversized, rectangular masses – Robbinn had intended to look as many men as he could in the eye, but saw now that this would be utterly impossible.

The two Daeemoris stood at the feet of a dragon each, two Greater Deathcallers, and watched him approach with similar aethereal expressions on their faces. Robbinn swallowed thickly as he tried to think of what to say to them all. When he opened his mouth, the Daeemoris shut the visors on their helmets, and commanded their dragons to hold flame in their mouths.

"Men." He called loudly, walking his horse towards the centre of the formation so that as many soldiers as possible would hear him, Luciaan trailing behind like a demented dog on a chain. "It is more than likely that we face war. I will not lie to you and tell you that I know what it is we face, for I do not. I believe it to be foolish to tell you any different. None of you have yet fought for me, I don't expect you to do so without good reason. Therefore if negotiations go poorly, I will lead the attack myself. I am prepared to lay down my life, just the same as you are. I believe we will emerge victorious if you trust me – you will have free reign when we take back the colonies he has tried to steal, you may do as you please under the watch of the Tapper of Mabin. Trust in me, men. I will bring you home."

Once he finished, he looked out on the sea of his soldiers, for there must have been hundreds of thousands of them, trained to be willing to fall on their swords if he gave such word when in formation. Robbinn didn't want them to feel like an expendable resource, and was trying to find some indication that it had worked and given them some degree of confidence in him that they wouldn't have had in his father.

Just as he was beginning to think he had embarrassed himself; his soldiers began to smack their swords against their shields, and a rumble of approval that quickly turned into a roar of cheering. Robbinn felt his heart thundering in his chest with the beating of every sword against every shield, and with it a strange sort of glee rose in him, as though some strange beast of war had reared its head and roared with the excitement of being allowed to fight.

"Do you trust me, men?" he bellowed above them all, his voice carrying in a strange, level way that it certainly shouldn't have done. His army thundered back as one in the affirmative, followed by one man speaking for them all.

"You carry Ydmirr with you, Your Grace! We trust that none other could lead us to victory the same way."

"I would throw myself upon my own sword for each and every one of you – would you do the same for me?"

Each and every man thrust his sword or bow in the air with his cheer, and his cavalry even asked their horses to rear up in their fierce response. This must have been what Ydmirr felt as he approached the field of battle, the anticipation, the blood thundering around his limbs at such speed he felt it in his fingertips and jawbone, even in his teeth.

"In that case, when the bastard washes up on our shores, you must show him yourselves at your most bloodthirsty. We will avoid bloodshed if we can, but it may not be possible. He will likely approach on the beach just a few miles behind you. If things do not go to plan, we attack immediately and without mercy – your signal will be this:" Robbinn raised his hand high above his head, outstretched, palm facing outward, and left it there for a moment before clenching his fist again. "I will show twice, first charge will be foot soldiers, when I give it a second time it will be the cavalry's. Do you all understand?"

There was a ripple of agreement as a dragon flew overhead to land surprisingly lightly for a creature so large beside Oseerys and mutter something to him in the low, gravelly voice dragons had.

256

"What is it?" Robbinn asked, looking between dragon and master curiously, he didn't care which of them answered, he just needed to know what the message was.

"The wind has changed, human. He'll be on that shore by midday," the dragon answered, turning its bright green eyes on him as it spoke. Robbinn felt his heart skip a beat in his excitement as his men shuffled and murmured between themselves, like a blanket of living beast hissing and churning at a threat.

"I see. In that case, men, we must march! Cavalry, your charge has been transferred to the tapper, you will follow his orders. Foot soldiers, you and Aldredd will get a head start now, march for your lives and I will lead you. You needn't charge the beach, wait a little back. Give me chance to speak with him. Your signal to attack will be as we discussed. Daeemori, I want your dragons on the beach if they would be so kind. Anyone belonging to the Northern loyalty will follow your general, and be at my side. Am I understood men?"

A great cheer met him, many swords clashing against shields one more time before weapons were thrust once more into the air.

"Good, get on then!" Aldredd and his horse met the foot soldiers to lead their march towards the beach as Robbinn held back to speak to his wife as Luciaan too turned to command his ranks. "Oserys my dear, this is not your fight, and if you are so inclined, you need not fight it. You don't need to be here."

She smiled, her head tilted up to meet his eye as she lifted her visor, amusement in her voice. Clearly she knew something that he'd missed. Robbinn's brow furrowed for a moment.

"I do appreciate the offer, my love, but you sort of need the general of the North to command their army."

As the words left her lips, the sky darkened as an enormous group of dragons sailed overhead, each of them wearing saddles, each of them Northern Greater Dragons, some black, some alabaster and some deep purple in colour, and landed in a line behind their commander.

"You're the general of the North?" Robbinn gaped as she smirked up at him. "Why on earth didn't you say so?"

"I have to keep some secrets now, don't I?" She laughed as her own dragon, the largest of the group, but clearly not a Northern Greater variety, lowered its head to allow her on its back. Its scales were far too dark and glossy to be one, and its snout too long, its claws were far sharper too, and its posture was different. While Robbinn knew that the Deathcaller wasn't the only dragon in the ranks of riders, he didn't recognise the species of this dragon at all. It looked at him with bright gold eyes with vertical, cat like slits of pupils. Oserys seemed to notice Robbinn's admiration as once secure on its back, she called down to him.

"My dragon is a Silent Death, Robbinn! Also known as a Northern Black dragon, far larger than the Northern Greater, but also much, much rarer! I'll tell you more about her when we have the time!"

And with that her dragon took off, letting out a call for the other dragons and their riders to follow as Robbinn turned Solmyrer towards his marching soldiers, joining Aldredd's side as he led the men.

Strangely he found very little to say to the men following as they marched, simply listening to the sound of their feet striking the earth in near perfect unison and at a fair pace – Solmyrer had to near enough jog to stay level with them.

Thankfully after keeping up the same pace for the journey, Robbinn's army made it to the beach first, the dunes of which were by now lined with dragons of various species, poised to attack as far as the eye could see. Robbinn again hoped his army was larger than Hermontt's as he organised his men to line the beach with their large shields together, forming a wall. Behind them stood his cavalry, each man and his horse armoured to the teeth, awaiting command. Just a little behind them on the dunes in front of the dragons, stood the archers, each with a nocked arrow, ready to draw when they heard the command.

Robbinn certainly thought they looked quite the imposing sight and was admiring them as his mother approached him, before the enemy ships could be seen, before their pirate allies lined their ships up a little out from the shoreline.

"Son, might I speak with you?" He slowly turned his head, dragging his eyes away from his men.

"Yes, of course." He moved Solmyrer a few paces away, so that he would avoid being overheard.

"Are you nervous?" She asked quietly, once just out of earshot.

"A little, but my men aren't to know that," he replied coolly, hoping his tone would cover the fact that he absolutely was quite nervous.

"You needn't be." Oleyyna reached out to rest her hand against Robbinn's cheek, raising his face to the sunlight. "Do you know why?"

"No, I don't." Robbinn looked at her curiously, albeit slightly down his nose due to how she was holding him. He saw a look of distinct pride as she admired him, and heard it quite clearly in her voice when she spoke.

"You, my son, carry war in your eyes. You carry him with you in your face and upon your shoulders. Your wife carries thunder in hers, and the commander of your cavalry carries death in his. Do you know what that makes the three of you together? Assembled, as you are?" There was no way she should have known that Luciaan was there, and yet she looked straight at him as her eye jumped between the three of them.

"No. What does it make us?" Robbinn asked, curiously.

"The omens of victory. When war, death and thunder assemble together, the earth hides its face. You will crush this silly uprising beneath your heel, my boy." She pulled his face back to be level with hers and she stared directly into his eyes with fire in hers that he had never seen before. "I raised a soldier, not a coward. You will do well to remember that."

Robbinn swallowed hard, and opened his mouth to respond, but a dragon's call broke the anticipated silence first, and directed his attention to the horizon before he could make a sound.

"They're here."

Chapter Twenty-Five

Robbinn muttered a soft 'holy shit' to himself as the sizable fleet raced towards them and his pirates flanked either side of his army. He took his horse cantering to the foremost central position and called for quiet. As per his orders, a hush fell upon the shifting, anxious men. Robbinn allowed Hermontt to disembark as his own dragons, or more accurately wyverns and amphipteres, the smaller, weaker cousins to dragons, landed in a line, mimicking Robbinn's Northern allies.

Hermontt stepped off his ship wearing a crown of bones, truly the spitting image of his executed brother, only as though he were ten years younger. Where Huxell had once been handsome and had fallen into a gaunt, disused, desperately thin appearance, Hermontt was still fit, handsome and almost bright in the face. There was an awful smile on his face as he strode up towards the army lining the beach, as though he knew he had the upper hand. Robbinn rode up to meet him, vastly more confident having now seen how much of an advantage he truly had.

"Hermontt, is it?" He didn't dismount Solmyrer before speaking – Hermontt didn't deserve to see him like an equal.

"Yes, I think you knew that didn't you little birdy?" leered Hermontt, blue eyes staring up at him with vicious anticipation.

"Are you intending to back down? Or are you going to spill more blood?" Hermontt's army was rapidly disembarking from their ships. Robbinn still seemed to have the advantage. "I'm giving you one chance to surrender."

"Oh? What makes you think I will? What do you have that I don't?" Hermontt bared his teeth confidently as Robbinn glanced behind him to point at Luciaan and beckon him forward with a finger. It was now or never for the Tapper of Mabin.

There was an awful silence as the Pereggnir's hooves beat into the ground behind Robbinn, whose eyes had now settled on Hermontt's once more. When the tapping started, it was quiet. Hardly audible over the breeze that chilled the men to their bones. A horrific quiet that got louder as men on Hermontt's side attempted to turn and run. Luciaan galloped Pereggnir up and down the beach, just tapping. It was a rhythmic sound, just fast enough to make the human heart try to match it, just enough to spark the panic.

Hermontt's face dropped like a stone in a lake and paled like the first frost of winter as his men began to shift with their fear, turning away, muttering about the tapper. One or two even threw themselves on their own swords to save themselves having to fight an army led by that man. Robbinn smirked.

"How? That shouldn't be possible, he's supposed to be dead!" Floundered Hermontt, trying to ignore the shift in his army.

"Clearly, he isn't. I shall repeat myself, you have one chance to surrender. Do you wish to do so?" Robbinn asked, coolly.

"Never. I came to rip that crown off your shitty little corpse, and I intend to do so."

"Your brother squealed like a pig when my wife killed him. I wonder, will you do the same?" Robbinn watched his face contort with rage as he stuttered for the words for an attack as he scrambled backward to protect himself. Robbinn raised his hand as the Hermontt's army began the foot charge to his own. He clenched his fist. With a cry of glorious fury shared by all his men, the charge began.

His foot soldiers advanced first, clashing with Hermontt's with screaming, the clashing of metal, the sounds of men hitting the floor, followed by screaming and gurgling as great spurts of blood painted his soldiers. Robbinn whipped his horse around, swinging his grandfather's sword as though he had already earned it at the men rushing Solmyrer, feeling their flesh cleaved from bone under his blade with sickening ease. He retreated to his next wave of men, calling out to his archers as he saw Hermontt find his.

"DRAW," commanding them to nock before the battle had given him a fraction of a second's advantage as he heard the bowstrings tighten just before Hermontt's, "LOOSE!"

Robbinn's roar came louder than the men being slaughtered just a little way before him, and the whistling of arrows came louder still. A cloud of arrows sailed overhead from his archers and hit their mark, hitting soldier after soldier in the eyes and arms. His split second's advantage was the difference – the returning fire was remarkably thinner.

Somewhere between the fire, Luciaan had returned to his side to ready the cavalry for their charge, but before Robbinn could give their command, Hermontt's dragons took flight with their riders, and he was forced to call for Oserys to lead a counterattack.

Thankfully, all it took was a glance in her direction before her magnificent dragon pushed off from the ground and tore straight for the largest of the wyverns, grabbing its delicate neck and rider in her jaws and rolling in mid-air, ripping off great chunks of flesh as the wyvern screeched mournfully to its death.

As Oserys left the ground, her father followed, leading the rest of the dragons to take flight with them and begin to battle the wyvern and amphiptere riders with a great gust of wind that

263

near unseated the cavalry. Many of the soldiers fighting paused momentarily – foolishly – to glance up at the battling reptilian beasts, to watch as Oseerys' dragon spat out an enormous jet of flame that destroyed most of Hermontt's waiting ships, killing all those on board, but it seemed more were coming, as many of the other riders joined him to attempt to destroy more.

Robbinn may have had the upper hand in terms of dragon power, but Hermontt had an army far larger than his own – a fact that only became apparent when he saw hundreds of ships appearing on the horizon, many of them burning, but an unnerving amount intact as the dragons battled above them. He bit his lip, and decided to lead his army back, the way they were being pushed.

Somehow, he had so far experienced very few casualties – there were bodies littering the ground, but only one or two were from his army, he could only assume that training was superior to numbers.

Oserys and her dragon lit up a wall of soldiers like torches between the ships and the dunes as the archers were shown their command to continue aiming behind it, to allow the rest of Robbinn's army a chance to back up onto the open grazing land between Mabin and its neighbouring city.

Robbinn addressed those who had made it with him quickly as they reformed their ranks.

"This will be a battle of attrition, there's only one way to get to us, and it's over the dunes. Give them your all, don't let a single one escape you."

He took Solmyrer behind the newly formed line with Luci-aan at his side as his archers too took their chance to join back to rain hell on the opposition, arrows nocked. There was a pause where even the earth itself seemed to hold its breath as each soldier watched the top of the dunes. And waited.

"Hold, men." Robbinn breathed, holding his hand up, above his hand, palm open. When it happened, there was hardly time to think as Hermontt's men advanced on foot towards them at a sprint, down the bank, and towards them with a furious battle cry. Robbinn let them come just a little before clenching his fist and roaring for his soldiers and cavalry to attack, putting himself at the front, Luciaan beside him swung his arm in a wide circle, crashing his great sword against his shield, sparking a similar excitement from the cavalry as he followed. Robbinn patted Solmyrer on the neck and muttered to him that it was all right as quite abruptly he imagined it to be bushes he was ploughing through instead of a wall of soldiers, swinging the sword of his grandfather, jumping ditches instead of fallen bodies, much as he had done what felt like a lifetime ago but the other way around as he tore through the treeline.

He led his cavalry around the hoard of men in two groups in a pincer movement, cutting them down left and right around him. He led his mounted troops to cut the advancing men off with their armoured horses like great battering rams, moving seamlessly to employ a well-practiced tactic where the horses would canter between one another in cross hatching paths, the men on their backs swinging swords down onto the poorly armed men below them. Out at the other side the unscathed cavalry reformed together at the back of the foot soldiers as they cut down anyone who survived. This particular tactic had been implemented and taught by Luciaan, who had hailed it as the reason battles had been won on numerous occasions.

Robbinn heard the men screaming and crying for their mothers but had found it horribly easy to numb his ears to the sound in favour of the dragons fighting somewhere hundreds of feet in the air, straining his ears for any indication of who had the upper hand. All he could hear was the roaring, snapping and snarling, aside from the odd sickening thud as a dead or wounded one fell to the ground.

Thankfully, a pattern of attack displayed itself to be more than a little effective, albeit unexpectedly: Robbinn told his archers to fire great clouds of arrows at the approaching soldiers, to thin the herd until there were enough running down the bank for his pincer to cross hatch attack massacred the vast majority with almost no fallout aside from the loss of one or two of his hundreds of riders every other wave, and his foot soldiers moved in to finish the remaining off.

On and on went this pattern, painting Robbinn's armour with blood over and over – he was nearing numb to the excitement as the sun began to set, at which point Oserys landed her giant dragon and commanded her to perch on the dirty dunes and torch the approaching men as she ran to speak with Robbinn.

"Their dragons are dead, all of them – there's still hundreds of soldiers, but he's worried. Our dragons are tired, they're all running out of fire." She was cut off suddenly as overhead her father's dragon plummeted towards the ground, crashing into the beach just below where her own dragon was concentrating fire. Robbinn had never heard a scream like it. It was as though she were possessed by the goddess of thunder herself as she drew her sword and ran for her father, ignoring horses and dragons entirely as she cut down man after man in her rage, her desperation. Somehow Robbinn knew he wouldn't see her again until the attack was thinning. He commanded his army to continue their work and told any dragon riders to mount horses instead if their beasts needed rest, this battle was now down purely to attrition, and this strategy was continuing to work. Distantly he wondered how much of his success was down to the gods' intervention, and how much of it was the true efficiency of his strategic choices. He hoped it was more the latter – but he didn't miss how the soldiers had slowed in their attempted advance once the sun had set.

Flame and smoke filled the land as the sun rose again, stuffing the throats of living soldiers with the stench of charred corpses of horse and human alike. The dragons which were not resting had continued raining fire on Hermontt's remaining army, and Robbinn still hadn't seen Oserys since her father was brought down. By the time daylight had truly broken, Robbinn had around three quarters of the army he had started with, but Arriella reported to him that now the numbers were quite equal. These words sparked a small lurch of hope in his stomach, now that his confident shield had been thoroughly battered. He pulled away when he saw Oserys returning on her dragon, asking for just a little more out of Solmyrer for the moment.

"Did you find him? Oserys, is he all right?" Robbinn pleaded, praying that this was not the cost of his victory as she lifted the visor of her helmet.

"He's dead." Her voice was numb, completely devoid of emotion. "I held his hand as he went." She looked to her hip as her words hit Robbinn like a punch to the gut. Although he had not known The Great Oseerys Daeemori all that long, he rather liked the man – he held far more affection for him than he did his own father. "His sword is mine now. It gave over loyalty."

Robbinn swallowed thickly. "My dear, there are no words I can say to ease your pain. I will not force you to stay here, but I will ask you to. This isn't over yet, and I need your help. Without you we have no chance of victory."

The cries of agonised men dying floated over as her bloodshot eyes hardened with determination, the colour mingling to make them seem to glow.

"I'm going to kill every last one of the bastards." She nod-

267

ded at him with her promise, and he nodded back as she replaced her visor.

"You will have the opportunity, I promise you that. Come, we must finish this." Oserys offered him a spot on the back of her dragon, which he accepted without hesitation, dismounting Solmyrer with a final, grateful pat and passed him to a passing healer on his way to tend to the wounded at base camp.

Robbinn climbed the scaly wing of the dragon, and no sooner had he done so did she move, diving across to the battle he had left – now the remaining soldiers were attempting a final charge on Robbinn's deadly cavalry, surrounded by dragons creating a ring of deadly fire to keep them held like fish in a barrel.

Suddenly there came a great roar, over the top of everything going on around him, from Hermontt. He stood there, in the middle of the battlefield, holding someone on their knees at his hip, with a dagger to their throat.

"ENOUGH!" It stopped every soldier in their tracks. The stench of blood filled the air. The ground was a carpet of bodies that melted into one another, leaving no space for mud or desperate blades of grass to see the light of day.

"HOLD, MEN." Robbinn snarled at his soldiers, to keep them there. There was no more snow where the bodies lay.

"Now let's all just calm down, hm?" Hermontt trudged further in, directly towards Robbinn and yanked a head of white hair up from armour Robbinn recognised. It was Luciaan. His mind and heart began to race, but his feet were glued to the spot. His mouth went dry as he saw Hermontt press the blade into Luciaan's suddenly very fragile throat hard enough for fat beads of hot blood to form. There was blood on his armour, at his side, either he was wounded or had cut someone down before being apprehended – there was steam billowing from the spot, the blood must have been fresh.

Hermontt had a terrible, deranged smile on his face. "Surrender your kingdom to me, your throne, your titles—all of it, and I will let you both live." His smile broadened when he saw Robbinn's eyes growing wide.

"Quickly now! I have your Tapper of Mabin, I know what he is to you!" Hermontt's voice was almost strained, his icy eyes near bulging out of his skull with the excitement as he pressed the blade harder into Luciaan's throat. His handsome face was so tired, his Luci wasn't even fighting the disturbed man who held him. Robbinn couldn't speak. He couldn't move, he could think of nothing but how he needed to do something. His mouth opened and closed to form words that wouldn't come. Hermontt's smile grew impossibly wider still.

Robbinn only became aware that somewhere behind him an arrow had been shot when it whistled past his head, and only realised what had happened when it buried itself between Hermontt's bulging eyes. His body gave a great jerk as he fell, dragging the blade across Luciaan's throat, at once spraying blood everywhere.

Robbinn screamed. He screamed the most blood curdling scream his lungs had ever produced as his body was suddenly able to move enough to race towards Luciaan as he fell, weak hands clutching at his neck. Robbinn collapsed to his knees at his side, pulling his beloved into his lap. He didn't notice the soldiers around him, he wouldn't have cared if he had. He didn't notice Oserys either, not until she spoke.

"Robbinn. This isn't over, you can't stop now." He looked at her. She was holding a bow. He listened to Luciaan's shaky, weak breaths. He looked at his army. He stared for only a moment at the corpse of Hermontt Hardweaverr as he heard his men starting to attempt a retreat. When Robbinn found his voice again, it came out more akin to a dragon's roar than a man's as tears rolled down his cheeks, cutting paths through the mud, sand and blood on his face.

"KILL THEM ALL! EVERY LAST ONE, SHOW NO MERCY, GIVE NO QUARTER." He roared, hunched over Luciaan as his precious blood spilled out onto the ground.

Chapter Twenty-Six

Robbinn heard his army cry out their final attack, heard feet and hooves thunder past his ears as his gaze dropped to Luciaan, clutched in his arms. He cradled that big stupid head and brushed filthy hair from his beautiful eyes, still shining out like crystals against the darkness of the mud and soot caking the skin around them, glassy with tears. Robbinn clamped his free hand against the wound in his neck to try and stop the blood. Oh gods the blood, there was so much blood. Too much for one injury, and as he searched, he found the split in his armour where something – perhaps a spear, perhaps an enormous dagger – had been jammed through, into his flesh.

Robbinn's voice shook and cracked as he began to mutter to Luciaan, the heart within his chest wailing out with his pain. "I'm sorry, I'm so sorry, Luci—Luci I'm so sorry." He repeated over and over as the clouds above split to allow the sun to light up the two of them, forcibly reminding Robbinn how beautiful Luciaan was, his blue eye lighting up like stained glass, his brown one warming to the colour of honey. It made him feel sick as blood rushed around his ears, his own frantic pulse all he could focus on as the screaming started anew.

That was until Luciaan lifted a bloody shaking hand to his face as he continued to apologise and tell Luciaan he never should've involved him in all this, that it was all his fault. The moment his hand touched Robbinn's face, he fell still and quiet, staring down into the pale face of his beloved as a small line of blood fell from his lips, down his cheek.

Luciaan sucked in a deep, shaky breath, forcing his lungs to obey his command, staring determinedly into Robbinn's face. "It's okay, it's okay. I promise, it's okay. Go, you aren't finished."

His lips twitched into a pained smile as Robbinn's tears cascaded down his face. "I love you." Robbinn gasped, hunching over Luciaan to press one last kiss into his lips.

"I love you too, Robbinn." And he fell still. Robbinns's entire body shook with the force of the sound that escaped him, the truest of anguish, the very real agony he felt ripped out of his throat. Hot, stinging tears flowed down his face as he forced himself to move, to leave him there, despite every fibre of his being wanting to stay and be buried with Luciaan, to melt into a pile of bones alongside him. His fury however, led him on foot to destroy the rest of Hermontt's pathetic army and ready his men to board his ships to be carried by the remaining dragons.

Robbinn felt his body give the command to retake all his lost colonies with every ounce of force they had, heard himself tell them to show now mercy and to make an obvious display of deterrence – to show any other would-be kings that uprising like this will not be tolerated.

Before he could bring himself back down to earth, back to the forefront of his own head, in the middle of preparations to travel, Clauude of all people shoved his way to the front of the group, a dagger in his hand and a disturbed expression on his face, holding Oleyyna squirming against his chest, his other hand covering her mouth. Robbinn stared blankly at the sight as his favourite servant held the blade to his mother's throat. Aldredd beside him drew his sword.

"I discovered the spy. I was about to tell you his identity, Your Grace, but he seems to have done that himself." Growled the soldier – one of the last of his true allies.

"I too had deduced it to be either Clauude or Father's old servant. Hermontt knew things only one of the two would know. Let go of my mother and I may spare your life, Clauude," Robbinn said, dully. Clauude's eyes bulged.

"What if to die was my duty? I passed information on for years and served you for longer! I know you. I know your limits, your weakness. I know what you fear."

"You know only what I have told you." Robbinn drew his grandfather's sword that he still hadn't won over. "I shall give you only one more chance to release her, or you will die." A chill ran up his spine when he heard his mother give a soft whimper against Clauude's grip. For a moment it looked as though Clauude was going to surrender, he even lowered his blade, but in a split second he had changed his mind and had dug the weapon into Oleyyna's torso, just under the ribs like he was gutting a pig. She screamed against him, her voice muffled as he twisted the knife in her body, cutting everything he could so that when he withdrew it, her organs all cascaded out with it.

Robbinn didn't think about what he was doing when he sprinted forward with his sword and swung it at Clauude, all of his rage and agony forcing the blade through his flesh, taking his head from his shoulders in one blow. At once the scarlet jewel in the sword's hilt lit up like a flame, and the whole sword lightened in his hands. Could it be he had won the loyalty of his legendary blade? Now, when his mother lay dying as he cast it aside, as his love was gone, as he collapsed to his knees beside her, had he won its allegiance?

He cradled his mother has she struggled over her last few breaths. She was clearly in too much pain to speak, but her eyes searched for his, stinging with tears as she found them. He saw her lips twitch into a small smile as she fell still in his arms.

273

Perhaps Oleyyna was seeing Falkonn's face in his once more, and it brought her comfort as she slipped away in his arms. He gently used his cleaner hand to brush flaming hair from her eyes as Aldredd kneeled on her other side to carefully push her eyelids closed. If Robbinn were to look from the chest up, his mother could easily have been sleeping. Somewhere behind him there was movement, then a soft hum of thought. Robbinn felt a hand on his shoulder, and heard Oserys' voice come with it, but didn't take his eyes off his mother's body as blood seeped onto his lap.

"Robbinn. You've won it, your sword. I can't lift it."

"Leave me. I want to sit here with my mother."

"You didn't leave me. We've both lost parents today. I wanted to give up, you didn't let me – so I won't let you, either. We can bury her and my father, together." Her voice was calm, but authoritative and firm. He didn't try to fight her as he stood and pulled his cloak off to drape it over her form, looking to Oserys with determination in his eyes. To his shock, she pulled the sword from her hip, and sank to one knee as she held her father's sword out in her hands.

"Robbinn, I hereby swear to you my blade and my body to wield it on your behalf. I will henceforth take orders from you, and you alone."

He knew what this was. She was swearing her allegiance like a knight, and he knew what he was to do in turn. He placed his hands over hers, and bent forward at the waist to kiss the blade.

"If you are certain, I swear to you in turn to use your strength only when truly necessary, and with due mercy. You in turn have my trust. Stand, Oserys. I declare you a knight of Ar-kordouur." Robbinn took a step back to allow her room to stand. The men around them had fallen into a hush of anticipation. It was likely she was the first female knight any of them had seen.

"Board the ships men, Oserys' dragons will take us to the Western continent. One of you, make certain that there is parchment, quills, and ink available to me. There are many laws that need to be rewritten, I sense wasting any time would be foolish." He didn't wait for a response before turning to leave, Oserys at his side.

It only took a few hours to prepare for their next journey, with men filling the remaining intact ships to bursting and the largest of the dragons gasping them carefully in their enormous talons to take flight, but for Robbinn it felt like a few moments, he turned his head and was on the back of Oserys' dragon, giving the order to move. Apparently, he had planned to burn the structures Hermontt had built using the dragons as the soldiers took out their defences, protecting the dragons from the ground. Robbinn remembered none of that, he felt as though he had been plucked from one moment in time and unceremoniously placed somewhere else, something which greatly unnerved him, but he decided not to confess to anyone. After all, who did

The next thing he knew, his nose was flooded with the stench of burning corpses and hair, smoke filled his lungs, he felt as though he was choking as the dragon beneath him spewed fire onto the towns below, the sounds of screaming filled his ears, the pleading, the begging for their lives rooted him to the spot. He was frozen in horror – but he knew he must have given the orders to fire, to burn the innocents, this wouldn't be happening otherwise.

Distantly he thought about the language Hermontt had used, specifically the term 'tyranny' and wondered if there had been any truth to it. Was what he was doing evil? Was there too much force? His father had long ago taught him that people must be taught not to question his rule, he must rule with force where necessary to teach important lessons. Part of him wondered if allowing his men to pillage like this and burn the settlements. 'Liberation,' Hermontt had called it. He thought about how sickened he would have been with himself a year ago. A year ago he had not known battle.

Quite abruptly he remembered wondering where he was supposed to fit into a story book, his life, his romantic endeavours, all of them were supposed to be some kind of guide as to what things were supposed to be. He had never considered the idea that he may have been the villain of his story.

Somewhere in between his thoughts far more time passed than he perceived, suddenly it was dark, he could see the stars around him as his mouth moved without him telling it to, he heard himself command that his soldiers tighten laws in every part of his kingdom. Prison time was to be increased, humiliation and torture penalties were given for more crimes, and the death penalty too was increased. When he was in more control of his own actions once again, Robbinn began putting prices on heads. The Tapper of Mabin was to be found at all costs. After sending someone to find Luciaan's body for burial, he had been told it was gone. There was almost no way Luciaan had survived, which meant it was likely someone had taken him to strip his carcass of its armour and steal his name. Quietly, Robbinn held onto the delusion that just maybe he had lived, and was being cared for by someone.

The next manhunt he started was for any and all members of the Hardweaverr house. Men, women, children – all of them he wanted. If both of their sons were so determined to kill him and take over, they must have got it from somewhere.

Robbinn signed off on hefty rewards for each of his wanted men, then turned his attention to laws he had wanted to change since he was a boy. Immediately he listed that women could become soldiers and become queens without the assistance of kings – meaning his wife would now be known as Queen Oserys, not Lady. He disbanded the law ruling homosexual behaviour illegal too, stating that since the Gods had no problem with it, there was no reason for humans to either. He anticipated backlash as Pereggnir's statues were replaced in church after church across the kingdom, and of course was correct – but he intended to crush this too. He placed resistance to the church on the same level as high treason itself.

At some point in the following days, Aldredd had asked him quietly if he was sure about what he was doing, warning him that if he continues on this path, his people may begin to lose hope in him.

"Perhaps in some cases it's better to be feared than loved, Aldredd." Was all Robbinn offered him in reply. He found himself unable to recall what had happened next, not only on this occasion but on a few others throughout the week. Soon enough he had begun to skip bits and pieces of time, starting with minutes, to hours, to days, until he was losing track of entire weeks.

The next time he returned to control over himself, he felt a soul sucking sense of despair and rage as he threw himself to his knees before Pereggnir's statue as it looked down on him with a strange sort of pity in its face. He pleaded with it, fury in his face, tilted up to look at the statue.

"You said – you promised – that I would emerge victorious. My love is gone, I will never again see him, or hold him, or hear his voice. My mother too is dead." His voice broke with tears as he pleaded with the statue. "She is gone forever, I will never see nor speak to her again. I see no victory in this."

"I said you would win this war. I did not say it would be

without loss." Robbinn gave an agonized cry as he turned away to leave, screwing his eyes shut to stem the flow of tears. When he opened them again, he was sitting in his throne room with a numb feeling in the pit of his stomach, which quickly turned to rage as he realised that once again, he had lost time. Ever since the battle he had found it increasingly difficult to retain memories, more so now that he was consistently losing time.

A man suddenly burst through the door, chased by Robbinn's guards, before he could be seized, the man sprinted up to Robbinn and smacked him hard around the face. Robbinn felt his head move with the force of the slap, felt his cheek sting, heard his loyal blade Oserys halfway draw her sword as the rest of his guard rushed to his aid. Robbinn held up a hand to halt them as the man stepped back panting, his eyes wild.

"The next time you try to misuse your hands, I will have them taken from you. Do I make myself clear?" The man's face contorted in fury.

"You bastard Carbeus have been terrorising the common people for generations! It's time for someone else to take the throne – that Hardweaverr was the best thing to ever happen to this kingdom!" He spat, reaching out to strike Robbinn again.

"Oserys, relieve this man of his hands – he clearly does not know what to do with them." Drawled Robbinn, his cold eyes staring the man in his furious face. He listened to the scrape as Oserys drew her sword, the sound of his guards seizing the man, but were cut sharply by a strangled shout.

"COWARD!"

Robbinn held up a hand to stop them once more.

"What did you just call me?" Robbinn hissed, his eyes narrowing as his own rage flashed.

"COWARD! Sending the Daeemori to do your dirty work, cut my hands off yourself!" The man snarled. A few seconds of deadly silence passed as Robbinn considered, his expression a horrifying blank as the tension drew like a bowstring until he stood.

"Good idea."

Robbinn felt himself step down from his throne in silence, draw the sword from his hip and lift it like it hardly weighed an ounce. The man began to plead and apologise, having the gall to ask for mercy after calling Robbinn a coward. He felt himself laugh. As easily as he had beheaded his beloved Clauude, he swung the sword down on the man's wrists, severing them from his arms in one smooth motion. It took a moment for him to scream, for his body to register there was something wrong as his blood began to paint the floor around Robbinn's throne which had gained a bone crown hanging off its frame.

Robbinn looked down on the man writhing and screaming in his guard's grip.

"Be thankful – I have shown you mercy." The wailing man slowly met Robbinn's eye and tried to swallow his tears.

"Mercy?" He asked, finally.

"I decided to use just one blow. You need only feel that pain once." He met the eye of one of his guards. "Take him away. Throw him in a ditch or something, I don't care."

"And the floor? Would you like us to send for someone to clean it?" The guard asked as he and his fellow tugged the man between them to his feet.

Robbinn considered for a moment as he looked at the drying blood on the stone floor.

"No, I think I'll leave it there."

And with that he swept from the room, his loyal wife at his heels, her father's three headed dogs trotting behind her.

Robbinn found he couldn't remember burying his mother, but her sarcophagus was beside Falkonn's in the crypt when he finally braved the visit, stuffing his ears with wads of fabric to ignore the ghosts and holding his lantern like a shield to keep them at bay. He was certain one of them was hers, the wound on her stomach matched the manner in which she had been killed, but he would never have been sure – the ghosts wanted him out of their resting place, that much was obvious. Only a fool would stay there long.

Robbinn next caught himself watching the snow melt as winter began to shift into spring. Time was passing him by too fast, far too fast, and there was nothing he could do to stop it or catch up, like a runaway carriage he had such little hope of seizing, but he tried to find anyway. The feeling of his grasp on reality slipping wasn't a pleasant one and before he knew it, he was losing weeks and months at a time in the blink of an eye, he felt as though the floor was crumbling beneath him into an icy ocean, and he had put off calling for help so long that now he couldn't, there was no time for anyone to throw him a rope. His head slipped under the crushing but familiar waves of loss – he couldn't find which way was up, he couldn't see where he was, nothing was clear.

Chapter Twenty-Seven

Robbinn couldn't tell how much time had passed when he came around – it felt as though he had been plunged into an icy lake and resurfaced somewhere entirely new. It was at least mid-winter, judging by the feet of thick snow blanketing the ground outside his window. Luciaan had looked so beautiful in the snow, it brought out the shards of icy blue in his brown eye, and his blue eye would shine like a diamond. The very thought pushed a horrible pain into his chest, he was reminded of how much he missed Luciaan, how he would give anything to just see him again, to look on that handsome face of his just once more.

He was soon greeted by Oserys, in her full armour, quiet and intimidating as was supposedly usual. He almost didn't know her any more, but he still felt he could trust her with any-thing, if their wedding vows were broken, or their previous blood pact, one or both of them would be dead by now.

"Oserys, might I ask you something? And I must ask you not to repeat any of this." Robbinn asked her quietly.

"Of course, I am sworn to you, your word is my com-mand." She replied, her voice slightly muffled through her hel-met.

"Be honest with me. How long ago did Hardweaverr at-tempt to invade?" His voice was cautious – he wasn't certain he truly wanted to know.

"Five years ago."

Robbinn's words caught in his throat. Five years. Five years had passed in the blink of an eye.

"Remind me, what else has been changed in terms of law?"

"Homosexual activity is legal, and marriage between same sex couples is legal under the church. There is a manhunt for The Tapper of Mabin, and anyone claiming to be him."

"Has anyone come forward?" He felt his heart in his mouth, heard the blood in his ears as the damp air of the castle corridors. He didn't know where he was going, but his feet seemed to.

"A few imposters. None of them were genuine." She replied coolly, falling into step at his side.

"I see. Is Arriella doing well?"

"She is. She has been my rock throughout the burial of my father, unfortunately you come second to her in that respect."

Robbinn huffed a laugh, but he didn't relax. "I understand."

Oserys hesitated for half a second. Robbinn tensed a little more as her hesitant voice filled the space between them once more, softly seeping out from her helmet like smoke from the nose of one of her dragons.

"Robbinn, might I offer you a word of caution?"

"I suppose so."

"In reference to Luciaan. You ought not to force what isn't meant to be. Some of those in our lives are only supposed to be temporary. Perhaps the time has come to let him go."

She spoke gently and without force, as though trying her best not to hurt him with her words, although they buried themselves into his gut like knives. His eyes began to sting and his vision blurred as he looked at her.

"I will never believe that. Not when it's him. I will not stop until he is in my arms again." He tipped his head back, closing his eyes to breathe a shaky breath. "Wait in the throne room for

282

me, I shall make my way there."

She nodded, bowed, and swept from the room in eerie silence despite her heavy, metal armour. The second her back was turned, Robbinn fled to the castle roof, tugging at the tunic at his neck, he couldn't breathe, his eyes stung as they welled with tears. Once he reached the cold, open air of his roof he gasped to catch his breath as his mind raced – he couldn't possibly have missed five whole years? What had he done during that time? He could easily have started wars and caused famine, he could have seen to it that his closest were killed – or done it with his own hands.

Robbinn felt sweat beading on his forehead and prick at his back and neck, his clothes were too hot despite the biting of the cold he was stood in. He hadn't felt panic like this since he had found Oserys and Arriella together in his library.

His hands gripped the stone walls before him so tightly his knuckles turned white and shook with his force, he tried to stare out at the first tree he saw, to calm himself, but he couldn't bring himself to do it as hot tears streamed down his cheeks and his vision trembled.

This was all far, far too much for him to handle alone. He sank to his knees in the snow and sobbed so hard his throat was raw and his lungs ached against the cold air until he could think of nothing but how cold he was after what could have been hours. And how lonely he felt. He had no mother to run to any more. No father to hide things from. No lover to confide in. He hardly had a friend in Oserys any more, she was practically a knight.

Distantly he remembered that nobody knew he was up there. If he really wanted to, he could stay there until he froze to death. Nobody would find him, nobody would be able to see him if he curled up like he had done. So what if he'd be leaving his kingdom to the next man to proclaim himself a king, if Robbinn were dead, he wouldn't have to worry about that – he would be with his Luciaan again.

Just as he was settling into this wonderful fantasy, he heard it. Frantic shouting and screaming for him. Footsteps tearing up and down the halls below him, so loud that a few pygmy dragons that were nesting on another section of roof startled, squawked, and flew off. He could pick out 'where's the king?' and 'this could be it' amongst the shouting. 'It'? What on earth did they mean, 'it'? He stood up as the realisation hit him like a slap to the face. His lips went cold. They could have found him.

Robbinn raced down the small, crumbling flight of stairs he had climbed and flew out into the corridors which were packed with people looking for him like ants fleeing a flooded hill.

"What? What is it? What have you found?" He demanded as they all skidded to a halt.

"The tapper, Your Grace! We think it might be the real one."

"Where is he?" The man didn't respond, he simply beckoned for Robbinn to follow him as he ran at full pelt down to the throne room.

And there he stood. Alive. Manacled at the wrists. Scarred. Clean. Alive.

Robbinn's breath caught in his throat as his eyes met with Luciaan's.

"Luci?" He whispered, stopping in his tracks. "Is that you?" His eyes stung with tears once again, but this time for a far different reason.

"It's me, Robbinn." He smiled, but it was slightly hesitant. Robbinn didn't care. The delight he felt reached every point of his body at the mere sight of the man he loved so much. It had been so long since he held the man bloody, bruised, and dying in his arms.

"Finally I found you, you're here—Guards—guards untie him at once." He demanded, stepping forward to touch Luciaan's arm. It really was him, not a vision, not his imagination. It was him. But his face had dropped even more. "What's wrong, Luci?"

"You're—You're not how I remember you." He said simply as his wrists were freed. "What have you done in your search for me?"

"Everything I had to." Robbinn replied darkly, deciding he did not like where this was going at all. "But it doesn't matter, does it? You're here."

Luciaan's smile returned to his lips, with the warmth of dragonfire as he pulled Robbinn against his chest to hug him tightly, as though he'd die if he were ever to dare to let go. "I'm here."

"I've missed you so much, Luci."

"I've missed you too. It felt as though there was part of my very soul missing without you at my side." Luciaan pulled back, tears making his beautiful eyes sparkle, to lift Robbinn's face with his hand and kiss him softly. Robbinn melted into him, all his fears and worry and loss banished from the moment he touched his soulmate.

All was well in the world with Luciaan in his arms.

But something was wrong. Luciaan gave a choked grunt. Robbinn's eyes flew open to see his face was pale. Then his knees buckled and he was falling, all his weight shifting into Robbinn's arms. He couldn't hold him, only guide him to the floor. There was a dagger in Luciaan's back. He stared up at the back of the murderer's head as he retreated.

Robbinn Falkonn Carbeu never really kept many friends. He found that people only hurt you as they left your life. How right he had been, he thought numbly as Luciaan slipped from his grip, blood pooling beneath him like spilled wine.

BESTIARY

NOTE BY OSEERYS DAEEMORI I: The Bestiary contains a brief overview of most of the species found in our world, used for teaching of children and young adults. This overview is not in detail, nor is it intended to be used as a guide for dealing with these creatures – the best instructions for dealing with creatures is to use common sense and light feet. Use this list wisely.

CLASS SYSTEMS:

DANGER: 1 (harmless), 2 (safe but capable of biting, capable of domestication), 3 (safe for most competent animal handlers), 4 (dangerous, requires specialist knowledge/magic), 5 (deadly, mostly untrainable, keep well clear and defend when necessary)

SIZE: small (horse size or under), medium (larger than horse, smaller than average fishing vessel), large (larger than average fishing vessel, smaller than a palace), mega (palace sized +)

INTELIGENCE: marked out of two. 1. Is of human intelligence or higher. 2. Is able to communicate with humans

DOMESTICATED: yes/no/in some areas

- Size class:
- Intelligence:
- Domesticated:
- Danger:

Lantern Collared Wyvern

(A black, medium dog sized wyvern with bioluminescent banding scales at the neck which glow yellow on males or green on females.)

- Size class: small
- Intelligence: 0
- Domesticated: in some areas
- Danger: 2

Skreghle

(Four-winged bird, black feathers green where the light catches them. The tip flight feather of each wing is gold. Sharp talons, capable of killing humans.)

- Size class: small
- Intelligence: 0
- Domesticated: no
- Danger: 4

Common Green Dragon (AKA Forest Terror)

(A large green dragon with yellow eyes. Not easily sexed unless observed laying eggs, parental work is spread evenly. They are aggressive only if challenged, though have sharp teeth and are capable of producing fire.)

- Size class: medium
- Intelligence: 0
- Domesticated: in some areas
- Danger: 3

Common Pixie

(Small humanoid with pointed ears, black eyes and blue, grey or green skin, generally benign but some humans are allergic to them, causing irritated skin. Found in most areas on the

map.)
- Size class: small
- Intelligence: 1
- Domesticated: no
- Danger: 1

Northern Greater Dragon (AKA Giant Deathcaller)
(Giant species of aggressive dragons capable of speech and fire. Dragonfire generally correlates to the colour of the dragon. Northern great dragons are black, alabaster or deep purple with eyes of almost any colour. Can form strong bonds with select humans.)
- Size class: mega
- Intelligence: 2
- Domesticated: in some areas
- Danger: 4

Merfolk
(Half human half fish or other marine creature. Females are noted to be most deadly, most of the time males will hide as they are far more timid. Not to be confused with their cousins, the Siren, Merfolk will actively search to tip small boats, and occasionally larger vessels if there are enough of them. Merfolk do not speak as willingly, though they have the ability.)
- Size class: medium
- Intelligence: 2
- Domesticated: no
- Danger: 5

Siren
(Cousin to the merfolk but less aggressive. Use song to lure in fishermen and pirates; noted to be more beautiful than mer-

folk and more willing to communicate with humans. Male Sirens are bolder than merfolk, and the primary prey of the siren is fish of any kind though humans are preferred.)

- Size class: medium
- Intelligence: 2
- Domesticated: no
- Danger: 4

Kraken

(Giant octopus-like monster, known to attack any ship it comes across, though its primary prey is whales. Generally grey or green in colour.)

- Size class: mega
- Intelligence: 2
- Domesticated: no, with few exceptions
- Danger: 5

Winged Horse

(Can be any colour that normal horses can with wings the same colour. More temperamental than average stallions, thus are more dangerous but can form very strong bonds with humans.)

- Size class: small
- Intelligence: 0
- Domesticated: in some areas
- Danger: 3

Domestic Pygmy Dragon (Carrier Dragon)

(Raven sized dragons widely used for carrying letters, intelligent enough to understand human direction, making them ideal for their use. Capable of breathing fire. Can be any colour. Generally have a sweet disposition, but will bite if provoked.)

- Size class: small
- Intelligence: 1
- Domesticated: yes
- Danger: 2

Unicorn

(Commonly white in colour with a typically golden horn, but there has been observed cases of the horn being black, alabaster, silver, or lilac. Typically stand between 15 and 18hh. Can be determined, have been known to attack humans that have 'wronged' them, will stop at nothing to kill enemies.)

- Size class: small
- Intelligence: 0
- Domesticated: in some areas
- Danger: 3

Phoenix

(Large bird with red and gold plumage that bursts into flame at the end of its lifecycle and is reborn from the ashes. Elusive, sought after for various remedial purposes, can be remarkably defensive.)

- Size class: small
- Intelligence: 1
- Domesticated: no
- Danger: 2

Manticore

(With the head of a human, body of a lion and tail of a scorpion. Highly aggressive. General population operates a kill on sight law for those able.)

- Size class: medium
- Intelligence: 2

- Domesticated: no
- Danger: 5

Gryphon
(Possesses the hind end of a lion and the body and wings of an eagle. Known to be fearsome and protective of its flock, but otherwise agreeable to humans if unprovoked.)
- Size class: small
- Intelligence: 1
- Domesticated: no
- Danger: 4

Kelpie
(A shapeshifting primarily water spirit that commonly transforms into the shape of a fine horse to entice humans onto its back to drag them to their deaths. This is not the Kelpie's only forms, it can appear as an attractive man or woman. It can be sticky to the touch, and is not limited to the water, only given away by seaweed in hair and/or mane.)
- Size class: small
- Intelligence: 2
- Domesticated: no
- Danger: 5

Gnome
(A dwarfish, earth spirit often described as looking like a wizened old man. These creatures are generally the size of a small dog. Known to frequent all areas of the planet.)
- Size class: small
- Intelligence: 0
- Domesticated: no
- Danger: 1

Hippogriff

(Half eagle, half horse, known to be capable of violence and some groups have been known to actively hunt humans. However, it is intelligent enough to occasionally cooperate with humans.)

- Size class: small
- Intelligence: 0
- Domesticated: in some areas
- Danger: 4

Silent Death (aka western black dragon)

(The largest known species of dragon, consistently black in colour. Capable of human speech, capable of vocalisation with other dragons but is also known to be perfectly silent, especially while hunting.)

- Size class: mega
- Intelligence: 2
- Domesticated: in some areas
- Danger: 5

Three headed dog

(Typically resembles sighthound breeds although shepherds, mastiffs and scent hounds, only with three heads. These heads generally have the same personality, as opposed to one for each head, however this is not always true, there are sometimes deviations.)

- Size class: small
- Intelligence: 0
- Domesticated: yes
- Danger: 2

Amphiptere

(A winged serpent, or legless dragon. Can be found in almost any colour, capable of breathing fire. Some subspecies are covered with feathers as opposed to scales. Elusive and intelligent, not often found in areas heavily populated by humans.)
- Size class: small
- Intelligence: 1
- Domesticated: no
- Danger: 2

Wyrm

(Wingless, legless flying serpents or dragons. Ancient adults can be the length of cities but typically burrow, and do not actively hunt humans.)
- Size class: large – mega
- Intelligence: 2
- Domesticated: no
- Danger: 4

Drake

(Four-legged, wingless dragon that breathes fire and hunts livestock but often avoids humans despite its intelligence.)
- Size class: small
- Intelligence: 2
- Domesticated: no
- Danger: 4

Treesnare

(The origins are not well known. Resembling trees, treesnares are known to snatch up passing humans and cover them with bark. The human form is cast like a statue in the tree, which appears to be unable to digest masses of hair.)

- Size class: small
- Intelligence: 2
- Domesticated: no
- Danger: 5